"I have the drive."

"Used to," Rosie corrected him.

"I'm very driven. And I have lots of friends who find me intriguing." Hudson hadn't meant to let Rosie get to him.

"I call them as I see them." Her voice was flat, as if she thought Hud's political career wasn't worth arguing about.

"And you know this by reading my file?" She didn't know him at all. "Maybe there are things that aren't in my file that might make you feel differently."

"I've been trained to be a judge of what works and what sells in the system. It's my professional opinion, nothing more."

Rosie DeWitt didn't know it yet, but her professional opinion was about to change.

Dear Reader,

I was excited to be included in the SINGLES... WITH KIDS miniseries. Having spent sixteen years as a working mom in the corporate world, I had a lot of history to draw upon, including that all-important network of other working moms who keep you sane. More important, I'd had these characters lurking in the recesses of my brain— Rosie and Hud, two driven, type A personalities who were used to being in the driver's seat and were craving a book of their own. It's a power struggle from the get-go and one neither intends to lose.

Only, these two didn't count on sparks flying from the moment they shake hands. Or the way falling in love necessitates revealing the best-kept secrets.

I hope you enjoy Rosie and Hud's story. I love to hear from readers, either through my Web site, www.MelindaCurtis.com, or through regular mail at P.O. Box 150, Denair, CA 95316.

Happy reading!

Melinda

THE BEST-KEPT SECRET
Melinda Curtis

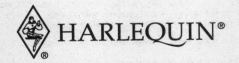

HARLEQUIN®

TORONTO • NEW YORK • LONDON
AMSTERDAM • PARIS • SYDNEY • HAMBURG
STOCKHOLM • ATHENS • TOKYO • MILAN • MADRID
PRAGUE • WARSAW • BUDAPEST • AUCKLAND

ISBN-13: 978-0-373-71416-2
ISBN-10:   0-373-71416-5

THE BEST-KEPT SECRET

www.eHarlequin.com

Printed in U.S.A.

ABOUT THE AUTHOR

Melinda Curtis lives in Northern California with her husband, three kids, two Labradors, two cats and a circle of friendly neighbors who eagerly weigh in on everything from the best way to cut your lawn to the best haircut for a fourth grader—just what good friends are for!

Books by Melinda Curtis

HARLEQUIN SUPERROMANCE

1109—MICHAEL'S FATHER
1187—GETTING MARRIED AGAIN
1241—THE FAMILY MAN
1301—EXPECTANT FATHER
1340—BACK TO EDEN

Don't miss any of our special offers. Write to us at the following address for information on our newest releases.

Harlequin Reader Service
U.S.: 3010 Walden Ave., P.O. Box 1325, Buffalo, NY 14269
Canadian: P.O. Box 609, Fort Erie, Ont. L2A 5X3

To my family, who understand what it means to have a working mom who might forget dentist appointments, singes the garlic bread and misplaces PE clothes. Your wit, eye rolls and unconditional love keep me going.

And to Thelma, who taught me about blended families, forgiveness and stuffing a bra. You will be missed.

CHAPTER ONE

"I NEED YOU TO DO something for me." A small favor. A phone call. Still, it went against Hudson McCloud's grain to ask anyone for help. It came down to this: swallow his pride and ask his mother for help...or wait. And Hud was done waiting.

"What is it?" Vivian McCloud turned from the sky-scraper's view of the turbulent waters of San Francisco Bay and the few sailboats that braved the post-Christmas Pacific Ocean tides. His mother had once been full of life, but the events of the past ten years had taken their toll.

And Hud was partially to blame.

He couldn't turn back the clock and prevent the mistakes and losses he'd suffered from happening, but after two years of biding his time there was finally a chance he could restore his family's honor.

Hud crossed the Oriental carpet in his mother's office to the cabinet that held the TV and filled the room with a sound he had come to loathe—a newscast.

"...sad news for the city. San Francisco's mayor was about to deliver a speech on the steps of city hall when he suffered a brain aneurism. The mayor was rushed to USF Medical Center and pronounced dead at ten a.m."

Hud was silent as his mother came to stand next to him. As a young senator's wife, she'd been a protégé of Jackie

Kennedy both in politics and fashion. Despite her silver hair, she was still a striking presence in her classic suit and pearls. Her influence as the widow of a fifth-generation U.S. senator stretched across both parties, but it was a power she rarely used.

There was a long silence between them, as the news changed to the weather. She had to know what Hud wanted and how important it was to him, to the McCloud legacy.

When his mother didn't speak, Hud smoothed his tie, cleared his throat and said quietly, "This is just what I've been looking for."

His mother gave him a sharp look. "Another chance for you to be hurt?"

"It's what I want." It's what he had to do. Hud muted the volume. He'd turned out to be the screwup in the McCloud family, not Samuel. How in the hell had that happened?

"You excel at running McCloud Inc. Any other man would try to be satisfied with the way things turned out."

"But not a McCloud." McClouds didn't give up. His father had taught him that, along with duty before personal goals.

She sighed heavily. They both knew Hudson had sacrificed his own dreams for the sake of the family.

"I know the public thinks I failed." These last words came out gruffly despite Hud's resolve not to care what anyone else thought. He cleared his throat again. "But I can make it right this time." Hud wanted his mother to be able to hold her head up once more, wanted to hear her laugh with unbridled joy rather than polite response.

"Mayor of San Francisco? The party would be foolish to consider you."

And Hud was a fool to believe he had a chance. Still,

he had one card left to play. "They won't turn me down if you ask them. No one refuses Vivian McCloud."

"ROSIE, YOU HAVE two calls waiting." Rosie DeWitt's assistant, Marsha, stuck her head in Rosie's office. "Line one is Walter O'Connell."

Just hours after the mayor's death, the news media and political world was in a frenzy over who was going to run in the election to replace him. Since Rosie was one of Walter's political strategists, he probably wanted her opinion. He might even want her to run the campaign for the Democratic candidate.

"Line two is Casey's day care."

Anxiety pulsed through Rosie's veins. She set down her coffee and quickly pushed the button for line two. "Is Casey okay?"

"He's fine, Ms. DeWitt." Rosie recognized the voice of Rainbow Day Care's principal, Ms. Phan. Casey attended the Rainbow center after school and during the holidays. "I just wanted to make sure we get our school play on your calendar in late January."

Ouch. She'd missed the last play when Walter had asked Rosie to accompany him to Washington to evaluate several candidates for office. She glanced at a photo of her and Casey from last summer. Heads close, they had the same black curly hair, dark brown eyes and energetic grins. Was she letting him down as Ms. Phan always seemed to imply? Sometimes Rosie felt as if she were trying to sail the SS *Motherhood* beneath the Golden Gate Bridge without a working rudder. No matter how hard she tried to be a good mother, life seemed to conspire against her.

Rosie dutifully penciled the play on her calendar and assured Ms. Phan she'd be there this time.

"And I'm sure you won't be late tonight to pick up Casey. It *is* New Year's Eve, after all," Ms. Phan added. "Once parents begin picking up their children Casey becomes a clock watcher."

To her credit, Rosie didn't snap a pencil or a sharp retort. She did, however, reach for her coffee. Just holding the warm ceramic mug settled her nerves.

Planning strategy, drafting legislation and writing speeches for candidates and incumbents often meant Rosie was late to pick up her kindergartener. She'd learned to leave money in her budget for the late fees she incurred from Rainbow on a weekly basis. What she hadn't completely mastered was the art of filtering all the advice she received about parenting without taking offense or feeling as if she and Casey needed to go to counseling. They were doing the best they could.

Rosie told Ms. Phan she'd be there before five o'clock closing, then paused to take a sip of coffee before she shifted back to professional mode.

Pressing the button for line one took her to California's power player. "Walter, how are you?" She caught the dinosaur Democrat in midcough. He was currently serving as the chairman of the Democratic Party for California. With Walter's approval—and increasingly Rosie's— candidates were groomed by the party for various positions throughout the state.

"A day short of the grave, as usual. Can't seem to shake this cough," he grumbled. "How's it feel to be a backup singer for Senator Alsace?"

"I'm just biding my time until the next political race."

"Ha! Your search for the right candidate is over. Win this one and you can write your own ticket."

"You're going to run for office?" Even as Rosie joked,

she was intrigued. Deals were how the American political system worked and how those involved got ahead.

Walter chuckled, a gruff sound that dissolved into another fit of coughing. "Perhaps you've noticed that San Francisco needs a new mayor."

"There's an opening for a squeaky clean candidate with aspirations of glory." Rosie fidgeted in her seat, excited by the prospect of something new. "Who did you have in mind?"

"You win this one, Rosie, and you'll have a spot on the presidential campaign."

She'd dreamed of working on a presidential campaign since she was a kid. "Who?"

"Hudson McCloud."

Rosie looked at the picture of her son again. The McClouds were the California equivalent of the Kennedys. Media followed their every step. Anyone who worked for the McClouds would receive the same scrutiny, and Rosie was fiercely protective of her privacy. She had to turn Walter down.

And yet, part of her yearned for the challenge. Pundits had dismissed Hudson McCloud's career. The campaign would make national news and, possibly, a strategist's career, as well. She would just have to work that much harder at keeping her professional life separate from her life with Casey.

"Rosie? Rosie, don't play games with me. You won't get another chance like this anytime soon."

"I don't doubt that." Had Walter lost his mind? Had she? Rosie couldn't quell her curiosity. "Why me?"

"Because you excel at advancing the underdog. Because you don't sugarcoat things." Walter coughed. "And because Vivian McCloud requested you."

Hud sat at what had once been his father's desk, in what had once been his father's chair, and perused a file of faded newspaper clippings by the light of a small desk lamp. Usually, his Queen Anne home, built after the 1906 quake, was never quiet. It groaned and shifted like a living thing. Tonight though, as if sensing Hud's somber mood, not a board in the one-hundred-year-old house dared creak.

Tomorrow he'd find out if the party considered him salvageable. He'd left the string-pulling to his mother once she'd agreed to inquire about the Democratic leadership's feelings toward him. But he had no idea who or what he'd face tomorrow. Would they welcome him back or challenge his interest in running?

Hud read the headlines of the articles he kept to remind him why he'd turned his back on his personal goals in the first place.

Hudson McCloud Flexes Power on First Day in Senate.

McCloud Accused of Conflict of Interest on Child Labor Bill.

Questions Increase, McCloud Influence Disappears.

Another Bill by Senator McCloud Crushed.

McCloud Stepping Down from Senate.

Who was Hud kidding? He may have saved McCloud Inc., the clothing conglomerate his great, great grandfather had founded, and their employees from ruin, but he'd done so at the sacrifice of his own career, tarnishing the family reputation in the process. The party wanted untouchable candidates who could influence policy. Hud's political power no longer existed. He'd best remember that and not get his hopes up about what tomorrow's meeting might bring.

SOMETHING SMELLED good enough to get out of bed for.

"I smell 'morning," Casey whispered from the other side of the bed. Sometime during the night, he'd padded into her bedroom complaining of a bad dream that only a dog or a little brother could protect him from.

Eyes still shut, Rosie rolled over and drank in the aroma of freshly brewed coffee. It was Friday. One more day until the weekend. An easy day. Casey was still on holiday from kindergarten.

No! She sat up and her head spun. It was *the* Friday, the day of her audience with Vivian McCloud. Rosie scrambled out of bed full of regret over agreeing to go in the first place. She was meeting Walter for breakfast at nine before their appointment at the Pyramid Center at eleven.

"Wake up, Case! We can't be late today."

Rosie dreaded what she had to do, but what choice did she have? To turn down Vivian McCloud outright was political suicide. So Rosie had done her homework. She had all the ammunition she needed to sink Hudson's political aspirations. Walter would find someone more suitable for the race and the tension that had been sitting in Rosie's stomach since Walter's call would disappear.

The next hour was a blur of activity in between gulps of hazelnut-flavored coffee and making sure Casey ate all his cereal. There was a small ceremonial moment—a lull in the morning chaos—as Rosie unwrapped a pair of new Jimmy Choo pumps. They'd been incredibly expensive but when she'd seen them at lunch on Wednesday, she knew she had to have them, so she'd used the money her parents sent her for Christmas. This morning they felt like success as she slipped them on her feet.

One last perusal in the mirror confirmed her springy

curls were still half-tamed, pulled back from her face and anchored simply by a clip just below her crown, and her clothes lacked major wrinkles or stains. Rosie loved the way her midnight-blue pantsuit projected confidence with a feminine touch provided by long, slightly belled sleeves.

Less than an hour after bolting from bed, keys jingling in one hand, her briefcase, umbrella and raincoat slung over her other arm, she was ready to leave.

"Case, let's go."

"Mommy, I can't go to day care today 'cause I don't have any shoes that match." He lifted his pants legs to show a sneaker on one foot and a sock with a hole in the toe on the other. "It's only a short day anyway."

Rosie slid out of her heels, dropped her briefcase to the floor, tossed her raincoat and umbrella onto a kitchen chair and made a mad dash around their crowded apartment to find a match for a blue-and-red Spider-Man tennis shoe.

"Not by the door. Not in the kitchen. Not in the bathroom." Rosie could feel herself starting to get sweaty. Could she send Casey in sandals? Unfortunately, no. The weatherman had predicted rain.

"Here it is," Casey singsonged. "It was under the couch cushion."

"What was it doing in there?" Rosie asked, setting a record for speedy shoe tying. She stuffed her feet back into her shoes, grabbed her briefcase and Casey's hand, and then they were out the door.

Rosie tugged Casey along as fast as she could, down the stairs past Chin-Chin's Pizzeria and Noodle House, spicy scents already wafting in the air, and along the familiar two-block walk to Rainbow Day Care. The wind swirled about them on the sidewalk and a glance up revealed heavy, gray clouds.

Predictably, the faster she tried to walk, the slower Casey became. "Mommy, can I have hot chocolate?"

Rosie glanced at her watch. "No." At this rate, she'd miss the bus.

"I'm hungry. Can we stop at McDonald's?"

"No, honey. You ate breakfast already." Rosie tried to at least appear as if she wasn't running a race, recognizing that Casey didn't want to be hustled off.

"Mommy, you forgot your coat and umbrella," Casey scolded her when they arrived at Rainbow Day Care. "Take mine." Casey dug his Spider-Man umbrella out of his cluttered cubby.

"I'm sure I won't need it." Rosie dismissed the dark clouds outside. The city had only been getting intermittent showers as they blew over toward the peninsula. Besides, anything with Spider-Man was precious to her son. What if the wind blew it away?

"It's going to get very messy later, Ms. DeWitt." Ms. Phan leaned out the office window. "What is it we always say, Casey?"

"Be prepared and take care of your neighbor!" Casey punched the neon bright umbrella toward the ceiling, eliciting a smile from Rosie.

Ms. Phan nodded with approval, and then gave Rosie a significant look. The day-care principal always managed to make Rosie feel like the worst mother on the planet.

"Thank you for your kind offer, sir," Rosie said as she took the umbrella, wondering if there was another day care in the neighborhood that offered after school services without persecution of its parents. This was just the impression Rosie wanted to make on Vivian McCloud when she rejected her son—a political strategist who liked Jimmy Choos…and Spider-Man.

"DON'T LET HUD BAIT YOU." The door to the Pyramid Center swung closed after Walter, almost hitting Rosie in the face. "He'll try to test your knowledge of the issues. This is an excellent training ground for the presidential campaign."

"Not a problem." *Presidential campaign.* Rosie latched on to the idea like a lifeline. She was about to meet one of her idols—the woman who'd shaken hands with at least six presidents, a dozen heads of state and probably a Supreme Court justice or two.

The woman who could make her life unimaginably miserable if things didn't go Rosie's way.

Rosie spotted the Starbucks in the lobby immediately and clenched the strap of her briefcase against the urge to grab a cup. One of her curls escaped and fell onto her cheek.

"You'll have to pass muster with his father's campaign manager," Walter continued, passing a hand over his bald head. "Stu Fenderson serves as Viv's assistant now."

She hadn't admitted to Walter that she didn't want the job. If Hudson turned out to be an ideal candidate—like that would happen—Rosie would recommend someone else work on his campaign.

"I've heard about Stu." Old, crotchety, a womanizer in his day. Rosie knew how to deal with him—never waffle on an issue, speak loud enough for his hearing aid to pick up and never let him have the last word.

"But it's most important that Viv approves of you. Make a bad impression and any chance you have at the national level will be slim to none. Everybody loves her and they'll do anything she asks." Walter pointed at Rosie.

"Including blackball you. So, let's not tell her you're having lunch with another candidate."

"She doesn't know about Roger Bartholomew?" Rosie balked as she was about to pass a large modern sculpture in the lobby. When Walter confessed this morning that he was interested in a second candidate, Rosie's grip on her coffee mug had turned white-knuckled. It was either that or let out a credibility-killing shout of relief. With another option, there was no way she'd get trapped into working on Hudson's campaign.

"I don't plan to tell Viv about Roger unless it's absolutely necessary. That's why I'm not going to lunch with you."

"But—"

Walter gave Rosie an odd look over his shoulder as he handed the security guard his ID. "I trust your assessment."

Rosie ignored the rush of excitement at the power he was giving her. "But you said Mrs. McCloud—"

"If you don't play both sides of the coin, you'll be empty-handed at the end of the day." Meaning he wanted Rosie to do his dirty work so his friendship with Mrs. McCloud wouldn't suffer.

She'd been planning to build a case against Hudson with Walter at her back, but now…

Certain she wore that deer in the headlights look, Rosie crossed the foyer and produced her ID.

They were followed into the elevator by a group of women each cradling a Starbucks cup. Trapped against the back wall, Rosie looked up at the small video screen playing news sound bites so she wouldn't focus on the coffee. She'd had coffee this morning. She was prepared for the meeting—even if her hair was starting to unravel, Rosie would not. She didn't need the prop of a coffee cup or the jolt of caffeine. But that didn't stop Rosie from ima-gining the surprised look on the face of the woman next to her as Rosie plucked the cup from her hand.

Since Walter hadn't given up his spot by the control buttons, he exited easily at the forty-second floor, while Rosie had to fight her way through the caffeine herd and was almost scrunched by the closing elevator doors. She trotted past several clear glass entryways, struggling on her short legs to catch up with Walter.

The doors to the McCloud offices had been replaced with paned, frosted ones so that no one in the hallway could see in. Walter marched through. Rosie's hand hesi-tated on the cool, pebbled glass. Tension buzzed in her ears.

Rosie backed up a step, her fingertips almost a memory on the door. If she left, she'd lose a chance to influence the agenda of the next president of the United States. What would she tell Casey the next time he asked about what she wanted to be when she grew up? How could she encourage him not to abandon his dreams without putting forth the effort if she didn't do the same? All she had to do was keep her mouth closed about Roger Bartholomew, not let Hudson get to her, control Stu and not even think about…

Don't.

With a deep breath, Rosie pushed the door open and stepped into an opulent, hushed reception area decorated in muted grays and deep burgundies, coming face-to-face with a large oil portrait of Hamilton and Vivian McCloud, flanked by their two grown sons, Hudson and Samuel. The men all shared a strong cleft chin. No one smiled. It was an ominous portrait, no doubt created as a legacy marker. All the wild charm had been painted out of Samuel's expression.

"There you are. I thought we'd lost you." Walter stood next to an old man with a grizzled appearance, whose rumpled suit was a far cry from Walter's fine wool one. "Rosie DeWitt, this is Stu Fenderson."

Rosie learned a lot about a person by the way they shook hands. Stu's hand latched on to hers like a tentacle, trapping Rosie's until he found a weakness.

"You're shorter than I expected," Stu noted.

It was odd how men in politics liked to throw insults. Rosie smiled, grateful her heels put her at the old man's height. She'd bet no one ever described Stu as tall, either. She looked him up and down. "Yeah, I hear that a lot, especially from men with a twenty-eight-inch inseam."

Hand still pumping hers, Stu glanced down at Rosie's shoes barely visible beneath the cuff of her pants. "Might be hard to keep up with us in those."

"They're a campaign necessity." Since he still pumped her hand, she leaned closer until she could almost smell the oil he'd used to comb over what few strands of white hair he had left. "You see, I double as campaign security. These heels are licensed to kill in ten of the fifty states."

"At the price you paid, they should be illegal in fifteen." Hamilton McCloud's widow leaned against a doorway to Rosie's left looking just as beautiful and composed in real life as she did on television…only taller. Her gray hair was cut stylishly short to accent the classic bone structure of her face. Vivian McCloud wore a conservative cream-colored skirt and jacket that showed off her statuesque figure. "Women in Jimmy Choos don't mess around, especially when those shoes haven't gone on sale yet this season. Let her be, Stu."

Stu reluctantly eased the suction on Rosie's hand.

"So this is who you brought us, Walter." Mrs. McCloud

towered over Rosie as she approached. Casey didn't get his height solely from the McCloud men.

Rosie was determined not to think about Samuel or the handful of days they'd spent together in Paris after her college graduation, but it was hard not to when she stood beneath his portrait with his mother bearing down on her.

"Only the best for our boy," Walter said, giving his raincoat to the receptionist. "She's strong on strategy and a compelling speech writer."

Grateful for the distraction, Rosie handed the receptionist Casey's Spider-Man umbrella, smiling sheepishly. Then she was shaking hands with Casey's grandmother. The strength of Vivian McCloud's grip rivaled that of a lioness protecting her young. This was a woman who'd be fearless against those who inflicted injustice and deception upon the McCloud family.

And yet, the guilt must not have shown on Rosie's face because the McCloud matriarch still spoke warmly. "Thank you for coming."

"My pleasure, ma'am. Rosie DeWitt, political strategist." Rosie prided herself on her composure. She was a pro, an up-and-comer with a solid reputation in politics. And a big fat li—

She would not define herself with the *L* word. Nor would she allow so much as a wobble in her high heels or succumb to the overwhelming desire to pass out. As long as Rosie kept her distance, stuck to her plan and didn't get chummy with the McClouds, she and Casey would be fine.

"*Ma'am?* That reference makes me feel old. You may call me Vivian. Later on you can tell me where you got those shoes."

"Thank you...Vivian." So much for keeping her distance.

Vivian beamed. "This looks like the beginning of a beautiful relationship. Don't you think so, Stu?"

"Let's see what she can do with him first," Stu said, gesturing to a door behind him.

With enviable composure, Vivian strolled past Rosie to the remaining closed door and opened it without knocking. "Hud, darling. Come see what Walter's brought you."

Stu and Walter followed Vivian, unaware that Rosie hesitated behind them glancing up at Samuel's portrait and wishing for a cup of coffee.

CHAPTER TWO

"COME IN AND SIT DOWN." Hud's mother held the door as the jury filed in with a verdict—salvageable candidate or not. The quality of the campaign manager Walter O'Connell selected would be telling.

Hud stood and came around his desk to shake hands with Walter, who held the fate of his family's political legacy in his hands. Hud nodded to Stu, but didn't see anyone behind the chairman's large frame. His shoulders sank. So, they'd decided Hud was unmarketable. He turned back to his desk.

His mother cleared her throat, inclining her head almost imperceptibly toward the door. Hud looked around to face a pixie with big dark eyes and long, wild black curls, including one artfully arranged on her cheek.

"Rosie DeWitt." Cheeks flaming, she thrust out her hand.

Hud took Ms. DeWitt's hand gingerly in both of his, afraid his normal grip might crush her delicate bones. Warm and soft, her hand fit nicely between his. Despite her solid reputation, there was no way Rosie DeWitt was capable of the cutthroat behavior that Hud needed from his campaign manager. Her hands were more suited to stroking a lover than greasing palms and salvaging careers.

As if sensing his assessment, her eyes flashed. She gripped his hand as firmly as any man ever had, gave it a good shake and pulled away. "You don't want to shake a woman's hand like that."

The absence of her warmth robbed him of speech.

A state his mother never experienced. "Why ever not? I think it's a sweet gesture."

"Women see it as something more subtle and…" Ms. DeWitt gave Hudson a sideways glance as she crossed the room to set down her slender leather briefcase. "A bit suggestive."

"I didn't mean—"

"I know you didn't." Ms. DeWitt cut him off, digging in her briefcase. She knew he was lying. He could tell by the lingering bloom of color on her cheeks that she'd felt the attraction between them and was as surprised as he was by it. "But not everyone else knows your touch is platonic." She pulled out a sheaf of papers and sank into a chair, gesturing for everyone to be seated as if this was her office, not his.

"Walter, what kind of game are you playing?" Hud asked, giving the woman a wide berth on the way to his chair. If he so much as brushed up against her she'd probably accuse him of sexual harassment.

"The kind of game you should have played when you were *Senator* McCloud." Ms. DeWitt looked past his shoulder in the direction of Alcatraz. "Play up your strengths, admit your mistakes and move on. Do you want me to continue?"

"No," Hud said at the same time his mother said, "Yes," arching her brows at him when he frowned.

Okay. Points to Mother. This was going to be painful just as she'd predicted. Hud was tired of hearing advice on what he should have done. He wanted advice to help him today. His father's clock ticked off the seconds Hud was wasting until Ms. DeWitt spoke again.

"According to a poll conducted by the party this week, one-third of registered voters believe Hudson did the honorable thing by stepping down, one-third considered his resignation an admission of guilt and one-third couldn't care less about him." Ms. DeWitt spoke directly to Hud's mother, as if she knew Hud would be annoyed that they'd conducted a poll already. It gave them ammunition he didn't have. "Now, if you look at women, two-thirds considered what Hud did honorable. We'll need to keep the female vote happy, but at a distance. We can't have as much as a breath of scandal."

That explained her aversion to his handshake. Hudson made a derisive noise and rolled his eyes. "Fortunately, I'm not the womanizer my brother Samuel was," he said before he realized his mother might be offended by his comment. Samuel had been her favorite.

But everyone ignored his outburst, including Ms. DeWitt. "We also asked who voters would prefer sitting down to dinner with—Hudson or the president—and they chose our commander in chief. Then we gave them a choice between Hudson or Samuel—and they chose Samuel." She seemed unexpectedly pleased that Hud had failed both questions.

"What kind of question is that?" And how had Hud lost to his irresponsible, dead brother?

"It's a standard question we ask," Walter explained. "If voters don't like you, they won't vote for you."

"I would have chosen the president, too," Stu inserted almost absently.

His mother shushed their family's longtime assistant.

Ms. DeWitt nodded. "If Hudson is serious about the election, he'll have to publicly address what happened in D.C.—"

"The past won't come into play here," Hud interjected. "This is about the future."

Ms. DeWitt's brow creased ever so slightly. She turned to his mother, no longer acknowledging Hudson's presence. "And create a more appealing persona."

Hud's jaw tightened. The verdict was in. The party didn't want him. In fact, Rosie DeWitt, who had a reputation for doing the impossible in politics, didn't like him.

"If the party chooses to back Hudson, we'd be taking a huge risk since the Republican opponent will most likely attack Hudson's Senate record relentlessly. That's what I'd do in their shoes." She gave Hud a look that dared him to contradict her. "So, Hudson, why don't you tell us why you think the Democrats should take this risk?"

"My son has the highest ethical standards," his mother bristled. Too late, Hudson realized how hard this must be on her. Perhaps he should have insisted she stay out of this meeting.

Walter started to speak, but Ms. DeWitt held up a hand. "To win, he'll need both voter trust and liking. How do you expect to increase your chances?" She didn't measure Hud with her stare but rather dared him to defend himself.

It had been years since anyone had challenged Hud, much less a miniature woman with too big of an ego. "I thought the party paid *you* to improve my numbers. Where do you categorize yourself on that poll you referenced earlier, Ms. DeWitt?"

"Excuse me?" Something flared in Ms. DeWitt's eyes. She may have dressed in designer clothes and spent hours to get that hair of hers to fall artfully over her face, but she wasn't an all-fluff, no-substance debutante. Her fact gathering proved that, and her nearly black eyes accented with a thick carpet of eyelashes and minimal cosmetics told him she was no nonsense.

No fun, either. Despite the unexpected physical spark between them. But Hud doubted if anyone dared contest Ms. DeWitt when the decision over their careers rested with her. For an instant, Hud considered retreating, but he was done sidestepping battles. "Did you vote for me to go to the slammer because of my handshaking style or did you think I should be acquitted of all charges?"

Hud half expected Ms. DeWitt to blush again, but she didn't. Her gaze hardened the way only seasoned backroom dealmakers could when someone got in their way. Hud spared a glance to Walter. What bonus had the party offered Ms. DeWitt to work on his campaign? She certainly wasn't one of his supporters.

"My personal opinion of you doesn't matter. It's my professional opinion you should be worried about. I don't back candidates that don't have what it takes to win." In that moment, her eyes blazing and her dark hair spiraling in wild waves around her face, Hud wanted to have her.

The reaction gave him pause.

"Walter?" His mother turned to the chairman.

Walter cleared his throat and Hud silenced him with a gesture before he could enter the fray. "What makes you think I don't have what it takes to win?"

SHE'D COME ON TOO STRONG. Hudson had gotten Rosie out of rhythm. From the get-go, his touch had thrown her off with his unexpected animal magnetism. She'd seen him speak before but never actually met him. Up close, he was tall—taller than Samuel—and so perfectly put together—

not a strand of black hair out of place or a wrinkle in his suit—with a penetrating gaze that challenged as intensely as it beckoned.

Yet she knew from what Samuel had told her that Hudson didn't care about others beyond how he could use them to garner more power. A man like that would never swallow his pride. She'd played to that, only she'd played a bit too hard and upset the McClouds.

Rosie stared at her hands, realizing she should have turned this meeting down and suffered the career setback. But in addition to fulfilling an obligation to Vivian McCloud and testing the waters that led to presidential campaigns, she'd wanted to see for herself if she was making the right decision by keeping Casey a secret from this side of his family tree. And by showing up and taking the offensive right away, she'd made things ten times worse.

Rosie stood, capturing Hudson's gaze, ignoring the stubborn cleft to his chin. "I'm no different than any other voter. I want to believe that you're a good person worthy of my trust. I'll even forgive you a few mistakes as long as you own up to them and apologize. But you haven't told me anything to keep those beliefs alive, not two years ago and certainly not today."

Hudson's mouth thinned into a hard line. He didn't say anything. Rosie's gaze drifted past him, but the spectacular view was hidden behind oppressive rain clouds.

"I'll tell you why you can't win. Voters want to back someone with a captivating personality. If you're intriguing, you don't let anyone see it." Disregarding a twinge of discomfort that she was being brutally cruel to Vivian's son in front of her, Rosie locked gazes with Hudson. "You're not married. You don't date. You don't show up at ball games or the beach. Everything about you, from this high-rise office suite to the domineering expression on your face shouts, 'stay away from me.'"

Chairs on either side of her creaked with disappointment, fueling the growing unease eating at Rosie's composure. Walter was letting her hang on this one. Her chances of being blackballed by Vivian now outweighed her chances at the presidential campaign. Ever.

She forced herself to face Vivian, hoping Casey's grandmother might understand, hoping she wouldn't hold Rosie's rejection of Hudson against her. But as a mother, Rosie wouldn't forgive anyone who stood in the way of her son's dreams. "I was hoping your son was someone honorable, someone I could trust to watch out for the interests of *my* son. I'd pour my heart into a campaign for someone like that, regardless of what his last name was." She'd said too much, looked too weak.

And there was no sign of forgiveness in Vivian McCloud's expression, only a sad resignation as if she was sorry to have to end Rosie's career.

Rosie picked up her briefcase. "Excuse me. I have another appointment."

"WELL, THAT'S THAT," Hud's mother announced brightly.

"You agree that my political career is over because I have no personality?" There was so much adrenaline pumping through his veins, Hud could barely sit still. He disagreed with everything Ms. DeWitt said, but the Democratic chairman hadn't supported or refuted her judgment, so Hud hadn't argued with her toward the end of her insulting diatribe.

"Rosie's assessments are usually right on the money," Walter said, showing his true colors.

"She's a regular firecracker," Stu said. "I'd pay to see that again. Do you want me to go get her?"

"No." His mother waved a weary hand. "At your age, you'd never catch a determined woman like that. It's for the best."

"Yes. Rosie is long gone." Walter looked apologetic. "She's having lunch with Roger Bartholomew."

"Is she dating him?" Stu asked before Hud could.

Roger Bartholomew lied and cheated his way through life and seduced women he had no feelings for. Among the social elite of the city, Roger made Samuel look like a saint. Although Ms. DeWitt dating Roger would explain why she and Hud didn't get along, Hud suspected something far worse. "You're considering Roger for mayor, aren't you? This was all a show. You were never seriously considering me."

"There's been many a politician who overcame worse than you've experienced, and their last name wasn't McCloud. Rosie told you what you needed to do. I've never known her to steer someone wrong." Walter stood. "It was an interesting idea, Viv. Now, just so I don't feel as if I wasted the trip from Los Angeles, would you like to go to lunch?"

The party didn't think Hudson was a failure? Ms. DeWitt thought he had a chance?

"I'm always free for lunch with you, Walter," his mother replied with an apologetic look in Hud's direction. "Perhaps we can talk about Hud's prospects over lobster salad at Aqua?"

Walter's laughter dissolved into a fit of coughing. "Maybe I didn't make myself clear. That little lady has never led me astray in my decision of who the party backs." Walter buttoned his suit jacket. "I imagine after

lunch at Plouf, she'll recommend the party back Bartholomew."

Without even a cursory shake of Walter's hand, Hudson
sprinted toward the door.

"WELL, I…" Vivian didn't know what to say as she
watched Hudson's retreating back.

"He's usually very steady." Stu filled in the void.

"I'm sure he is," Walter said. "I'm still free for lunch,
Viv."

From the day her husband had introduced Vivian to the
tall, broad-shouldered politician, Walter had called her
Viv. She'd always been Vivian to Hamilton, yet there was
something about the way Walter said the nickname that
she'd always liked. "Do you think Hud went after her?"

"If he wants to reenter politics, he better be hightailing
it after her." Walter gestured for Vivian to precede him out
of Hudson's office, then called his driver requesting he
bring the car around.

"I'm sure he'll set things right." She still wasn't sure
she wanted Hud back in politics. Vivian was proud of
Hud and the choices he'd made, but even she had to
admit he came across as a stuffed shirt. It would take a
lot to get him to loosen up.

Walter helped Vivian into her raincoat. After he
smoothed her collar, his hands drifted down her arms in
an intimate manner and then fell away.

Vivian froze. Walter was always such a gentleman.
She'd probably misread the moment. They were friends.
That touch…that touch was just supportive. What had
they been talking about? Uh… "It takes a strong woman
to go out in Jimmy Choos on a day like today with only
a Spider-Man umbrella."

"Most admirable." Walter held the door and bid goodbye to Stu.

Vivian passed Walter, her walk unusually self-conscious. "How are your kids?"

"Healthy. Still married. Financially sound." Walter reached in front of Vivian to press the elevator button. He had solid, strong fingers. "Now that the grandchild is talking, I've found he's actually interesting."

"Really?" Vivian suppressed her envy. With her husband and Samuel gone, her life was too empty. Not that she wanted it filled with politics again. She'd lost most of her friends in D.C. after Hudson stepped down, which just proved they weren't really her friends. Vivian forced herself to smile. Walter didn't deserve her melancholy mood. "You're too young to be a grandfather."

He chuckled, the textured sound filling her chest in an odd way. "I'm old enough to be a widower, as are you. Fifteen, twenty years ago when our kids were in high school we were old enough to be grandparents. We were just lucky, that's all."

"You don't fit the mold of any grandparent I know," Vivian said, stepping into the empty elevator, noting how thoughtful he was to have a hand on the door.

"Let me tell you about today's grandparents." Walter crossed his arms and leaned against the wall. He was one of a few men from their generation who was considerably taller than she was. "Grandparents nowadays still vote, but they travel and go out to eat at nice restaurants, and every once in a while, if they're lucky, they have sex."

Just the word *sex* was enough to send Vivian's pulse racing. She'd given up on the idea years ago and now Walter had reawakened a need. Vivian was going to have to check her medication because she had to be having a hot flash.

"IT'S A PLEASURE TO MEET YOU." Many women probably found Roger Bartholomew attractive, but his highlighted blond hair and average chin didn't make near the impression on Rosie that Hudson's presence did. Roger cradled Rosie's hand in both of his smooth, pale ones without shaking it at all.

Rosie extracted herself and tried to lift at least one corner of her mouth in a weak interpretation of a smile. Still reeling from the awkward scene with the McClouds, Rosie needed Roger to be a stellar candidate. And quickly, because she had to pick up Casey early today. Once she settled into a chair across from Roger, Rosie looked up to find Hudson McCloud at the maitre d' stand. Their gazes collided, sending her heart pounding.

He knows about Casey. Why else would Hudson be here except to demand visitation and subject Casey to the kind of media circus he'd grown up with?

Because he's a conceited nuisance who wants to be mayor. Sanity returned, along with a steadier heartbeat.

"Would you excuse me, Roger?" Rosie hurried to the front of the restaurant, grabbed Hudson by the arm and tugged him over toward the restrooms out of Roger's line of vision should he look. "What are you doing here?"

"You're not finished with your assessment of me." Hudson thrust his hands into his raincoat pockets. "We didn't talk about my ideas for the city."

"Don't be a sore loser." Even in her heels, Rosie had to tilt her head back to look at Hudson, to take in his determined expression on his much too handsome features framed by crisp, well-behaved dark hair. Although her time with Samuel had been brief, she'd appreciated the fact that the hair at the nape of Samuel's neck curled uncontrollably and his nose was a bit crooked. Perfection like Hudson's was intimidating.

"I won't lose. I'll just wait by the door for you to realize I'm a better risk than Roger." True to his word, tall, dark and annoying went to stand in the foyer.

His political career was so over.

As she walked past him, Hudson leaned close. "What did you think of his handshake?"

Rosie didn't want to admit that Roger's handshake gave her the heebie-jeebies. With only two candidates on Walter's radar, if Roger had other qualities that were marketable, Rosie was recommending him. Handshakes could be fixed. Personality flaws like Hudson's could not.

"I'm sorry for the interruption." Rosie arranged her napkin in her lap and looked about the table. "Didn't we have menus?"

"I ordered for you while you were in the ladies' room."

Rosie tried to mask her irritation at Roger's presumptuous behavior. "We've never met before. How did you know what to order?"

"I know what women like." Something sexist dripped from each word and Roger's smile was condescending.

If it wasn't for Hudson McCloud standing watch, Rosie might have left. Instead, she vowed to get the upper hand. "Never presume, Roger." Flagging down a waiter, Rosie requested a menu.

"I apologize." Roger looked quite unattractive when things didn't go his way.

Rosie was familiar with the French seafood bistro and knew what she wanted, but she still gave the menu a cursory glance before ordering an endive salad and lobster ravioli. "Why don't you tell me why you want to be mayor?"

"My family settled in the city nearly one hundred years

ago and it seems like a good place to start a political career."

That wasn't an answer. Rosie knew Roger lived off his family's wealth rather than working, as Hudson did. According to Walter, his charitable contributions paled next to Hudson's. She needed to uncover any advantage Roger had over Hudson. She tried again. "If you were mayor…" Rosie trailed off as she caught Roger's attention drifting after a twiggy woman in a too-short skirt passing their table.

Roger gave Rosie an unrepentant grin, as if this were a common occurrence a female campaign manager wouldn't find both insulting and problematic. "I'm always on the lookout for the next Mrs. Bartholomew. I've heard it's easier to get into office as a married man than as a single one."

Oh, pul-ease. Why had Walter set up this lunch? Roger was not politician material. Rosie didn't need any more time to make that judgment, but she couldn't bail with Hudson waiting. If she had to grin and bear Roger through lunch, she was going to need a glass of wine. Rosie held up a hand and signaled another waiter. At least the service at Plouf was excellent.

"Rosie?" Hudson appeared next to their table with a practiced, easy grin. Heaven forbid he show too many teeth. "I thought that was you. And then you waved and—"

"I did not wave at *you*." Rosie glared at Hudson. "Did you think I was asking you to join us?" No one could be that obtuse.

"May I?" Hudson greeted Roger, shook his hand and sat beside Rosie, ignoring the look she gave him and nodding his head toward the awestruck woman at the next table. "The place is packed."

"We're having a private conversation," Roger said, his brows pitching downward.

Hudson pointed at the two of them. "I'm not interrupting something romantic, am I?"

"No!" Rosie felt like jabbing an elbow in Hudson's rib cage.

"Good. Just pretend I'm not here. I need to check e-mail anyway." With that, Hudson pulled out his Black-Berry and started scrolling through his messages.

Where was that waiter?

CHAPTER THREE

ROGER LOWERED HIS VOICE. "The lady wants you to leave."

"Given your track record, I prefer to stay. The lady needs protection." From both Roger and her own mistaken impressions. Hud leaned back in his chair and put his arm across the top of Rosie's chair. Somewhere between his office and Plouf she'd become someone who believed in him, however reluctant that belief might be, and he'd started thinking of her as Rosie.

"Gentlemen, please." But Rosie only stared at Hud and bobbed her head in the direction of the door, freeing another wayward curl in her effort to get rid of him.

If Rosie wasn't going to willingly give him a second chance, Hud had no choice but to create his own opportunities. "I hear you're interested in running for mayor, Roger. I'm curious. What would you put on your agenda?"

"Agenda?" The other man frowned.

Thank you, Roger, for making this easy. "What issues would take priority for you? Education? Health care? Transportation?"

Roger shrugged. "They all seem important to me. Doesn't the city have a lot of programs in place already?"

"Yes, we do." Hud smiled and brought his head closer to Rosie's because he knew it would annoy Roger. "There are several great programs in San Francisco. The problem is red tape. People don't know how to get the help they need or they can't work their way through the bureaucratic paper trail."

"Like you know what's going on in San Francisco," Roger sulked.

"I know that with the most attractive health care and services programs around we attract more than our fair share of homeless." Hud sensed Rosie's appraising gaze upon him and hoped she realized how passionate he was about serving his community. "And that our city is overly dependent upon tourism. Our infrastructure is strained and the new bay bridge still won't be large enough to handle all the traffic during rush hour."

"What? Are you applying for the mayor's job?" Roger snapped. Then he looked from Hud to Rosie and swore. "You are!"

"That's enough," Rosie interjected.

Hud shrugged. "I'd like to think I can make the city a better place."

"That's bull." Roger shook his head. "No one can change a thing. The best you can do is ride shotgun and hope for no earthquakes or terrorist attacks."

"I think you're wrong." And now, hopefully, Rosie would, too.

"You're not going to impress her with that." Roger's voice turned sour. "Politicians are realists. Aren't they?"

"I think," Rosie said after looking the two of them over, "things have gotten out of hand here and—"

"You should go," Hud told Roger, moving his hand closer to Rosie's shoulder with a grin.

Roger stood. "Don't make any hasty decisions about Hudson. Everyone knows he's a quitter." Tossing his napkin on the table, Roger left.

Hud didn't realize he'd gripped Rosie's shoulder until she loosened his fingers from her jacket. "Please tell me that more people wanted to go to dinner with me than with that pompous jerk," he said.

The waiter placed a glass of white wine in front of her while Rosie scooted her chair away from his. "I have never seen such a childish display in my life," she said finally. "You barge in here—"

"Pull out your charts."

"Sit down in the midst of what is clearly a business meeting—"

"Or I'll do it for you."

"And bully Roger into leaving."

She was breathing heavy and so was Hud. He hadn't experienced a good fight in a long time. He was angry and frustrated and trying not to be desperate. But what was most surprising was how alive Rosie DeWitt made him feel, how he wanted to twine his fingers through her long springy curls while they sparred. Hud could tell from the intensity of her glare that she felt the same way. Adversaries sometimes made the best lovers. Not that pursuing a relationship with his campaign manager would help Hud's image. He'd learned over the last few years that short-term attraction distracted him from his long-term goals. But that didn't mean Hud couldn't use this spark between them to his advantage.

Hud grinned. "I can wait all day." Because he was going to get Rosie's endorsement for mayor if he had to follow her home.

"PERHAPS I SHOULD CALL HUD." Vivian fiddled with the stem of her wineglass as she sat across from Walter in one of San Francisco's most exclusive restaurants.

Walter put his chin on his hand and studied her intently, much the way he'd been doing all through lunch, as if he'd just met her and was trying to figure her out. "Why? He's a grown man."

"I know, but I want him to be happy."

"After age eighteen, they have to be in charge of finding their own happiness. I think I told you as much twenty years ago."

Vivian attempted a smile. "I didn't listen then, either." She'd spoiled Samuel because Hamilton had been so hard on Hud. It had taken Samuel a long time to grow up, but eventually he had, going so far as to receive a graduate degree from Berkeley before joining the army. When he was killed in Afghanistan, Vivian was glad she'd made his short life so special.

"Adversity builds character," Walter pointed out, reaching for her hand. He was so supportive, always there when she needed him. A decade ago Walter had stood by her side when Hamilton passed away from complications created by his diabetes. He'd helped Hud see her through the loss of Samuel nearly five years later and had been one of the few people who didn't disappear when things went sour for Hud in the Senate. When she'd called earlier in the week to discuss Hud's options, Walter had been the one to suggest Rosie and she'd readily agreed, knowing he'd use Vivian's name to smooth things over for Hud.

With her hand enveloped in Walter's larger one, Vivian felt safe. "We've had enough adversity in our lives. Hud doesn't need any more."

"Hudson is young enough to weather a few more storms." Walter stroked his thumb across the back of her hand, sending an almost forgotten thrill skittering across her skin. "You're the one I want to see happy."

She tried to ease her hand back, but Walter only held on tighter. If she had any sense, she'd think her old friend was making a move on her. But Vivian knew better. She was nearing sixty-five with skin that had lost its elasticity and body parts that drooped. Powerful men like Walter pursued young, nubile bodies.

Vivian patted Walter's hand and gently extricated herself, because she knew what he wanted even if he seemed not to at the moment. "I am happy."

With a significant glance at his empty hand, Walter's dark eyebrows went up a centimeter or two. They both knew that was a fib. She'd spent the last two years moping around her office and home. A change of subject was in order.

"Why on earth are you considering Roger Bartholomew? He was one of Samuel's friends." One of his wilder friends and someone Vivian considered an extremely bad influence on her son in college. "And he's too young."

"I chose two candidates that I'm certain will make Rosie's recommendation an easy one." And that was as close as Walter would come to admitting he'd stacked the deck in Hud's favor. "I thought you didn't want Hudson back in politics."

"I've grown accustomed to the peace and quiet."

"You've retreated from the world but you can't quite give up influencing it. You can't have it both ways, Viv." Walter gave her a half smile.

She laughed. "When you've done all I've done, why be bothered with all this?" Vivian gestured to the room full of men and women in suits.

"Do you want me to buy you some support hose and a rocking chair?"

"I don't consider myself elderly." Vivian bristled.

"Then don't act like it." There was that spark of male interest in his eyes again.

Vivian didn't want to admit that she longed for a rocking chair and a lap filled with babies more than she longed to stand behind Hud while he gave speech after speech. Anybody could do that. "Maybe I want some-thing different. Maybe I want to be…" *Needed.*

"What?"

But Vivian wasn't ready to tell Walter that she had no reason to get up in the morning and no reason to climb into her empty bed at night.

ROSIE'S PHONE BEEPED. Somehow in the midst of all the arguing and male posturing, she'd missed a call. A quick check of the screen revealed the words Rainbow Day Care. Caught up in the excitement, she'd lost track of time. Using her bad-mommy antennae, Ms. Phan had probably sensed Rosie would be hung up and called to remind her.

It was one-fifteen. Rosie was going to be late and Casey, bless his heart, was going to forgive her like he always did. "I've got to go."

"Wait," Hudson said. "Tell me if my figures are stronger than Roger's."

"I have to pick up my son." Grabbing her things, Rosie wended her way to the door. On her way out, she left money with the maitre d'.

"Do you have an umbrella?" the maitre d' asked. "It's really coming down."

Glancing up, Rosie saw the downpour. *Idiot.* She'd left Casey's Spider-Man umbrella in Hudson's office. She'd have to admit to Casey that she'd lost it. He'd find this in-fraction harder to forgive than her being late. It was two blocks to a bus stop, and at least four to BART. Getting a taxi during lunch hour in the city was always challenging, but during a rain shower would be next to impossible. She'd show up late, drenched, without Casey's umbrella.

Rosie called Selena, who had a car and as an artist had a more flexible schedule than most of her friends. She'd picked up Casey before when Rosie got in a jam. But Selena's phone rolled to voice mail.

A hand touched her shoulder. Rosie jumped and twisted her ankle as her slender heel gave way, not noticing a steadying grip on her arm until she regained her footing.

Hudson's brown eyes were the color of strong whiskey, a potent, overwhelming force. "Let me give you a ride."

She'd never liked whiskey. "I'll get a taxi." Rosie tried to remember where the nearest hotel was. That would be her best bet for a cab. The last thing she needed was Hudson hounding her all across town. In addition to the flaws Samuel had pointed out to her all those years ago, his brother had no manners.

"You'll need this." He pulled Casey's small Spider-Man umbrella out of his inner raincoat pocket. "My assistant realized you left without it."

She was saved. "That was very nice of you." He'd carried it all this way. Rosie couldn't imagine Samuel doing such a thing.

"Unexpected, I see."

"It certainly is. You could have given it to me in front of Roger." And tried to humiliate her.

Hudson shrugged, grinning as if he didn't often get caught being nice. "You don't pull any punches, do you?"

"Neither do you."

The rain came down so hard it sounded as if there was a train outside.

"How about we declare a truce?" Hudson rubbed the back of his neck, looking contrite. "You'll never get a cab and my driver is just around the corner."

"Fine." Even with Casey's umbrella, there was no way Rosie would find a taxi in time. While Hudson called his driver, Rosie stepped out of her Jimmy Choos and stuffed them into her slender briefcase, managing to zip it closed. The money she'd paid for those shoes would have been better spent on Casey's college fund. Chalk up another bad decision on the long list of her parenting mistakes.

"INNER SUNSET, PLEASE," Rosie said, bending forward so that Graham, Hud's driver, could hear the rest of her directions. Then she sat back, opened her briefcase and pulled out her precious shoes, dragging out a file bursting with clippings, photos and papers in the process. The file tab bore his name.

Hud recognized the edge of one of his Senate campaign photos. His fingers twitched as he wondered what else was in there.

"They didn't get wet," she murmured, reverently placing the shoes on the seat between them before sinking back and closing her eyes. She curled her wet toes, shimmering with pink polish, into the carpet. "I'll just sit here and pretend I'm invisible and that the past two and a half hours didn't happen. Can you wake me when we get to my son's day care?"

Most women Hud knew would have harped on about what he'd just done. But then, most women didn't have an inch-thick file on Hud or such a disappointing set of beliefs about him. There had to be a way to change Rosie's mind. Caving in to his curiosity, he flipped her file open to an editorial on his Senatorial campaign viewpoints.

Rosie had written "fair assessment" in the margin as well as underlining a passage claiming Hudson was passionate but too young and green for the responsibilities of office.

"What are you doing?" She turned her head slightly to look at him.

"Trying to find out what you think of me."

"I believe I made that clear in your office."

"I can still wonder why you think I'm a poor choice, can't I?" Hud shrugged.

Rosie stiffened, then faced forward again and closed her eyes, but her eyelashes fluttered as if she was trying to peek at him.

She'd printed off his voting record. There was a defense bill he'd voted for that she'd written "mistake" next to, but a medical bill he'd helped write had "good piece of work" scribbled next to it. Hud relaxed against the seat, agreeing with her. He'd voted for the defense bill in exchange for a vote on a childcare bill from a Texas senator although the defense bill was loaded with pork.

He flipped to a clipping of his debate team winning the state championship his senior year in high school. There was a small picture of him in action looking as if he could conquer the world. "That was a lifetime ago."

"I suppose it was hard to face the reality that everything you touch doesn't turn to gold." Her finger twitched on the door handle as if she were impatient to get away from him.

She was a piece of work and Hud was going to enjoy making her see things his way. "Everyone goes through a teenage phase of immortality."

"Yours just lasted longer than others." She cast a sideways glance in his direction, a smile tugging at the corner of her mouth.

"I hadn't realized putting me in my place had become a blood sport. Or that one of the aides to the Democratic chairman would enjoy it so much."

Without a word, Rosie looked out the window as if he'd struck a nerve. Why was she so determined to point out his flaws? He returned his attention to her file in case it held the answer.

Just behind the article was a picture of that year's debate team. Hud's eyes weren't as good as they used to be and he had to lift the photo closer to look at the once familiar faces, including his own naively confident visage. Standing next to him was Samuel, looking as bored and out of place as he'd ever been at anything that their father cared about. Hud passed his fingers over the photo.

"That's my brother," Hudson said when he trusted himself to speak. Thinking of Samuel was sometimes like that. There were days when Hud could talk about him easily and others when his throat trapped all the emotion inside him.

"People loved him," she pointed out, as if rubbing it in that Hud was the less popular brother.

"He liked making friends, but he had no interest in politics." Much to the family's dismay. And Hud's. It would have been easier on him if he didn't have to shoulder all the hopes of the family.

"He didn't have the drive."

"Like I do."

"Like you used to have," Rosie corrected him, giving him a view of the curls on the back of her head.

"I am very driven. And I have lots of friends who find me intriguing." He hadn't meant to let Rosie get to him.

"I call them as I see them." Her voice was flat, as if she thought Hud wasn't worth arguing over.

"And you know this by reading my file." She didn't

know Hud at all. "Maybe there are things that aren't in my file—that might make you feel differently."

"I've been trained to be a judge of what sells and what works in the system. It's my professional opinion, nothing more."

He wasn't going to take this setback lying down. Rosie DeWitt didn't know it yet, but her professional opinion was about to change.

"MOMMY!" Casey stumbled away from the table where he'd been sitting and watching the clock. He ran to Rosie on coltish legs that seemed to get longer every week. "Did you forget today was an early day?"

The doctor predicted Casey would be at least six foot five, which shocked Rosie, who only stood five foot three on bad hair days when the fog or rain frizzed her hair an additional vertical inch.

Casey loped past the one other boy still waiting to be picked up, leaping over the action figures he'd spread across the carpet and landing in a way that almost sent him crashing to his knees. Instead of falling, her son hurtled into her, hugging Rosie as only a child can hug.

"I'm sorry, pumpkin."

On the other side of the glassed entryway, Hudson waited in his car, unaware that Rosie planned to walk home in her bare feet if the rain let up at all. Would he see anything of Samuel in Casey? Or was he too self-involved to notice? She was betting on the latter.

Unwilling to release the love of her life, Rosie half carried, half dragged her son toward the door. Casey squealed with joy and clung tighter until she set him down at the wall of cubbies so they could grab his backpack and a stack of notices.

"It's Friday. Pizza night! Pizza night!" Casey moved in a jolting rendition of a dance he'd seen advertising an amusement park as Rosie retrieved his coat. Casey raised his arms to the ceiling. "Pep-per-oni! Pep-per-on-i!" Then he looked at her expectantly.

The Friday night pizza dance was one of their rituals and considering she was late again, Rosie didn't dare short her child on anything else. "Ve-ge-tables. Ve-ge-tables." She pumped her arms and moved her hips. If Hudson was watching from his car, maybe now he'd understand how much he lacked in personality.

Casey's lip thrust out. "Gross, not mushrooms."

"Yum, and green peppers." Not daring to look behind her at the street, she kept dancing. Now would be a good time for it to stop raining so they could ditch Hudson and walk home.

"No, Mommy," Casey said, putting a hand on her arm, as serious as the uncle he'd never met and Rosie didn't want to introduce him to. "I'm gonna tell Chin-Chin only pepperoni on mine."

"Deal." Rosie stopped dancing and brushed her finger over his nose. "But only if you eat salad first, Case."

Rosie wished Ms. Phan a good weekend and turned to find Hudson holding the day care door open for them with one hand and an umbrella in the other. With a smile at Casey, Hudson gestured toward his open car door, barely visible through the steady curtain of rain.

Holding her breath, Rosie searched Hudson's expression for any indication that he saw some resemblance between Samuel and Casey. Not that there were many. Other than his height, Casey took after Rosie's side of the family.

"I asked Graham to turn on the radio," Hudson said,

obviously trying not to laugh, but the effort only empha-
sized the cleft in his chin. "In case you wanted to rock
out in the car."

Instead of sinking against the wall in relief because
Hudson hadn't recognized any of the McCloud attributes
in Casey's features, Rosie gave Hudson *the look,* the one
perfected from years of being a mom, the one that said,
"You have got to be kidding me."

"Who are you?" Casey asked, backing up a step and
rolling his head back so he could see Hudson's face.

"I'm Hudson McCloud. Your mom's going to get me
elected mayor."

Ms. Phan made an excited noise and came over to
shake Hudson's hand.

Hudson snuck a triumphant glance at Rosie that
seemed to say, "See, people like me."

"I love your mother," Ms. Phan gushed, causing
Hudson's smile to falter.

"Most people do," Rosie acknowledged, grateful that
it was only two blocks to Chin-Chin's Pizzeria and Noodle
House and their apartment above it. Her toes were cold
and—hallelujah—the ride with Hudson would be too
short for much conversation.

Once they were belted into the car and Graham had
been given instructions, Casey pressed his nose to the
glass and asked, "Can we go to the video store?"

Trying to keep her thigh from touching Hudson's,
Rosie inched closer to Casey. "Let me change first." And
get rid of Hudson.

Casey noticed his breath fogged the window and after
emitting several gusts of air, he drew circles on the glass.
"No, I want to ride in the car."

"We'll drive you," Hudson offered too eagerly.

"Awesome." Casey wiped his drawings away, then began blowing on the glass again.

"I'm sure you have business you need to attend to," Rosie said, tucking her left arm closer to her chest. The less time Hudson spent with Casey the better.

"I don't bite," Hudson said, chuckling.

"I'm not going to find out," Rosie retorted, leaning farther away from him as they turned the corner.

With a glance over his shoulder at Rosie, Casey asked, "Can we go? Plea-ea-ease." He gave her a toothy grin. "We never get to drive anywhere."

"There's a video store a few blocks up," Graham pointed out, inclining his gray head.

"That's the one!" Casey bounced in his seat. "This is so cool. I wish we had a car like this."

Hudson leaned across Rosie, brushing his shoulder against hers as he spoke to Casey. "You could have a car like this at your disposal every day."

"That's slick." Rosie spoke through gritted teeth, trying to ignore how his eyes sparkled when they looked at her. "Now you're bribing me?"

"It's not a bribe." Hudson smiled. "It's a perk."

They passed Chin-Chin's and Rosie suppressed sounds of annoyance.

"I want the cartoon with the mermaid. The one you like." Casey swung his feet, trying to reach the seat in front of him. "Mommy likes it because the mermaid falls in love. We don't have a daddy."

Rosie put a hand on one of Casey's thin legs. "Settle down. You have to be on your best behavior in the store. No running, use your quiet voice and stay with me."

Graham pulled into a small parking space in front of

the video store. The rain was still coming down. And down. And down. Today wasn't Rosie's day for breaks.

"You can wait here," Rosie said to Hudson, trying to make it sound more like a command than an option.

"And miss out on mermaids? Not a chance." Hudson's grin was unexpectedly mischievous.

That couldn't be. Hudson was the somber, straight-laced, unlikable McCloud. And Rosie wanted him to stay that way.

CHAPTER FOUR

"CASEY MENTIONED you're having pizza for dinner," Hud said as they pulled up in front of Rosie's apartment. "I like pizza."

"Are you trying to come over for dinner? 'Cause my mom says you need to wait to be asked." Clutching his movies, Casey's eyes were *uh-oh* wide at Hud's transgression. "Besides, those are work clothes. We don't eat in work clothes."

Strike one.

"How about if dinner is my treat? There. I asked you to dinner, not the other way around." He turned, his face inches from Rosie's and let his gaze drift to her lips. They were incredible, kissable lips. Surely, she knew that.

Without looking at him, Rosie ran her tongue across her bottom lip and shook her head.

Strike two.

Pointing at his mother with his thumb, Casey explained in a whisper, "That usually means no."

Strike three.

Hud wasn't much of a baseball fan, but he needed a second chance at bat. As soon as the car stopped, he leapt out and opened his umbrella, then bent over to help Rosie out, taking her petite hand in his. She lifted her head to look at him as they stood huddled together in the shelter of the umbrella, the rain a curtain around them. And there it was—the spark.

"We can't leave things like this," Hud blurted. He meant the endorsement of the party, of course.

There they stood, staring at each other as if they were lovers and this was the last time they'd see each other. Her riotous curls had become even wilder during the day and framed her face in a way that made her dark chocolate eyes seem huge. If he hadn't been holding her hand between them, he might have reached up and brushed a curl off her cheek. All in the name of keeping her off balance, of course.

With a shriek of excitement, Casey hopped out and ran across the sidewalk into the apartment building foyer. He held the door open by leaning at a forty-five degree angle. "Mommy, come on."

Rosie blinked and let go of Hud's hand.

"He's a great kid," Hud said. He'd always heard moms were suckers for a compliment about their children.

"Nice try, but the answer is still no." She started for the door, leaving him no choice but to follow with the umbrella.

Hud took over doorman duties from Casey. Rain bounced off the ground angrily. Barefoot, Rosie stood in the foyer clutching her bag containing his file and those shoes of hers she protected like the crown jewels. Casey bounded up the stairs while their gazes locked once more.

"We'll meet again," Hud promised.

"I think not." Rosie turned and headed toward the stairs.

Turn around. If she looked once more, he had a chance. At what, he wasn't sure.

Turn around.

Rosie hesitated on the fifth step, but she didn't look

back. And then she continued to climb. Hud let the door swing shut and retreated to the car.

"Where to?" Graham asked.

"Home." To change. It was pizza night and, according to Hud's source, nobody ate pizza with work clothes on.

LESS THAN AN HOUR LATER, Rosie pounded across her apartment's hardwood floor in blue jeans and a T-shirt, mumbling, "That better not be Hudson McCloud." She yanked open the door.

An umbrella with ducklings on it clattered to the parquet floor. Looking like a gypsy with her dark hair beneath a scarf, Selena held up hands splattered with neon blue paint, dropping a leash as she did so. "We come in peace."

Something big, furry and four-legged bumped Rosie out of its way.

"Wet dog! Wet dog!" Selena ran inside the apartment after him, clumping across the floor in purple plastic rain-boots adorned with leaping frogs. "I'm sorry. I should have held on to the leash."

Casey was giggling even though Axel had him pinned against the couch and was trying to eat what was left of his cookie. Rosie ran to get a towel. When she returned, Selena was still trying to control the overly friendly beast.

"Here." Rosie tossed a towel over the dog's back just as he started to shake the water out of his fur.

Chaos erupted and Rosie ran to get more towels amidst Selena's apologies.

"Now that Drew is *too old* for anything that isn't played with a ball, I brought over the finger-paint set that used to be his. It's great for rainy days," Selena explained. Rosie envied the way Selena handled everything with Drew confidently, as if he were her second, not her first and only, child. Selena coaxed Axel into laying down and began rubbing his belly. "I didn't mean to unleash Axel on you, but he had to go out and I thought I'd kill two birds with one stone."

"No harm done." Holding a towel, Rosie scanned the living room for more water to wipe up.

"Really? You looked like you were going to kill me when you opened the door."

"She thought you were the mayor," Casey said, tossing a towel on the floor.

"Oh, wow. Today was the day you met the McClouds. How did that go?" Selena dropped her voice. "Was Hudson as handsome in person as he is on camera?"

Rosie chose to overlook this last question. "I turned them down."

"Then who were you expecting?" As soon as Selena stopped rubbing Axel's stomach, the near pony-sized dog rolled to his feet, ready for action.

"The mayor," Casey repeated as if Selena was missing something obvious.

"Hudson gave us a ride home and told Casey— repeatedly—that I was going to help him get elected mayor."

"And my mom doesn't lose." Casey spoke with pride, making Rosie smile and hug her little champion.

"You know, Rosie," Selena began, rising to her feet. "A lot of the candidates you take on have a strong sense of ethics and truly want to help people, but just once, for me, could you back someone single and gorgeous, like Hudson McCloud?"

Rosie laughed despite the drama of the day. "How can you expect me to offer you tea after a remark like that?"

"Just because we're single parents doesn't mean we don't date." Selena paused to smile slyly. "Oh, I forgot. You took an oath of celibacy when you had Casey."

"What's sell-basey?" Casey asked with a confused expression.

Selena bent down to Casey's level. "It's another word for loneliness—"

"Stop, stop, stop. Don't you have a dog to walk?" Rosie pointed to the door.

"I'll go, but remember one thing." Selena held up a finger. "Because you didn't back Hunky McCloud, you missed out on the perfect opportunity to date him and for him to introduce your friends to all his single, rich friends." Selena batted her eyes.

"I don't want to date him or his friends. He's not my type or yours, either." Hudson was off-limits in more ways than one. She hadn't told her friends who Casey's father was, so she didn't expect Selena to understand. "Hudson didn't pass the criteria for a candidate. What makes you think I'd date a guy like that?"

"The way he looks, I'd let that criteria slide."

"I'll see you Thursday at Margo's." Thursday night gatherings at Margo's Bistro had become a ritual for a handful of friends who shared the challenges of single parenthood. Well, at least until recently, when three of the friends—Margo, Nora and Derrick—had found someone special to share love and parenting with. Rosie opened the door for Selena, knowing she hadn't planned to stop long anyway. "Thank you for the paints."

"And the advice. Don't forget to thank me for the advice." Selena grinned as she dragged Axel out the door and down the back stairs to the alley where she'd parked her car.

"TIME TO PLACE our order, Case." Rosie dug her wallet out of her purse. Pizza night meant descending the stairs to Chin-Chin's to place their dinner order.

"All right." Casey rolled off the couch where they'd been watching a movie together and where he'd contracted a severe case of bed-head.

"Go brush your hair." Rosie pointed to the bathroom. She'd pulled hers back into a simple ponytail.

"Mrs. Chin doesn't care how I look," Casey pouted, dragging his feet down the hallway.

"But I do," Rosie called after him. When Casey wasn't presentable, Rosie felt as if every parent judged her and found her lacking.

They placed their order, but not before Mrs. Chin, grandmother of twelve, chastised Rosie for not making Casey eat something more nutritious—"Maybe squid? Or shrimp on his pizza?"—which caused Casey's stress level to ratchet to Defcon 4, more commonly known as wailing-and-close-to-tears. Drained, they climbed up the creaky wooden stairs with their salads to their apartment with the promise of a phone call when their pizza was ready.

As they began eating their ordinary lettuce with ranch dressing, Rosie started to regret missing her meal at Plouf, which made her think of Hudson once more. The man had hardly left her thoughts all afternoon. Why couldn't Hudson see he had no future in politics if he didn't open up and explain his past? And why had Hudson awakened her hibernating libido?

"Mommy, why can't I have a little brother? Everyone else has one." Casey blinked in faux innocence as if it was the first time he'd asked.

The question was loaded with pitfalls, so Rosie set

aside thoughts of Hudson and considered her words carefully. "First off, not everyone has a little brother. I don't."

"You don't count." Casey was quite good at pouting. If she wasn't his mother, she might have fallen for that look and felt sorry for him.

"Secondly, you need a daddy around to get a little brother. I'm afraid it's just you and me." She'd told Casey his daddy had gone to heaven. Thankfully, he hadn't ask many questions about Samuel. Rosie dreaded the day when she had to explain she hadn't known Casey's father well enough to find out if she loved him or not. Marriage had certainly never been discussed. She wasn't going to be Casey's best role model for abstinence.

"Why do you have to be so *old?*" Casey slumped and fingered a chess piece he'd brought to the table.

Considering Rosie was only twenty-nine, she gave her son the look of disapproval she'd learned upon seeing it so often from her own mom. It was the same look she'd given Hudson earlier.

"You're not a kid, Mommy." Casey squirmed, not willing to give up just yet. "I don't have anyone to play with at home, not even a dog."

"Oh, so it's a choice between a dog *or* a little brother?"

"I'm bored all the time." Casey caught her gaze as it drifted over to the window sill where the paintings they'd made this afternoon dried, and added petulantly, "And you're always working."

That was so unfair. Rosie pushed the lettuce around with her fork, refusing to let Casey see he'd upset her. She'd turned down numerous assignments because she couldn't accompany candidates on most evening or out-of-state appearances. She tried not to work until after Casey went to bed. Rosie put her son first as much as possible and despite that he was still able to make her feel guilty.

Casey wasn't about to let up. "Mo-mmy—"

Someone knocked on the door. If they weren't busy downstairs, Mrs. Chin sometimes delivered.

"That's our pizza. Why don't you get out the plates, Case?"

"I hate setting the table." Casey crossed his thin arms over his chest.

"It's only two plates. You'd hate it more if you had another place to set…say for a little brother."

"PIZZA'S HERE." Hud held up the take-out boxes when Rosie's face didn't register a warm smile of welcome. She wore relaxed blue jeans and a short T-shirt that hugged her curves, but Rosie seemed wound up tighter than the curls she'd caught in a ponytail at the nape of her neck. "I ordered breadsticks and noodles, too."

"Is that the mayor?" Casey peeked from behind the door.

Rosie scowled at Casey's reference, while Hud's smile widened.

"Hey, you don't have work clothes on." The boy wiggled past Rosie's leg and took in Hud's jeans and sweater with an approving nod. "We already watched the videos, so you missed out."

Given Rosie's closed expression, the boy was going to be his best bet to get inside. Hud bent his knees to bring him closer to the kid's level. "I offered to buy you dinner. But when I stopped in downstairs they said you'd already ordered, so I did the next best thing—I delivered it."

"You shanghaied our dinner?" Rosie crossed her arms over her chest.

Kneeling at her feet, Hud gave Rosie his most charming grin. "I told you we had to talk. I'll let you have your food if you let me in."

"Are you someone's daddy?" Imitating his mom, Casey crossed his twiglike arms over his chest. Hudson recognized the calculating expression on the little guy's face. "I don't think you are 'cause daddies don't steal people's pizza."

"I'm not a daddy," Hud confirmed with a wink. "And it would only be stealing if I ate it all myself."

"Good, 'cause my mommy's sell-batey and I don't have a little brother." Casey's long face split into a grin as he gazed up at Rosie. "I like the mayor."

Hud straightened and tried to look innocent, wondering what "sell-batey" meant in adult speak.

"Casey," Rosie warned. She seemed more tense than when she'd first opened the door.

The kid stood at attention and tried to tow his mother's line. "Leave him outside, Mommy. We can call the cops. Stealing isn't nice."

"I agree," Rosie said, reaching for her pizza with a dangerous gleam in her eye. "Hand over the food slowly and no one gets hurt."

Hud took a step back, his mind racing. He could see the small table behind them with two take-out containers with salad, glasses of milk and a chess piece. Gambling, Hud appealed to Casey again. "Tell you what. If you let me in, I'll play a game of chess with you."

"You play chess?" the little guardian asked with interest.

"I haven't played in a long time, but I still remember how." Things were looking up. "It was one of my favorite games as a kid."

Casey tried pushing the door open wider but Rosie held firm. "You can't con your way in by sweet-talking my five-year-old."

In spite of the stakes, Hud was enjoying their wrangling.

"What does *con* mean?" Casey asked before Hud could regroup.

"He's trying to trick you. I doubt he knows how to play chess."

With a gasp, Casey shook his finger at Hud. "Lying and stealing aren't nice. Mr. Stephanopolis at the park is good at chess. He doesn't lie and he's better at chess than you."

"Probably." Hud looked at Rosie. "I bet Mr. Stephanopolis never stole someone's pizza."

Rosie shook her head, but her expression wasn't as foreboding as before.

"Mr. Quan at the senior center is better than you," Casey continued.

"Most likely." This had not been the best of days for Hud's ego.

"I could beat you in less than ten moves."

Hud didn't skip a beat. "You could probably beat me in five."

Rosie's little doorman grinned. "That would be *so* cool." Taking Rosie by surprise, Casey stepped back and opened the door wider. "Come on in."

"I'LL GET THE CHESS SET." Casey scampered down the hall to his room as Hudson elbowed his way into her home and shut the door.

Rosie blocked Hudson's path to the table. He loomed above her wearing the victorious grin of the devil wrapped in a rain-splattered jacket and blue jeans. "Of all the low creatures on the planet, you have got to be the lowest. Manipulating a little boy like that—"

"Any manipulating was purely on Casey's part. That boy definitely inherited your political savvy. You didn't see that coming, did you?" Hudson moved to the left, but she sidestepped.

Rosie didn't want to think where Casey's skills came from or fall prey to the impulse to laugh with Hudson at Casey's cleverness. "Why don't you just hand over the pizza and make your apologies?" She reached for the box again, but Hudson lifted it out of her grasp. With a glance behind her, Rosie lowered her voice. "He's sharp, but I'll look like the bad guy if I ask you to go. A gentleman would leave."

"I think we've already established that you don't believe I'm a gentleman." Hudson moved to the right, but so did she. "I didn't have lunch and I've been holding this very tasty-smelling pizza so long, I could eat the box. So if you could save your remarks until I've had a couple bites, I'll be more able to defend myself."

"I don't want you to be able to defend yourself." It was bad enough she was constantly on guard around him.

"Afraid you won't be able to argue your way out of this? All you've done today is run away."

Rosie was so flabbergasted that Hudson managed to get past her. She followed him to the kitchen. "I had to leave our meeting because I had a lunch appointment. I had to leave *my* lunch meeting to pick up Casey."

"You forgot to mention how you fled upstairs instead of standing your ground with me after the video store. See? Running." Hudson put the food on the counter and began opening her cupboards. "Where are the plates?"

"I'm not getting rid of you until I hear you out, am I?"

"No."

With a sigh, Rosie admitted defeat and gave Hudson a plate. "We drink milk with dinner. You aren't allergic by any chance…?"

"No." His triumphant smile transformed his otherwise stern face. "We'll talk after I play chess, right?"

"What choice do I have?"

"YOU'RE NOT GOING TO let me win, are you?" Casey scratched his head, sending a lock of hair sticking out as he leaned over the chess board.

They sat at the small oak kitchen table with the undersized living room to one side and the miniscule kitchen to the other. As big as Hud was, he should have felt cramped. Instead, it felt welcoming. Rosie's home was an eclectic mix of San Francisco's cultures—from a tie-dyed tea towel in the kitchen to a Chinese calendar on the wall to a large abalone shell on the mantel—set against more traditional furnishings.

"Do you want me to let you win?" They'd only just started the game and Hud wanted to know the rules early. Although Rosie was in the living room reading the paper, Hud could tell she was listening.

Casey looked up from studying the board. He'd inherited his serious brown eyes from his mother. "No. I can't get better if you let me win."

"You need to earn it," Hud agreed. Still, he hoped the kid was sharp enough to beat him if he played sloppy.

Casey nodded and returned his attention to the board.

After some consideration, Hud moved his queen—in this case the salt shaker since Casey couldn't find the white queen—out onto the board. He'd already advanced a couple of pawns and a knight. Five moves in and Hud hadn't lost yet.

"You don't think ahead," Casey noted, inching a pawn forward.

"I'm not afraid to put my power pieces into play." Hud sent his bishop out to take Casey's pawn.

"That won't win games." Casey took Hud's bishop with his knight. "Check."

Hud hadn't seen that coming. Was he going to be defeated in ten moves?

Later, after Casey had beaten Hud twice in less than twenty moves, Hud was that much closer to a straight conversation with Rosie. She poured coffee into mugs and tried to send Casey to the bathtub.

"Just one more game, Mommy." Casey sat in a chair at the table with his head on his arms, looking up at Hud as if he was Casey's hero. It felt nice.

"Bath tub." Rosie put an edge on the command. "This is the second time I've asked."

Casey slid out of his chair and ambled toward the hall, touching the couch, the curio cabinet and the television as if searching for a reason to pause.

"Go," Rosie ordered. When he was gone, she admitted, "Sometimes I feel like such a bad mom. I'm constantly nagging and worrying and late…" She trailed off.

"He seems like a good kid to me. I haven't seen him throw himself on the ground in a screaming fit or pick his nose."

The sound of water thundering into a bathtub was muffled by a door closing.

"Let's hope you don't see that." Her smile included Hud, which was a refreshing change from the dagger-filled expressions she'd given him earlier today. "How do you take your coffee?"

"Black." She looked worn out, more in need of a glass

of wine than coffee. "Should you be drinking that stuff this late at night?"

"Are you kidding? After Casey goes to bed my second shift starts. I work every night until about midnight." Rosie's admission came as no surprise. She'd gotten far for one so young. She brought him a mug with a Chinese proverb on it—A fall into a ditch makes you wiser.

Well, he'd already fallen and considered himself bruised, but less gullible.

"You can't get ahead without putting in the extra time." Rosie sat across from him.

"I know that." Here was the opening he'd been looking for. "I've spent all week looking critically at the situation in the city. I have several ideas—"

"Before you go any further, let's go back to the two obstacles you'll need to overcome—the allegations behind your resignation from the Senate and—"

"If you insist on telling me that I have no personality after the day we've had, I may have to call in character witnesses." Hud couldn't believe how closed-minded Rosie was being about this.

"You're missing the point completely." Rosie covered his hand with hers ever so briefly, but long enough to stir his pulse. "In the public's mind you've become this icon of wealth and power. You're a myth, a fairy tale." Avoiding his gaze, she added cream to her coffee. "You lock yourself away in a tower, don't grant interviews, don't admit to missteps or misfortunes. Of course, the voters can't identify with you."

Hud's face felt wooden. "So you think Roger Bartholomew is a better choice?"

"It would be more to my liking if Roger switched parties and ran for the Republicans." Rosie still wouldn't look at him, paying careful attention to the sugar she was adding to her mug.

Relief deflated some of the fight out of him. Hud sat back in his chair and reached for his coffee.

"What is wrong with getting up close and personal with the public? You've been in my face all day, and let me tell you, that was quite a surprise." Rosie laughed softly, almost to herself. "I had no idea that you were so…"

"Determined? Driven?"

Rosie looked at him levelly then said, "I was going to say creative and ballsy. I wouldn't have approached a rejection quite the way you did."

"But it worked." At least, so far. Promising things were lurking just beneath the surface between them.

She shook her head. "I didn't think you were like your brother in any way, but you are."

"You knew Samuel?"

"Mommy, come shampoo my hair."

Rosie held her coffee mug midway to her lips, as if she realized she'd said more than she should have.

CHAPTER FIVE

"DID THE MAYOR leave yet?" Casey asked, sailing a pirate ship in the bubbly water.

"Not yet." Rosie lathered Casey's curls with strawberry shampoo.

Distance. Rosie needed distance between herself and Hudson. Physical space would be nice because she couldn't stop noticing things she shouldn't be noticing. Like the easy way he talked to Casey or how broad his shoulders were beneath that sweater. Shoulders like that could support more than his share of burdens, adding to Hudson's appeal as a candidate for a woman wrenched between work and family responsibilities. Hypothetically, of course.

"I like him." Casey steered the boat around a large clump of bubbles. "He doesn't play chess good."

"He's easy to beat. Is that what you're saying?" Rosie picked up a plastic measuring cup and handed Casey a washcloth. She waited until he covered his face with the small towel before she began rinsing the soap from his hair.

Blinking, Casey blew raspberries to get the excess water from his mouth. "It's fun to win."

Rosie couldn't argue with that, but said, "We're not keeping him."

Casey looked up at her with his pouty lower lip thrust out.

"Don't even think about it." Rosie had best heed her own advice. Hanging out with Hudson, considering she didn't plan to tell him he was Casey's uncle, was wrong.

Rosie couldn't figure out the attraction. Hudson was pompous and arrogant, his actions as a senator questionable. With a sigh, Rosie left Casey to face the man she knew was going to have questions about Samuel. Questions she had no intention of answering. If it came to telling the truth or lying, Rosie was determined not to say anything.

Silently, Hudson's eyes bored into Rosie as she crossed the living room. He cradled his coffee mug as if it was the only thing anchoring him to his chair. With a tilt of his dark head, cleft chin at a determined angle, he watched her take a seat. His shrewd whiskey-colored eyes took in every breath, every movement as she sipped her coffee.

"You dated him," Hudson blurted, practically spitting with anger.

"How did—"

"And he broke your heart." Hudson's eyes narrowed. "So now you're taking it out on me."

"I'm not—"

"Do you know how many women come up to me and tell me they once had sex— Excuse me." Hudson closed his eyes briefly and when he opened them he seemed calmer. "*Dated* Samuel?"

"Lots?" It seemed the simple answer given his state of mind, although it hurt her to say.

Hudson's lip curled in disgust. "In college, my brother and Roger kept a running total of women they slept with. One year the loser had to buy the winner an airline ticket to Paris."

"Paris?" Rosie's skin crawled. She hadn't known anyone Samuel hung out with in college. She'd only known the famous McCloud attended Berkeley at the same time she did. And then they'd both been part of the college sponsored trip to Paris after graduate school ceremonies. Samuel's reputation as a player preceded him, but she'd been starstruck by the fact that he was a McCloud. What they shared may not have been love, but it hadn't been just sex, either. Samuel had respected her. Rosie clung to the belief as tightly as she clung to her coffee cup.

"I'm surprised more women don't come up to me claiming to be raising my niece or nephew," Hudson continued harshly.

"More? How many woman have claimed to…" If there had ever been a time in Rosie's life she'd wanted to faint, it was now. Hudson's face swam out of focus.

He didn't seem to notice. "A few. Our lawyers kept it quiet. I don't know how we got so lucky."

Is that how he would have treated her? Rosie pinched her leg and rubbed her forehead before she gave herself away. She knew the McCloud brothers hadn't been close, but until now she hadn't realized Samuel's lifestyle may have hurt his family. She couldn't begin to imagine what Vivian had been through or how she felt.

"Yes, we dated," Rosie admitted. "No, he didn't break my heart. Samuel was not the kind of guy a girl saw a future with." Especially not this girl. She'd vowed not to be *that brainy girl* on her trip to Paris. She hadn't packed a sensible item of clothing. Yet, despite short skirts and hints of cleavage, she and Samuel had spent hours just talking. They'd had conversations about politics, music and the snobby French, the war, meddlesome parents and San Francisco's persnickety weather. If Samuel had wanted to get a jump start on his tally for the new year, Rosie would have only shared one night with him, not three.

Hudson's scrutiny was intense as he waited for more information.

Uh-huh. She'd said more than she'd intended. Besides, who did he think she was? A vindictive woman who was going to kiss and tell? Ick.

"I'm offended that you'd assume I'd allow my professional opinion to be colored by something that happened years ago." Rosie needed Selena's froggy boots because she was in muddy waters here. Casey was the reason she didn't want to work with Hudson, but she wouldn't be in this predicament if it weren't for Samuel and condoms that weren't one hundred percent effective.

Hudson slowly turned his coffee cup around, gazing into its depths as if he could obtain some kind of guidance. When he finally spoke, his voice had a raw, defeated quality to it that she hadn't heard all day. "I jumped to conclusions I shouldn't have. I'm sorry. It's just…" He lifted his gaze to hers. The anger was gone, but the hurt lingered at the corners of his eyes. "I'm tired of being prejudged."

It was a huge concession for Hudson, but Rosie knew he had to open up even more to win an election.

And she wasn't sure he could do it.

"THE ONLY WAY to change how people feel about you is to start a dialogue of some sort, even if it's only one-sided through selective interviews and advertising you control. Saying nothing changes nothing." Rosie tilted her head as she waited to gauge Hud's reaction.

She had an expressive face that conveyed her emotions too easily—not the best trait for a career in politics. He'd watched her react with shock and embarrassment when he confronted her about Samuel. Yet despite being indignant by the episode, she hadn't kicked his butt out to the pavement which gave Hud hope that she was finally coming around. The more time he spent with Rosie, the more he wanted her guiding his campaign.

"I won't address anything from my past," he said. "I want this focused toward the future."

"The McCloud name will only take you so far. The Republicans will find you fair game if you stick to your vow of silence." As if the finality of her words wasn't enough, the look in her eyes seemed to pity him.

"Why jump the gun? It may not be an issue." Wishful thinking on his part, but Hud wasn't ready to give in just yet.

Rosie rubbed her temple. "This is textbook Campaign Tactics 101. Attack your opponent's greatest weakness."

"I say we wait it out." Yes, *we*. She sounded as if she'd softened and was willing to endorse him. He didn't have much more time. Casey wouldn't be in that bathtub forever.

Her gaze became guarded. "I haven't said I'll back you."

"But…" After the day they'd spent together… After the bond he'd made with her son… She hadn't said no. "You're going to."

Rosie shook her head. "It just doesn't seem right. We argue about everything, about the basics of how your campaign should be run. I know how to win and I manage my candidates accordingly."

"We wouldn't argue once we settle things." He put on his best smile. "Well, at least not all the time."

She averted her gaze, making Hud nervous. Next she'd be asking him to leave.

"You only take on impossible candidates. I'm perfect

for you." He tried to keep the desperation from his voice. "You're my best shot. Without you..."

"You're not ready." She cut him off gently, touching his hand once more. "There will be other races, other handlers. Don't quit politics just because I won't endorse you this time."

"I am not a quitter!" He'd held his peace for two years, but he couldn't hold back from her. "I left office because I had to."

Rosie set down her mug. "Someone forced you out of office?"

Was Hud really going to tell her? He shouldn't say anything. If he said too much... "This is not for public consumption."

"If you were forced out, people deserve to know." Her gaze drew him in with its sincerity. She wanted to believe in him. "Everything in your life is public domain and—"

Hud pounded the table with his fist. "Not this."

Rosie studied him in that intense way of hers that made Hud feel as if she wanted to find what made him tick, even if it wasn't all good news. "Okay, tell me."

His eyes were drawn to a framed photo hanging on the wall nearby of Rosie and Casey at the beach. She had her arms around him and they were both grinning as if there was no place else they'd rather be. His childhood had been filled with photo ops and campaign junkets. There had been very few lazy days in the park or hugs so tight Hud knew nothing he'd ever do could stop his father from loving him. "I was never involved with the family business. My parents always had other responsibilities for me."

"Like backing your run for city council at age twenty-five?"

He nodded. His father pushed hard for Hud's early

success. If only he'd paid as much attention to the family business. "And serving on several charitable boards. The success of McCloud Inc. guaranteed I'd never have to work a regular day job." Or so he'd assumed. "The company had been set up to fund the political ambitions of the McClouds. It was run by businessmen, not by the family. I don't think a McCloud had made a daily management decision for the company since my great-grandfather's time."

"There's nothing wrong with that."

"There's nothing *right* with that." Hudson paused. He was getting ahead of himself, giving too much away. "When the rumors first broke that our company had benefited from legislation that I authored, I didn't believe it. I went back to my office in D.C. that night and scrutinized the bill, comparing what I'd written to what had finally been signed."

She nodded approvingly, making his partial confession that much harder to make.

Hud glanced once more at the picture of Rosie and Casey. "There was a rider on the bill that was attributed to me but that I hadn't written. Lobbyists sometimes draft legislation as a *favor* to busy politicians and their staff."

"So you looked into it."

Knowing he should have looked into it *before* he signed, Hud kept his gaze averted. "Yes. I had been in touch with a lobbyist for the garment industry who had taken the McCloud CEO and me to lunch a few times. He had submitted several suggestions for legislation, but I wasn't familiar with this piece. It lifted sanctions from companies who were using child labor in other countries." The slimy bastard.

"I read about that, but it was never proven that McCloud followed those practices."

"Never proven, but the damage was done. Nothing I put forth in the Senate after that went through. Democrats distanced themselves from me in case something surfaced that confirmed the rumors. I was dead weight for the party."

"You could have stayed in office. After a year, maybe two, you could have formed alliances." Rosie made it sound cut-and-dry when there were no easy choices.

Anger pulsed in his temple. "Power is a terrible thing to waste. The leadership *encouraged* me to step down. It was even suggested that they'd protect my family's legacy if I did the right thing." What a sucker he'd been to believe them. "My mother had never quite recovered from Samuel's death and it seemed best to get out before she suffered more."

After a long silence, Rosie said, "You felt boxed in so you stepped down."

"Yes." Hud's shoulders relaxed. "So, now you see."

"See what?" There was a slight crease to her brow that worried him.

Hud enveloped her hand in both of his, aware yet not caring that she'd disapprove of the intimacy. "Why I can't trust this campaign to anyone else but you. You're the only one who can turn this around. I'm letting five generations of McCloud senators down if I allow our legacy to end like this."

When she stared at their hands without speaking, he pressed on. "Rosie, you can help me restore the McCloud name to greatness. You have a reputation as a straight shooter. I know you won't hide things or sell me out for your own gain."

"I THINK YOU SHOULD GO." Rosie stood, breaking away from Hudson's touch.

She could keep things from Hudson when she believed he'd bent the rules in the Senate. But knowing he'd been a victim of a double whammy—family circumstances and sharks who called themselves lobbyists—she couldn't do it. She couldn't work for Hudson and keep Casey's heritage a secret, not when he'd shown such high moral standards, that he was willing to give up his career to uphold his family's honor.

And here was Rosie, who'd let her professional goals put her personal responsibilities in jeopardy. She'd been willing to risk the way she was bringing up her son for a chance at working on a presidential campaign. Sickening. Hudson made Rosie feel inferior. Another blow to her less-than-perfect-mommy record. Wasn't that just what she needed?

"I need to finish my coffee." Hudson lifted his mug, his expression inscrutable.

"I need to get Casey out of the bathtub and in bed." Rosie plucked weakly at any excuse.

"Let's talk about what you can do for me first." Hudson's words conjured up much more than she wanted them to, of bedrooms and heated touches. Another reason she couldn't do this. "I'm convinced you're the best chance the McClouds have."

"You've taken up too much of my time." And he'd occupy Rosie's thoughts long after he'd gone.

"I haven't taken enough time." Hudson came around the table, grasped her shoulders and brought his face close to hers as if she were a lover he was about to kiss. "What's your answer, Rosie? I need to hear you say yes."

Somehow, Rosie was able to look Hudson in the eye. "I'll recommend you to the party, but they'll assign you someone else."

"I don't want someone else." Heat radiated from his fingers and his warm breath wafted over her. Who knew Hudson McCloud was this passionate?

Rosie stepped out of his grip. Hudson made her feel like a woman. No one had done that in a long time. She'd been a mother and a good party member and a loyal employee, not a physical being with needs.

He paced around the table, around her. "Do you know what it's like to believe that you've struggled to do the right thing only to find out that nothing was under your control in the first place? To watch your world being turned upside down while you stand by helpless to stop it?"

Boy, did she ever. Like standing in the shadows of a tree at the edge of a cemetery watching the father of your child be buried. Or starting her first job out of college by asking about maternity benefits instead of vacation time.

Hudson came to a stop in front of Rosie with a gaze so raw and hurt, so filled with resigned disappointment it created an almost physical ache within her. She knew how he felt. "All my life I've tried to do the right thing and I realize now I probably acted for the wrong reasons. This time, *this time*," he repeated clenching his fists, "I won't be doing the right thing because it was expected of me or because I have aspirations of glory. I'm just going to do the right thing because it needs to be done."

The fight seemed to drain out of him then. Hudson rubbed the back of his neck and lowered his voice, so that Rosie had to take a step closer to hear what he said. "If I could do it alone, I would. But I can't." Hudson lifted his gaze to hers and Rosie expected him to ask her to help, but all he said was, "I can't."

"WHAT ARE YOU GOING TO SAY?" Hud's mother straightened his tie as they drove to city hall Monday morning to announce his candidacy.

"Rosie wrote me a speech." As of last night, she hadn't finished it, which was worrisome. Hud had offered to work on it with her this weekend, but she'd refused. Since Hud was uncomfortable that it had taken a near meltdown to get Rosie to consent to manage his campaign he hadn't pressed the point, but now he was sorry he hadn't.

"Did you tell her about…?" His tie was suddenly cutting off his air supply.

Hud removed his mother's hands from his throat and wiggled his tie loose, which meant she had to straighten it again. "I told her as much as she needed to know." Hud pushed aside the guilt he had for not divulging everything about what happened two years ago.

"Was that wise?" Stu asked from the front seat.

"I'll take care of it." Hud wasn't sure whether Stu questioned his wisdom for sharing anything with Rosie or for his lack of full disclosure. Noting the worry lines around his mother's eyes, Hud squeezed her hand reassuringly. "That blue suits you."

She smoothed the lapel of her blue raincoat content to pretend along with Hud that they weren't on their way to something vitally important for the McCloud family. "Navy blue was your father's favorite color. I don't know what I would have done if he'd have run for office in a country with a green flag. I suppose I would have looked sickly for years."

"You used to tell that joke ten years ago." Hud remembered when the quote had appeared in *People* magazine.

"I haven't had much to joke about lately." She fiddled with her purse strap.

"That's my fault."

"You had no way of knowing what your father and grandfather had done." She sighed. "And you couldn't have prevented the loss of your father and brother."

"But this hasn't helped." Hud couldn't fill the void in his mother's life. "If you miss Dad so much, you could—"

"Don't even say it. Ladies my age don't date. I'm waiting for grandkids."

"The pickings are looking pretty slim in that direction." Even as he spoke, Hud could picture a leggy, toothpick of a boy holding the hand of a diminutive woman with soft dark eyes. The image was inconsequential. Now that Rosie was on his team he wouldn't jeopardize his campaign by pursuing anything more than a professional relationship with her. Still, it wouldn't do to ignore the attraction altogether. He needed something in his arsenal to keep that ego of hers in line.

"Somebody just ran their Hummer into a city bus. Traffic's not moving," Graham told them. "We might be stuck here ten, twenty minutes."

Hud glanced at his watch. They could walk eight blocks in the rain or sit in traffic.

"I'll go on ahead and hold down the fort," Stu offered.

"MCCLOUDS DON'T STAND OUT on the steps talking to reporters prior to a press conference." Taking Rosie by surprise, Stu swept her inside city hall with a stilted gait and across the crowded Tennessee-pink marble toward an alcove beneath the rotunda.

Feeling the eyes of the press upon her, Rosie lowered her voice and freed her arm. Hud had drawn press and paparazzi befitting a rock star…or a McCloud. "I was just working the crowd. I know some of the reporters and—"

"Reporters are to be managed, otherwise, they can

make your life purgatory." He walked hunched over beneath a drab raincoat, using his umbrella like a cane.

The old man didn't understand the way Rosie needed to run Hudson's campaign and she didn't have much time to argue. "But—"

"I've stood by the McClouds through several elections, and this is the way we do things. You've got heart, but you need to toughen up a bit." Stu stopped at the alcove, a bit out of breath. "We can't have this press conference out in the rain on the steps. It's too gothic."

"I've set up the microphones inside on the rotunda." Rosie stepped out of the alcove and showed the older man before slipping out of her hooded raincoat. Everything had come together too easily over the weekend for her peace of mind.

"Perfect." Stu shook out his umbrella. "Where's Hudson's speech?"

"I've got it right here." Rosie opened a leather portfolio and withdrew two sheets of paper. She'd finished close to midnight.

Stu nabbed it. He was quick for an old guy. "It's not very long," Stu observed before beginning to read. "And you can't mention anything about Hudson's experiences in Washington." Stu withdrew a stubby, chewed pencil from his inner coat pocket and began crossing things out.

"Please don't do that." Rosie's shoulders tensed. Thankfully, she had a second clean copy in her portfolio. The worst that could happen was Stu's feelings would be hurt when Hudson read Rosie's original speech. "Where's Hudson?"

"Stuck in traffic." Stu pointed to a line on the page. "Is this supposed to be a joke? McClouds don't joke. They're not funny."

"Hudson has a strong sense of humor." He'd need one

to put up with Stu. But being late for a campaign kickoff was not funny.

"Hud is a man of stature." Stu crossed out another few lines. "Given his background, I don't think humor is appropriate."

"Why don't we let Hudson decide?" If Hudson got here on time. Rosie's impression of Hudson from Samuel and his press interviews was cold and calculating, a man with his emotions buried so deep he'd forgotten he had them. Hudson had been anything but that on Friday night. She'd been unable to resist his request once he bared his soul. Now all she had to do was figure out how to channel his personality through the media.

"Hudson has so much to worry about already. It's my job to keep things on an even keel and not bother Hudson with trivial details."

"Like speeches," Rosie murmured, watching the crowd of reporters gather in the rotunda.

Stu's cell phone beeped. He squinted at it. "Right on time. Hudson will be here any moment." Stu caught Rosie by the arm again and headed toward the podium. "The three of us should close ranks behind him in a show of support. Vivian will stand behind Hud's left shoulder with you to her left, otherwise, even in your heels no one will see you. I'll stand behind Hudson's right shoulder."

"I prefer to work behind the scenes." Rosie's smile felt strained and she knew her lipstick could use a refresh. They were on a collision course with Hudson and his mother, who waved as if they were royalty, arriving at the dais at the same time as if it had been choreographed. "The last thing I want from this is celebrity."

"You're pretty. The more your face is associated with the campaign, the more useful you'll be." Stu's eye twitched and Rosie worried that he'd scare children watching at home with his caretaker-of-the-cemetery appearance. "Here they are. It's time to start."

Before Rosie could stop him, Stu handed Hudson the hacked speech.

CHAPTER SIX

UNSURE OF THE REACTION he was about to receive, Hudson stepped behind the podium. Would the press embrace or reject him? And how would he handle the inevitable questions about what had happened two years ago? The traffic had been so snarled, he'd been late arriving at city hall and now had no time to review the speech Rosie had prepared.

A glance behind him showed his mother's composed smile, Stu's steadfast look, and Rosie's...slightly annoyed expression. She held a few pages out to him.

"I've got a copy," he whispered, not catching whatever she whispered back as he turned to face the music.

"Thank you all for coming," Hudson adjusted the mic and looked out over the sea of faces watching his every move. He hadn't expected so many to come. Hudson stared down at his speech, surprised to see the number of deletions—the words *while a senator* among them—and the tiny notations in the margins. He hesitated, glancing back at Rosie once more.

Her lips were pursed. Her eyes furious. She shook her head slightly. What in the hell was going on? This was rinky-dink, amateur stuff. Had she waited until this morning to write the speech and crossed out what he'd been reluctant to address at the last minute?

Stu cleared his throat, a signal to proceed. But with

what? The few uncensored lines were inconsequential. His father would have insisted Hud read what he'd been given, stick to what his paid experts recommended. *Don't think, don't question, just do what they tell you, son.* Wasn't that how Hud got into trouble before?

Rosie stepped closer, but Hud stopped her with a slight shake of his head. She'd let him down. Damn it. He'd been so sure Rosie was the right choice, too.

Flipping the pages over, Hudson faced his fate alone. "I imagine most of you know why I'm here." Now if Hud only knew what to say. "Recently…" A lot of shit happened. "San Francisco lost a beloved mayor to tragedy. We're in the process of grieving—" the body was barely cold "—but the agenda for the city must move on."

Reporters scribbled on their pads. A few of the cameramen turned their lenses either for a wider angle or an extremely painful close-up which would capture Hudson ad-libbing his candidacy announcement. There was a lull as they all waited for him to say more.

"As a native of the city, I feel I'm up to the challenge of helping San Francisco continue to move forward, to provide its citizens with a better quality of life and its corporate tenants with an environment for prosperity, while guarding the charm and natural beauty that makes our city unique." Hudson drew in a breath of much needed air. He hadn't fallen on his face yet, no thanks to his new campaign manager. "Therefore, I have decided to run for mayor."

The room dissolved into chaos. Bulbs flashed. Microphones were thrust closer to his face. Hud tried not to cringe.

"Hudson! Hudson!"

"This way! Over here!"

Hudson pointed to a familiar face, a reporter from the *San Francisco Examiner.*

"Can you tell us more about your agenda?" he asked.

"Barry, we'll get into the specifics next week."

A columnist from *San Francisco Living* caught his eye. "There are rumors that one of the Bartholomews is going to run for the Republican party. Any comment?"

"I grew up with Natalie and Roger. Good luck to them." Hudson hoped the surprise didn't show on his face. It was just as Rosie predicted.

"Hudson! Amy Furokawa, Action News." The woman was too thin, lacking curves to soften her sharp edges. And her eyes were hungry, more like a tabloid reporter than a respected newswoman. "What can you say to reassure voters that you won't give up the way you did in the Senate?"

Less than five minutes into the campaign and trouble had already reared its ugly head. Smooth, this wasn't. Out of the corner of his eye, Hud noticed Rosie shift her weight. "I've heard that America is about new beginnings. That's what we're here to talk about today."

It wasn't long afterward that Hud took Rosie by the arm with a taut grip and escorted her down city hall's steps. She and Hud were meeting a Realtor to view empty offices that were potential locations for his campaign headquarters. The rain had let up but the sky was still threateningly gloomy. The reporters had dispersed, and his mother and Stu were headed back to the company's offices, which was a good thing. Hud didn't want any witnesses when he skewered Rosie.

Rosie paused on a step and glanced around, presumably to catch sight of the Realtor. She wore another dark pantsuit, but this time she had on sensible boots and a raincoat. "That wasn't at all what I expected but—"

"Not what you expected?" Hud cut her off. "I was expecting a complete speech, not your notes."

Her eyes narrowed in on him and a lock of hair fell over one eye. She brusquely swept it behind her ear. "I tried to—"

"No. I see how it is." He'd boxed her in on Friday and then she'd had second thoughts all weekend. "You wanted me to look stupid, didn't you? That way you could bail on me with just cause. Well, it didn't work."

Rosie pushed past him down the steps, but Hud was right behind her.

"Hey, I thought I was the one with the reputation as a quitter," he said. "You never even gave me a fair chance."

She spun around and tapped him on his tie clip. "First off, I tried to hand you the right speech but you were just a little too preoccupied with the limelight to pay attention to me." Rosie leaned in closer staring up at him with a stormy gaze that rivaled the clouds above them. "And secondly, never—ever—take a speech from anyone else but me. That was my speech in your hands, but Stu had decided it needed fine tuning. Never mind that you came in at the last second like a prima donna without even checking with me."

He could have been mistaken, but it looked like smoke was coming out of her ears. Hud opened his mouth to say something, he hadn't quite determined just what, when they were interrupted.

"Hudson, can you spare a minute for an interview?" It was Amy Furokawa. The reporter hurried over, gaze locked on Hudson, microphone in hand. It was probably already turned on.

"Amy, I'm so sorry." Moving in front of Hud, Rosie cut the reporter off, friendly but firm. "We've got a tight schedule this morning. Perhaps later today."

Amy's steps slowed. "Certainly. I've got your number," she said with a forced smile.

Now it was Rosie who took Hud's arm and steered him down the steps toward a large, black Mercedes. A classically dressed older woman waved at them through its open window.

Rosie opened the car's back door for Hud. "We'll continue this discussion later." Her eyes flashed with intent to maim, but her tone was strictly business.

If Rosie expected him to roll over and be silently obedient, she had another thing coming. "I see your point, but remember mine." He bent down so that only she could hear. "You could have stopped me at any time if you really wanted to."

Rosie rolled her eyes, then slid into the front seat and started chatting with the realtor as if she'd had the most pleasant morning, leaving Hud to fume alone in the backseat like a misbehaving child while they wove through the city.

Okay, so his speech had been appropriated by Stu, but Rosie could have been more aggressive in trying to stop him from using it. Rosie was just trying to make the point that she was in charge, but no matter how much Hud valued her opinion, he wasn't letting someone else take the reins of his future. Not this time.

Rosie didn't even get out at the first stop. She just pressed her nose to the window and said, "No."

"What's wrong with it?" Hud asked. The marble entryway was imposing and the address near the Embarcadero Center was impressive.

"Too sterile."

So it was on to the next one on Market Street.

Rosie got out for that one, walked around the lobby,

keeping a careful distance between herself and Hud. "Let's see what else is out there." Obviously, she didn't want or care for Hud's opinion.

Still too angry to make nice, Hud decided to wait until they walked through the office itself, not the lobby, before he'd weigh in on the decision.

The next space was on the bottom floor of a converted warehouse in SOMA. It had scuffed linoleum, shabby cubicles, beat-up desks and floor to ceiling windows that the press was going to love. Clearly, it wasn't going to meet Rosie's high standards, nor would it pass Hudn's. He moved closer to the door.

Rosie emerged from a corner office with a radiant smile. "This is perfect."

"This place?" Hud looked around again to see what he'd missed. Nope, it was still the same transparent dump.

"It's on one of the main sidewalks office workers take to get to the bus or Market Street. Commuters drive by here five days a week. Everyone who wants to catch a glimpse of you will." She gazed out the window. "It's ideal."

Hud said, "I don't know." When he really meant no. Couldn't she see that?

"We're taking it." Rosie nodded to the realtor and began punching numbers on her cell phone.

"Could you give us a minute?" Hud asked the realtor, waiting until she was outside before confronting Rosie. "What happened to asking for my approval?"

"You gave that up when you practically begged me to run your campaign."

There was something about the way she didn't back down that made his pulse quicken. It was like when he'd been on the high school debate team and the world was his for the taking. It would have made him smile if he didn't need to get the upper hand with her. "I wanted you running the campaign *with* me, not for me."

With that slight furrow to her brow he was getting used to, Rosie flipped her phone closed and tucked a curl behind her ear. "Are you or are you not a man of the people? Because if you're not, we'll hide you away in one of those glass-and-marble buildings where no one can get past security to see you."

"You aren't afraid of stalkers? Paparazzi?" Hudson shuddered just thinking about his lack of privacy.

"I'll get security, don't worry. And the photographers will tire of having you available all the time. We'll have to put up with them for a week, maybe two." Rosie pointed to the street, her features aglow as if she'd found buried treasure she wanted to share. "Can you just see the photo opportunity when you deliver a press release on your solutions to traffic congestion? You'll be standing next to one of the most overcrowded roads on the planet."

Damn if she didn't make sense. He didn't want her to be right. There had to be some other reason the place was unsuitable. "We're not in a high crime neighborhood, are we? I don't want to be photographed being mugged on the way home at night." That would be hell to live down.

"It's one of the safer districts," Rosie assured him. "Quit trying to veto it just because you're paranoid that I'm out to ruin your career."

Paranoid?

But Rosie wasn't through. "If this is going to work, we're going to have to learn each others' styles. I'm a tad stubborn, especially when I feel someone I'm trying to help isn't listening to me." She blew a curl off her face and Hud realized she was talking about this morning's fiasco.

"But I vent and I get over it. I can see by the cloud that's been hovering above your head all morning that you like to stew about things. Trust me when I say that I don't accept any position that might take me away from Casey unless I'm in it to win. I'm serious about your potential and the potential of this place."

Rosie moved closer and shook his arm as if he were her big brother. *As if?* Not in this lifetime.

"And best of all—" Rosie grinned slyly "—Margo's Bistro is right down the street."

"What's at Margo's Bistro?"

"Great food…and coffee." Rosie's smile was devilish, creating impulses in Hud she had no idea she ignited and he knew right then that Rosie had won this round.

"HANK, I NEED A FAVOR." Rosie closed the door to her new office, which was next to Hudson's. "We're putting together a campaign for Hudson McCloud for mayor."

"So I heard. It was a big news story on *Saturday* when you leaked it to me and every other channel in town," Hank complained. He worked at the third-highest-ranking news station in the city. "I need big news today."

"Would you be interested in assigning someone to the story on a regular basis?" Rosie crossed her fingers. She'd been turned down by two other stations.

"We may have gone to summer band camp together, Rosie, but you know I have to clear everything through the senior staff before I devote resources."

"What about exclusive access to the campaign? Interviews with our candidate…" Hank wasn't biting. Rosie took a chance. "Interviews with his mother—"

"Mrs. McCloud?" The interest in Hank's voice was unmistakable. "She rarely grants interviews anymore."

"That's right. That's got to be worth something." There had to be a way to get the elusive McCloud matriarch to agree to an interview. Rosie would figure that out later.

"We've got a new reporter here that's hungry for a story. You probably saw Amy this morning. Let me see what I can do."

Rosie thanked him and flipped to the next contact on her list, an Internet blogger. Campaigns were all about sound bites and buzz, and Rosie was good at creating both.

"I'M NOT AN ACTOR," Hudson grumbled with his back turned to the street. Rosie made him take off his suit jacket and loosen his tie, but when he balked at rolling up his sleeves, she stepped forward to do it herself.

"Nobody gets work done in a suit," Rosie replied, trying hard to keep her fingers from trembling against his skin. There were thousands of men with striking good looks in the world. Why did Rosie have to be drawn to the one that was least appropriate for her and Casey? Yet that didn't keep her adrenaline from rushing whenever Hudson was near. "I'm just making you more comfortable."

When Hudson remained suspiciously silent, Rosie stole a look at him. He was grinning from ear to ear. "There are paying customers a couple of blocks from here waiting to see a woman in a window make a man comfortable. If that doesn't draw someone's interest, nothing will."

Oh, my. Heat washed into her cheeks. He was referring to the untouchable window dancers at clubs where men stared at women in outrageously skimpy outfits. Someone hurried past in the hallway behind her and the murmur of voices on phones reminded Rosie they weren't alone.

"Quit kidding around." A bit out of breath, Rosie

backed away. "You need to review a proposed schedule of events and a couple of press releases I've written." She thrust a pile of papers from the desk at him and retreated to the outer office, grateful she'd spent so much time pulling things together last weekend that she had something to show him.

They hadn't left the office since they'd found the place that morning. A cleaning crew had been the first to arrive, followed by the office supply company. Graham returned soon after with incidentals from Hudson's high-rise office that would give this one his personal stamp.

Every once in a while, Hudson caught Rosie's eye as she marched past trailing an ever growing ensemble of McCloud supporters. Most of the world saw only the handsome, uptight politician, not this bright, sexy man with vulnerabilities. Her biggest challenge would be encouraging Hudson to let his guard down.

They'd only been at the office a few hours but it was already bustling with activity. It helped that Rosie's contacts included local political science professors who offered extra credit to those who volunteered. She'd asked Hudson to help her assign duties, simple stuff like handing out phone lists to recruit more staff and stacks of signs that needed to be put up around the city. Surprisingly, he'd jumped right in.

Headquarters was bustling with noise and activity, yet Rosie was all too aware of her candidate's presence. Rosie's intensity and high energy usually wore people down, but she'd had no such effect on Hudson's quick wit and dogged determination. He wasn't going to let her run the show without a fight, but Rosie almost looked forward to it.

"Are you ready to be let out of your cage?" Rosie poked her head in Hudson's office midafternoon and asked sweetly even as another car honked on its way past. The honking was becoming irritating to everyone, even Rosie. Hudson was being a good sport sitting on display in his corner cell.

"You didn't put a sign out there that says Honk If You're Horny, did you?" Hudson glanced out at the traffic as if he'd had enough. It was three o'clock and Folsom was starting to get congested.

"Actually, it says, Honk If You Support McCloud," Rosie admitted. "You should be happy. A lot of people are honking."

He rubbed his temple, looking annoyed. "Oh, I'm happy, all right."

"Good, because your favorite reporter from Action News just made a surprise visit."

Hudson reached for his jacket. Rosie stepped between him and the coat rack.

"I think you should go out like that." She wanted him to show his muscles to the voting public. She found them compelling and bet others would as well.

A good foot above her, Hudson's eyes narrowed.

"Man of the people, remember?" She led him toward the door. "Now, don't go into what you stand for unless they bring it up, then refer to the traffic behind you and say something brilliant. They don't want any long-winded list of our agenda, just a sound bite or two."

"The McClouds have always been so private. What made you choose this location for your headquarters?" Amy Furokawa shoved a microphone in Hud's face. She'd used enough hairspray to keep her short hair submissive despite the brisk January wind.

Without his jacket, it was nippy outside, and yet Hud was starting to sweat. Appearing in front of the camera without so much as a brief review of an index card with talking points on it rattled him. He exchanged a glance with Rosie, who nodded encouragingly. Trying to not look too cold, nervous or uncomfortable, Hud put what he hoped was a pleasant smile on his face.

"We chose this location because the last time I ran for office, I was locked away from my constituents. Here—" Hud gestured to the glass office behind him, relieved when the camera man panned over to it "—people can see me working. They can stop by and share what's important to them on their way to and from work. We're also looking for volunteers."

"So you'll have an open office policy?" Amy moved within kissing distance of Hud, her eyes trained on his lips.

What the…? Willing himself to hold his ground, Hud somehow managed to keep his smile in place. "Yes. And it's also close to a small café that makes a great cup of coffee for someone who works long hours like I do."

"I didn't know you frequented coffee shops." With the back of her head to the camera, Amy's smile was a sultry invitation Hud was sure her viewers would be surprised to see. He certainly was shaken at the sight.

"Well, this one is different. It's…"

Lips pursed, Rosie was shaking her head, which wasn't helpful since Hud was having a memory lapse, further hindered by the proximity of the reporter.

And then Hud remembered. "Margo's Bistro. Great food, too." Stepping back, Hud looked into the camera as if sharing a special secret, hoping viewers wouldn't think his special secret involved female reporters.

The interview continued for a few more minutes, but Hud didn't breathe easier until someone called "cut."

"How'd I do?" Hud asked Rosie when the camera

crew had left. He'd survived without making a fool of himself. "Do you think anyone noticed that reporter was coming on to me?"

But Rosie didn't answer. She just dragged him out the door. The soft skin of her hand was warm against his, but Hud wasn't crazy about her vise-like grip on his fingers.

"Hey, what's the hurry? Where are we going?" Neither one of them had a raincoat.

"Margo's Bistro. You've never been there. Now you've got to be a regular." Her heels clicked an angry cadence on the pavement. The wind lifted her curls toward him. "We don't have time for this."

She was mad at him? After what he'd just gone through? "Maybe you should have thought of that when you tossed me to that piranha without warning. I would have liked some prep time first."

"Prep time?" Her voice rose. "Prep time? This from the man who didn't show up until the minute he was scheduled to give a press conference today."

"I got stuck in traffic," he pointed out.

Someone honked. Rosie dropped his arm and hissed, "Wave."

Hud obliged. "So now I'm not only an actor, I'm a trained dog who performs on demand."

"You are so far from trained, it's not funny."

This campaign was nothing like what he was used to. Hud's patience and pride was tested at every turn. And yet, he'd never felt so involved. Between editing speeches, coming up with ideas for appearances and working with the volunteers, he was an integral part of the process. "Why don't you tell me how you really feel?"

"Disappointed. Frustrated. Ticked off." She stopped walking and sighed.

Had Rosie paused midblock because she was resigning? "Hold on. What happened to learning each other's styles? Don't quit yet."

Rosie gave him an odd look and pointed to a hand-painted sign behind him—Margo's Bistro. Below the sign was a chalkboard with the special of the day, Cauliflower Leek Soup, written in loopy script. "We're here."

"Get inside and order something." Rosie's smile didn't reach her eyes. "Make friends with the staff and I'll make sure Margo covers your ass if anyone asks."

CHAPTER SEVEN

"HEY, NEIGHBOR." Margo, composed and with every blond hair in place, greeted Rosie with a cup of coffee topped with whipped cream. Rosie had called her friend earlier with the news that Hudson's campaign headquarters was down the street. "I saw you walking this way and figured you were your usual sleep-deprived self and due for a caffeine boost."

"You don't know how badly I need this." While Hudson walked around the colorful café, Rosie took a tentative sip, but Margo's coffee was neither too hot nor too cold, so she took another. "By the way, if anyone comes by, Hudson is a customer here. And if you could greet him with whatever he orders today as his usual order, I'll advance purchase my coffee for the next year."

"You have a spare three hundred dollars lying around?"

"Don't joke with a desperate woman." Just holding the rich liquid laced with caffeine settled Rosie's nerves. It was nonfat, but the whipped cream wasn't, just the way she liked it. "Besides, you shouldn't shortchange yourself. I probably spend closer to four hundred dollars here."

"Trouble with the senator?"

"He's the most irrational man I've ever known. I just want to—" Rosie fisted one hand at shoulder height "—shake him."

"So he's not perfect. But he is even more gorgeous in person than in his photographs." Margo snuck a peak at him. "My advice? Dazzle him with your brilliance. And if that doesn't work," Margo said, grinning, "try a candlelight dinner followed by a drive to North Beach."

Knowing Margo was joking to lift her spirits, Rosie tried to laugh. "Like he'd be interested in parking action with me."

"Don't sell yourself short," Margo said half under her breath before breaking into one of her sunny smiles as Hudson approached.

"I've discovered your weakness," Hudson said, his arm nearly touching Rosie's shoulder as he grinned down at her. He introduced himself to Margo and nodded toward Rosie. "I'm not big on cream and sugar, Margo. What would you recommend to someone who drinks coffee straight up?"

"I see you do know our Rosie well." Margo was her usual gracious self. Rosie would have preferred she put Hudson in his place. "Our feature this week is Rwanda Blue—a rich, exotic blend that will keep your motor running the rest of the afternoon."

"Perfect. I love traffic." Hudson turned to look out the window.

He was unmanageable and Rosie refused to fall prey to his charm. "Margo, Hudson will be paying the bill today and leaving a generous tip."

At first glance, Hudson looked relaxed and nowhere near as shaken as Rosie was by their third battle of the day, but there was something almost forced about his smile upon further inspection that telegraphed things were not as they should be. "I always come to the rescue of damsels who charge onto the street without their purses or cell phones."

Rosie made a little squeaky noise most unbecoming of a campaign manager. She'd left her cell phone back at the office and a gazillion people were supposed to call.

"That order is to go," Hudson said, turning back to Margo.

The short return walk to headquarters started out blissfully silent considering nothing about Hudson's campaign was easy and Rosie needed a few minutes to regroup, but she had no time to sulk and neither did he.

She drew him to a stop away from the curb. "We need to clear the air."

"Before we get back to the glass prison?"

"Yes." Rosie tried not to grind her teeth at his reference even though she'd been jokingly referring to it in much the same way. "You act as if you're sixty-five and set in your ways, not thirty-five with your entire life ahead of you." That's what bothered her about Hudson. Most politicians she'd taken on were willing to embrace her way of working if it attracted the hearts of voters.

"I sat at the knee of my grandfather and then my father during their campaigns."

"I'm sure they told you exactly what to do every minute and that's why your image today sucks."

His chin would have jutted in the air if he hadn't had to look down at her.

"You can rent opulent offices for headquarters. You can read from pristine speeches and hire an assistant to coach you through them." It was what she knew he wanted.

Hudson wasn't falling for it. "What's the catch?"

"I won't be working on your campaign." Just saying it saddened Rosie when she should have been feeling relieved. Casey's normal childhood would be guaranteed and she could tuck her unruly hormones back in the closet.

She didn't like the way Hudson hit her "Annoy Me" button one minute and her "I Want You" button the next.

"You can't quit on the first day."

"Really?" Her life would be so much easier if she did. Safer. Controllable. Quitting should have felt more appealing. "Then we have to come to an agreement about something. Maybe it would help if I explained the world of politics according to Rosie DeWitt."

She waited until he nodded.

"There are basically two kinds of politicians. I'm not saying one is any worse than the other. The kind of politicians you're used to are prepackaged, handled with kid gloves and show well in their designer suits. They don't worry about the electric bill or how to pay for their daughter's college education. They spend Sunday afternoon at the yacht club drinking champagne. It's hard for the voter to differentiate one of those from another."

With a grim set to his jaw, Hudson waited her out.

"Then there's the man of the people, rougher around the edges, more like the guy who lives down the street, the one who you catch retrieving the Sunday paper in his boxers every once in a while. The guy you look forward to hanging out with. He pitches in when you fix your fence and he makes friends with your dog. He's not always politically correct, but that's a good thing because you know he's going to shake things up and not become one of *them*. You remember a guy like that."

Hudson glanced up at the clouds hanging overhead. The wind ruffled his dark hair. "You think I'm one of *them?*"

"I think you were groomed that way." Raised to fit the mold. Hudson's upbringing was just another reason Rosie wanted Casey's identity to be a secret. She wanted her son to be whatever he wanted to be.

"So I'm a lost cause." The pain she'd seen in his eyes last Friday was back, threatening to melt her heart.

"I take on tough sells, not lost causes." Rosie found herself patting his shoulder reassuringly. Avoiding looking at him, she withdrew her hand and then tucked both hands safely in her armpits. Not only had she forgotten her cell phone, but her coat as well and it was chilly.

"I'm everything you described in the first group." Hudson didn't sound pleased. "My father wouldn't let me utter a word he and Stu hadn't reviewed and perfected first. I'm not comfortable with off-the-cuff interviews. Even opening up the floor to questions bothers me."

Because he'd been bullied into thinking he'd flub up if he opened his mouth. And from the get-go Rosie had hit the proud, stubborn McCloud's vulnerabilities head-on. She shivered from more than the chill air. No wonder Hudson so staunchly refused to open up to the public.

"I'm in a quandary here because the McClouds lean more toward the private side, while voters respond to the baring of souls." Rosie may have her secrets, but a politician couldn't afford any. "Neither the press nor the voters will wait for you to get over whatever hang-ups you've got. They want honesty and sincerity and they want it quickly."

"You want me to talk about what happened in the Senate. We both know if I don't deliver that message with the right tone, I'll drag down the family name more than it already has been." Hudson rubbed the back of his neck. "Honestly? This thing's been wearing me down for two years. It'll be a relief to get it off my chest, but I cringe just thinking about it. For now, can't we just…hint at it?"

"It's near impossible to cover up the truth long-term." Rosie couldn't look at Hudson when she said that because she wanted to hide Casey's identity forever. "As soon as you open up a little, the reporters will look for that can of worms you've been holding and from then on you can either dig yourself deeper or set yourself free."

Rosie couldn't tell anymore if she was talking about Hudson's secret or hers. She needed distance, yet her rebellious side was intrigued by the fact they both were hiding something. "So, am I still working on your campaign?"

"Yes." He didn't hesitate.

"Why?" Rosie told herself she'd only asked to hear him confirm they were on the same page. She was not fishing for compliments, but still she couldn't look at him.

"Because…because…" Hudson lifted her chin with a gentle touch, his gaze so grave she couldn't look away. "I think with your help I could be that guy that you want to hang out with, the one you can't forget."

A passing car honked.

Holy smokes. Mere inches separated them. Rosie stumbled back in alarm. She was no less susceptible to him than the Action News reporter.

Hudson smiled at her as if he knew they'd almost done something she'd regret later. "That honk was for you."

Rosie changed the subject, cheeks burning. "What you said about Margo's would have been charming if it was true. Maybe next time we'll plug Plouf." Rosie started walking.

"I'll buy you lunch there tomorrow." She heard the smile in his voice and refused to take it in. Hudson's smile could enchant the stripes off a zebra. "That ought to be worth a couple points."

"Having lunch with me won't earn us points in this race."

"Who said I wanted points for the race?"

He couldn't be flirting. Hudson McCloud didn't flirt with short, curvaceous single moms with chaotic lives who lacked a social pedigree. Rosie pretended Hudson was teasing her for nearly making a fool of herself. "I understand where you're coming from now. Maybe I can have one of the volunteers practice interviewing you to help you gain confidence. Meanwhile, I'll try to draft a speech that dances around the issues of what happened in the Senate."

"Thank you." Hudson stopped, captured Rosie's hand with both of his and shook on it.

Rosie didn't know if he was making fun of her or making a pass. Either way, she wasn't amused.

OUTSIDE HUD'S OFFICE WINDOW, the six-o'clock traffic was gridlocked. He couldn't tell if the beeping horns were for him or to relieve driver frustration.

He'd been giving phone interviews all afternoon, sticking close to the script that Rosie had provided in one of her press releases. Spontaneous, he wasn't. Rosie was nowhere to be seen. She'd been avoiding him since that moment they'd shared on the street. If they hadn't been interrupted, he was sure she would have kissed him.

Would her kiss be innocent or full of the intensity she brought to her work? He was determined to follow the attraction to its natural conclusion and just as determined to wait until he'd been elected to do so.

"Good night, sir." A volunteer wearing jeans and a Berkeley sweatshirt gave a tentative wave on his way past Hudson's office. He had a purple streak in his dark hair and a silver stud through one eyebrow.

Hudson replied in kind, even though he couldn't remember the college student's name or what he was there to do. They'd gotten too many volunteers over the course of the afternoon for him to remember all of them, most of them surprisingly young. Rosie probably knew everyone. She seemed the type who could juggle several balls in the air while reciting every capital city in the union. Sure it was an odd skill, but it was an interesting mix.

Hud caught a grandmotherly type just as she was about to swing the outer door open. "Excuse me. Have you seen Rosie?"

"She left for the day about half an hour ago, poor dear. She looked a bit ragged around the edges."

Hud thanked her and called Graham to bring the car around. This had to be a record for the shortest day a campaign manager had spent in the office working for him. Hoping Rosie might be free for dinner—to talk strategy, of course—he retrieved the piece of paper she'd scribbled her cell phone number on, but before he could dial, a familiar figure entered campaign headquarters with her nose wrinkled in distaste.

"Oh, my heavens." His mother's appearance created a stir among the remaining volunteers as she walked toward Hud's office, trailed by Stu. She recovered her composure enough to smile at them and lower her voice. "I saw you on the news. Tell me this is only temporary."

Her disapproval stung. She probably would have cut Samuel more slack. Hud closed the door behind them, resolved to make her understand. "We've been getting a positive response here. Twenty volunteers showed up already." Horns honked behind him in a loud cacophony. "Wave, Mother."

"At who?" She glanced behind her.

Hud gestured to the jammed road beyond his window with barely contained amusement. "At them." It was good to see someone else suffer from the exposure.

His mother stood up and craned her neck. More

honking ensued. She gave a weak wave and sank back into her seat with pursed lips. "Where is Rosie?"

"She's gone for the day." Hud couldn't keep the annoyance out of his voice. His campaign manager should be sticking to him like glue—something she'd almost done earlier on the sidewalk.

"Get her on the phone, please." His mother settled her purse in her lap, her gaze going everywhere but the windows. The displeasure in her voice was more than evident. "I'm sure she has a cell phone." She wasn't going anywhere until Hud made the call.

"Rosie, I've got my mother and Stu on the line. We're here at campaign headquarters," Hud began once Rosie answered. He tried to give her fair warning. For all he knew, Rosie could have left for a long standing dentist appointment...or a date.

"Hello, everyone." Rosie sounded flustered and out of breath. "Did I miss a meeting?"

A horn honked over the phone line. Hud looked around the intersection expecting to see Rosie outside carrying coffee and soup from Margo's. "Where are you?" Even though he'd been told Rosie left, now would be a good time for her to show up.

"I'm about to pick up Casey from day care."

"Ahh...so, this is a bad time."

"If you have a question that can't wait until the morning, ask away," Rosie said briskly. "Otherwise, I'll see you at the Rotary Club meeting at nine."

Hud shot his mother a questioning look.

"Fine." Lips pursed, his mother stood, gathering her tiny purse.

"I'll call you later, Rosie," Hud said, breaking the connection.

Vivian turned up her nose as she looked at the scuffed linoleum. "Is this the impression you want people to have about our family? About you?"

"The place makes a statement," Stu piped in, adding when Hud's mother frowned, "In a bad way."

Hud tried to smooth things over. "I admit Rosie's ideas are different, but I'm comfortable with her."

His mother raised her eyebrows. "I don't expect that behavior from you."

"I'm not Samuel. I don't think of her *that* way," Hud lied. Distracting fantasies didn't count if Hudson didn't act upon them. "Give me credit for knowing when to separate politics from personal pleasure."

"I want you to rethink this…" She floundered, waving her hand in the air as if encouraging the words to come more easily. "Don't think being here changes anything. We still have standards and a demanding campaign that needs to be run. If Rosie makes snap decisions like this, her mind is elsewhere. A mother may not be the right person for the job."

"Does that include you?" Hud tried to tease her.

"Don't be impertinent." Clutching her purse, she sighed. "I'm trying to be realistic. If she's got a child, you know we'll come second. If this is so important to you—"

"Rosie DeWitt wins elections," Hud reminded them. "You can't let Rosie go because of her family status. They call that discrimination."

"I call it losing," Stu said with a frown.

"We'll give her a chance." His mother nodded at Stu. "The same as we would anyone else."

"This is my time, my campaign." Hud hadn't spent the past two years cleaning up McCloud affairs for nothing. "Times have changed for the McClouds."

"Clearly." Blinking back tears, his mother backed out the door. "If you want me to withdraw my support, just say so."

Hud hurried to embrace her. "You're my staunchest supporter. I need you." He hugged her tight, unable to shake the feeling that he could never make her happy.

"You need the money I could raise."

"That, too." Hudson winked. A horn sounded behind him. "Smile at the people and then go get yourself a vodka tonic."

"She'll need a double," Stu grumbled as he shuffled out the door.

"THIS IS NOT THE WAY the McClouds usually run things, Walter." Vivian stood in the foyer of her Pacific Heights home beneath a portrait of her in-laws, cell phone in hand.

Walter heaved a sigh that gave Vivian a twinge of guilt. She'd come across as a shrew. Walter didn't need another one of those in his life.

But he didn't realize what was going on. "I support your choice for Hud. Rosie is very bright, but I will not have her denigrate the McCloud name. Things are far from satisfactory." She fingered her pearls and tried not to look at the visage of her mother-in-law. When Hamilton McCloud first met Vivian she'd been working as a maid at the Palace Hotel. Try as she might, she'd never completely won over her blue blood mother-in-law.

"Take a breath and tell me what we're talking about." Walter sounded tired.

"It's *her.* She's put Hudson on display on Folsom Avenue." Maybe now Walter would understand how inappropriate this was.

Silence. "Like a street performer?"

"No, no." Walter just didn't realize the gravity of the

matter. "Rosie opened campaign headquarters in a former retail store in one of those converted warehouses right next to where the traffic backs up to go onto the Bay Bridge. Hudson is in a fish bowl."

"Really?" Even in the heat of Vivian's embarrassment, she could hear the admiration in Walter's voice. "I told you she was good."

"People honked at me." Vivian was aghast. What if someone from the yacht club saw her there? "As if I was a woman on the street. I'm trying to protect the family image and you're not taking me seriously."

Walter cleared his throat. "Every demographic has a different way of expressing their fondness, Viv. It's not all tea parties and black-tie balls."

"But they're so…close. I could see this man's teeth." Or where he should have had teeth.

"When did you become such a prude?"

Vivian's skin flushed with heat. Prudes were less interesting, less powerful, less womanly. "I am *not* a prude!" She glanced up at Mama McCloud's stern features before turning her back on the portrait completely.

"Feeling your age?" Walter didn't sound tired anymore. He sounded ready for a night on the town.

"I have a call on the other line," Vivian lied, shaken by the odd way Walter made her feel.

His rich laughter echoed in her ears long after she'd hung up. With rigid steps, Vivian climbed the stairs to her room, feeling more confused than ever.

"HOW WAS YOUR DAY, CASEY?" Rosie's day had been less than a success. Just as she predicted, the press was going to make Hudson's past a vote-stopping issue.

"Jeremy poked me." Sitting at a table where he could

see the clock on the wall, Casey fingered his red nose gingerly. Then he looked up at Rosie revealing a black eye almost swollen shut. "He did it on purpose."

Rosie sank to the floor in front of her baby and pulled him into her arms.

"I tried to call you earlier, but your cell phone kept rolling to voice mail. I need your signature on the accident report." Ms. Phan materialized at Rosie's side with a clipboard. "Somebody didn't get enough sleep last night. Tempers were flaring here."

Ignoring the clipboard, Rosie stood, keeping one arm around Casey. "You're talking about Jeremy, right?" Why couldn't Ms. Phan have left her a message?

"Both boys seemed out of sorts today. The holidays will do that to you." Ms. Phan glanced at her watch as if disapproving of Rosie's arrival time.

"It's six o'clock." Much earlier than she normally showed up. Rosie was ready to poke someone herself. Instead, she seized the clipboard and signed the accident report.

"It's the first day back after vacation, that's all," Ms. Phan said. "Rest up, Casey. We'll see you tomorrow after school."

Taken down a peg or two, Rosie helped Casey gather up his belongings as she bid Ms. Phan good-night. Rosie handed Casey his umbrella and opened her own as they stepped out into the drizzly night.

"Did you see the mayor today?" Casey asked over the splash of cars passing them on the street. "Is he coming over tonight?"

"Yes and no." They trudged up the hill toward home with Rosie contemplating Ms. Phan's words with every step. "Ms. Phan is probably right. You stayed up too late last night." And she'd let him because there'd been a movie on television about a boy who was a chess champion.

"Only a little bit. And I didn't do anything to him, Mommy, honest," Casey said. "He told me to stop watching the clock and then he hit me and now it hurts. I have to keep my face frozen, like this." He turned and pursed his lips, looking pitiful.

"We'll take care of it when we get home." Never having had a black eye, Rosie wasn't sure if she should call the doctor or take Casey to the emergency clinic. She'd check her reference books and call someone—maybe Selena, who had a preteen boy—for an opinion.

Hand in hand, they walked in silence across the street. Rosie was unable to shake the feeling that Casey's black eye was all her fault.

"Do you have any happy news, Mommy? I need some."

Her poor baby. "I was on television today, standing behind your mayor." And later she'd almost kissed him.

"Lucky." Casey sighed. "Can I have macaroni and cheese for dinner? It would make my eye feel better."

CHAPTER EIGHT

"THE DOCTOR HAS ARRIVED." Selena swept into Rosie's apartment with a bagful of medical supplies. "Where's my patient?"

"You're not a doctor. You're a painter." Lifting a bag of frozen peas off his face, Casey twisted in his position on the couch to look at Selena.

"I'm an artiste," Selena replied with a flamboyant gesture.

Casey smiled. "Painter."

"Why does he insist on calling me that?" Selena unpacked her bag on the small dining room table.

"Maybe because you have purple paint in your hair," Rosie pointed out. "And what happened to your skirt? It looks like it got caught in a bicycle chain."

"Axel wanted a taste. He has a surprising appetite. He's eaten Drew's dirty PE socks, our remote control and a box of tampons." Selena shook her head and then added in a whisper. "Casey doesn't look so bad."

"One in ten facial injuries turn into something more serious." Rosie waved her reference book in Selena's direction. "And look at his eye. It's as purple as your hair."

"Honey, he's a boy. You better start getting used to it. It may look bad, but it's nothing compared to the scrapes, strains and broken bones he's going to have later. Remember how he wants to play football?"

"Don't remind me." Rosie shuddered. "Ms. Phan made me sign an accident report, as if it was Casey's fault."

"Everyone has to sign so the facility doesn't get sued. Don't you let her intimidate you." Selena smiled brightly at Rosie's son. "Casey, come over here and let me look at you."

Padding over in his pair of holey socks, Casey plopped into a chair. The bag of peas tumbled onto the table. "What's for dinner? I'm hungry."

"Is it after seven?" Rosie sat next to him. "I've been pouring through my children's health books for nearly an hour. I guess it's Chin-Chin's noodles tonight."

Casey made a face. "I wanted macaroni and cheese."

"Could be worse. I fed Drew leftovers and left him doing homework." Selena handed Rosie a bottle of chewable children's pain reliever. "Good thing you told me you were out of these. Turns out I didn't have any aspirin at home, either."

"Thanks. I forgot we used the last of it when Case had a fever before Christmas." Rosie opened the bottle and shook out two cherry-flavored pills, handing them to Casey.

Selena took Casey's chin gingerly in her hand. "I don't see any cuts. Muhammad Ali didn't do too much damage."

"His name is Jeremy," Casey said patiently. "He just hit me. I didn't do anything."

"Maybe you should take karate lessons," Selena suggested.

Casey perked up. "Like Jackie Chan? That would be cool." He popped off the chair with more energy than he'd exhibited all night and began making ninja moves in the living room.

"Oh, I don't think so. It's too dangerous."

"It's self-defense and…" Selena lowered her voice. "With no man around the house it might do him good. I didn't send Drew to karate, but he was always the leader of the pack."

"And Casey isn't even a follower." More like a misfit loner. He hadn't made many friends in kindergarten, and Rosie worried that he'd never fit in. "Where did I go wrong?"

"You didn't go wrong. Every kid is different. I know how hard it is to be a single parent. Everyone else seems to know more than you do, so take my suggestion with a grain of salt. Research it like everything else you do and find something you're both comfortable with. You're doing fine."

Friends like Selena and Margo made Rosie feel less of a failure as a mom.

"Next time Ms. Phan gives you grief just tell her you appreciate her concern but you're raising Casey the best you can. And while you're at it, give old Grandma Chin a piece of your mind as well."

"I can't do that."

"Why not?"

"They might take it out on Casey. And besides, it'll hurt their feelings."

"I liked your first reason better. I'm going to leave you with these supplies just in case the karate kid takes a tumble." Selena raised an eyebrow. "So, how did it go today? I heard the sexy senator making his announcement on the radio."

"It was a mixed bag. He didn't read my speech." She didn't go into how she'd lost control of the situation. "Hudson balked at my choice for headquarters and then he was quoted on camera as saying he was a regular at Margo's even though he's never been there."

"Maybe it's just first-day jitters. He's too good-looking to be a permanent putz."

"He is full of surprises." Who would have suspected

Hudson's perfectly cool veneer was just a facade for such a vulnerable man? Samuel had been wrong about his brother, but then again, Samuel had still been young.

"Persistent and assertive." Selena's smile was all too knowing. "That man has potential after all."

Rosie feigned ignorance. "As a candidate?"

"As a L-O-V-E-R," Selena spelled the word with a significant glance at Casey. "You really need to get out more."

"I'll be getting out quite a bit on this campaign, but S-E-X is the furthest thing from my mind." Or at least it should be because Rosie was going to have a hard enough time bringing the infamous McCloud to heel.

"I HOPE YOU LIKE orange chicken and moo goo gai pan." Unable to twiddle his thumbs at home, Hud held up the take-out containers in one hand and a tray of coffee from Margo's in the other as a peace offering.

"Do you own a cell phone?" Though her home was warm and hospitable, Rosie's frown was not. Wearing jeans and a baggy Cal Bears football jersey with her black hair cascading in waves from a high ponytail, Rosie looked like she was ready to study for college finals. She tugged the hem of her shirt self-consciously, as if wishing for one of her polished suits. Hud preferred her like this.

"We didn't get a chance to go over some things before you left." Hud pushed past her with the food. "Even if you've eaten, I haven't."

"Is that the mayor?" Casey ran over and hugged Hud's leg while he tried to set the coffee down without spilling. "Can we play chess?"

"If you promise to do all that bath stuff, I think we can fit in a game." Hud rubbed Casey's hair into further disarray and looked down into his eager little face. "Whoa, did you get hit by a truck or something?"

"No, just Jeremy. I wasn't doing anything and pow." Casey's little lip thrust out as if he might cry, and Rosie looked as if she might, too.

"I'm sure you gave him one back," Hud said, squatting to examine the red, puffy skin that forced the boy's eye almost closed. "I know I would have."

Rosie's intake of breath was hard to miss, and she glared at him with disapproval shining in her eyes.

"I'm not supposed to hit anyone," Casey said, as if repeating a mantra drilled into him by his mother. "You don't hit people do you?"

"Me? Nah. I just challenge them to a game of chess." Hud winked at the boy.

Casey giggled, his eyes wandering to the bounty on the table. "Did you bring macaroni and cheese?"

"I brought something better. Orange chicken." The woman at the Chinese restaurant downstairs had assured him little boys liked it. "And a hot chocolate from Margo's."

"A pairing fit for a connoisseur. Why don't you go back to the couch with your hot chocolate?" There was no mistaking the worried way Rosie hovered over Casey as she escorted him to the couch. "I'll bring you a plate."

Intruding upon her personal space wasn't as amusing as Hud had imagined. She was a single mom dealing with life's ups and downs alone. "Can I help with anything?"

"No." Rosie seemed frazzled. "I probably should have told you that I need to leave every day promptly by five-thirty because Casey's day care officially closes at six. I've got everything spread out here next to my laptop. What do you want to review?"

"Uh…" Busted. Hud didn't have anything to review.

"Let's eat first and talk business later. You look like you could use a break."

"Try understanding the five-year-old male psyche when you've never been one yourself. Do you know that boys are five times more likely to be in accidents involving toys than girls are?"

He'd never dated a woman with kids before. He'd always considered the extra baggage unappealing. Yet with Rosie, her attitude and responsibilities didn't diminish her appeal. She carried the role with weary dignity and a sly sense of humor.

Hud looked around at the immaculate apartment with its comfortable furniture and homey colors. "Ahh, that explains why the kid has a chess set instead of a baseball bat."

"My friend, Selena, told me I should take him to karate lessons to toughen him up." Rosie set a plate down in front of Hud.

"His father doesn't spend much time with him?" Hud sensed it was the wrong thing to ask when she made an unintelligible noise. "I'm sorry," he said, backpedaling. "It's none of my business."

She stared at Hud oddly, her body rigid. "His father died before Casey was born."

Ah, hell. He'd assumed the lack of a husband meant her son had been fathered by a loser she'd since dumped. Hud knew he compared well to most ex-boyfriends and ex-husbands. But dead exes were another thing entirely.

"What was it you wanted to talk about?" Rosie's tone was all business. "Do you want to review what I've written so far for your speech tomorrow morning?"

Questions unrelated to the campaign pinged about his head. Had she been serious with this guy? How had he died? Did she still think about him at night?

Respecting her privacy, Hud tried to match her detached tone. "I'm no good at speechwriting. Tell me more about your ideas on the plight of the homeless."

"I SAW YOU DEBATE ONCE. A long time ago." Somehow, despite Hudson's uninvited encroachment into her home, Rosie and Hudson ended up sitting on her couch mulling over the attributes of a not-so-great bottle of wine that had been in her cupboard for months. It didn't feel so strange to be sitting in her quiet apartment talking to a man. It felt— surprisingly—comfortably intimate, despite her grungy appearance and wild hair and him sitting there in his slacks, monogrammed shirt and tie and every hair in place.

Rosie pulled out her background file on Hudson and pointed to the newspaper clipping of him winning the state championship. "I was there."

Hud peered at the faded photo and then back at her. "In this photo?"

"No, but I was there. Your debate team beat my high school team in the semifinals. I was just a freshman that year but everyone was in awe of you. You had a reputation for always being prepared with arguments as bulletproof as they come." The debate had been the first time Rosie had seen hordes of photographers, some of whom stood directly in front of Hudson and Samuel to get their picture as the boys tried unsuccessfully to exit the podium. Not exactly a normal childhood.

"Do you have a picture? From school, I mean." When she hesitated, he cajoled her. "Come on. You probably have naked pictures of me as a baby."

She so did not want Hudson to see how she looked in high school. Calling it her awkward stage was an understatement, especially when she'd never seen a picture of

Hudson when he wasn't almost unbearably gorgeous. Then again, maybe he needed a dose of reality to squelch his interested vibe.

Rosie went over to the bookshelf, grabbed her yearbook from the bottom and flipped to the page with her debate team. "That's me."

Hudson peered at the page. "You look really young."

"I'd been home-schooled and skipped two grades. I was the only freshman on the team." Hudson was being nice when he should have recoiled from the horror of her picture. With hair so thick and curly it stuck out horizontally, a sacklike dress and a smile accented by a mouthful of braces it was no wonder Rosie hid out in the library at lunch. Thankfully, her teeth had straightened out, she developed fashion sense and discovered hair gel, but not until long after she'd moved out of her parents' hippie home.

"That hair was atrocious," Hudson noted. "I can see why you developed that thick skin of yours."

"Hey." Rosie tried to take the yearbook back, but Hudson kept it out of her reach. "You wouldn't know anything about *not* fitting in during high school, would you?"

He sighed. "I meant that as a compliment but you didn't take it that way, did you?"

"No."

He read an inscription on the page. "Are you sure this is your yearbook? This says, *To Barb.*"

Uh-oh. She'd forgotten about that. "Barb was my nickname."

"Care to elaborate?" His grin invited her to come out and play.

"No."

"Ah, come on. Is it your middle name?"

"It's stupid." And painful.

He flipped to the front inside cover and scanned the messages. "You don't have that many and they're all written to Barb." Hudson pinned her with his gaze.

"I didn't have many friends. Home-schooled, remember?" Rosie squirmed. "The kids never said what they meant. Their slang was like a foreign language. I focused on things I could understand."

"Math? History? Debate?" When she nodded, he asked softly. "And what about Barb?"

"It's stupid. Some smart aleck lost a debate to me early on and started calling me that because a rose has thorns." Rosie tried to laugh but didn't have much success. "Anyway, it stuck but that was a long time ago. No blood, no foul, right?" This time when she reached for the yearbook he relinquished it without a fight.

Hudson leaned forward, elbows resting on his knees. "What was his name? I'll track him down and have him meet me after school to settle this."

Maybe it was the wine. Maybe it was Hudson's boyish enthusiasm. Rosie found herself giggling.

"You should laugh more often," Hudson said. "You look…it makes…"

Rosie's cheeks heated. Now who was affected by the wine? She set down her glass and tried to smooth over the moment. "Let's just agree that I was an ugly duckling who grew into something more presentable and leave it at that. We'll just feel awkward in the morning."

The word *morning* seemed to hang in the air. As in he stayed the night and it was awkward in the morning. And it would be. Incredibly awkward. But looking into Hudson's eyes, Rosie suspected it just might be worth it.

Until Casey called her from the bathroom, reminding her that she couldn't take the chance.

THE EVENING HAD almost gone too far. Hud was grateful for Rosie's save. He couldn't afford any distractions, no matter how diverting Rosie was. When she returned from putting Casey to bed, he tried to make sure she'd understand. "If you read my file, you would have seen I prefer leggy blondes who've always been swans." Not that he'd taken the time to date in the past two years.

"Actresses, musicians and athletes. Don't you date anyone normal?" Her grin faded and she looked at the clock on the wall.

"Sometimes it's easier to date someone who's used to the media circus. Not everyone can handle the challenges of the press hounding your every move." Although those women seemed to pale next to Rosie.

"Your personal life is nobody's business but your own. Although the right celebrity would get you points with voters." Her grin was sad. Even her hair seemed to lose some of its spunk. "Sorry. The switch gets stuck in work mode. That's the reason I don't date. I turn off work only for Casey. I'm not much of a conversationalist if I'm not talking shop."

Hud changed his mind. He didn't want to talk about other women. He wanted to watch Rosie relax into the couch cushions next to him and make her laugh again. The fascination Hud felt for her was an odd mix of physical interest and emotional longing for her admiration. But what did she think of him?

Hud sat forward, ready to read her expression. "You never did tell me which way you would have voted for me in that poll. Did I do the honorable thing?"

She swirled the wine in her glass. "I was disappointed. Weren't you?" Rosie looked at him with that defiant gaze she'd used the morning they'd first met, as if she were challenging him to fight for her respect. "You let a huge opportunity slip through your fingers."

That wasn't the answer he'd been looking for. "Why is it that you…" Hud searched for the right words. "Most people tend to tell me what I want to hear."

"I'm a single working mom. I'm too tired to create an alternative reality for you." She rubbed her forehead, keeping her gaze averted. "You deserve the truth."

The funny thing was, coming from her, he believed she wouldn't lie to him. "Don't ever change."

That elicited a small smile. "Yes, sir."

"I'd rather you called me Hud. Or if you prefer, we can call each other *sir* and *Barb*." Hud waited until she looked at him again. It struck him how pretty she was, how he longed to touch her unruly curls and learn the feel of her lips on his. "I'd really like to take you to dinner sometime."

Rosie opened her mouth to reply, then closed it, and searched his expression. "I think it's time to call it a night."

Unable to explain what had come over him, Hud decided she was right.

"GOOD MORNING, ROSIE." In her most intimidating suit and pearls, Vivian walked briskly past the men of the Rotary Club to greet her son's campaign manager.

Rosie's smile didn't fade when she caught sight of Vivian and Stu. It should have. Perhaps Vivian was losing her touch in her old age.

Never. She'd channel Mama McCloud if she had to.

"Thanks for coming," Rosie said with a bright smile.

"We are here to fund-raise, aren't we?" Vivian tried not

to let resentment cloud her words, but it was hard. Fund-raising was all anyone thought she was good for. Well, she had a surprise for Rosie. Vivian had spent over half her life making sure she lived up to the upper crust McCloud heritage and helping the McCloud men come across as the power elite. All of which would surely be ruined if Hudson spent any more time in that glass office. Vivian wasn't going to be the quiet team player Walter so clearly wanted her to be.

"Where is Hudson's speech?" Stu asked, a bit out of breath as he caught up to Vivian. She needed to remember to walk slower for him.

Rosie turned to Vivian. "That's a lovely ensemble. Are you planning on spending time today at headquarters? We could sure use you."

"More fund-raising?" Vivian frowned. With the party's backing, how much money did the campaign need?

Rosie shook her head. "No, I'd like you to—"

"We're used to getting Hud's speeches." Stu cut her off, leaving Vivian wondering what Rosie wanted. "You haven't been sending out advanced copies."

"We don't have a speechwriter on board yet. I've been writing Hud's speeches late at night." Rosie's smile seemed strained. "Is there a reason you want to review his speech?"

"Because no one knows how the McClouds should be portrayed better than we do." Stu gestured with his coffee cup that Rosie should hand over the speech. "It's clear from the speech you wrote for yesterday's announcement and your *recommendation* for campaign headquarters that you don't understand who the McClouds are at all."

Rosie's lips compressed at an odd angle, as if she was trying to hold her temper. "Given my poll figures indicate the voting public sees Hudson as elitist and out of touch with their concerns, I think that gives me a pretty good understanding of who the McClouds are and what I need to do to get Hudson elected."

"I agree that Hudson has hurdles," Vivian began, trying to be diplomatic as personal interests warred with protecting the McCloud code. "You need to recognize that the McClouds have standards that your office space isn't meeting. I realize you've convinced Hud, but I'm not sure he's seeing the long-term impact of the place."

"Planning on having him make appearances at the local mall next?" Stu saluted Rosie with his coffee and winked. "You said yourself he's got a powerful handshake."

"What a good idea." But Rosie's features had become stiff. She nodded at the men and women filing into the meeting room. "It's getting crowded in here. Why don't we meet later to review the context I'm using for all his speeches?"

Rosie was good. Vivian would give her that. She didn't give in easily and knew how to be diplomatic and not make a scene.

"Good morning," Hud came up behind Rosie and put a hand on her shoulder.

His campaign manager flinched away. Something passed quickly over Hud's features before he greeted Vivian with a kiss on her cheek. There was more going on between the two of them than politics.

Hamilton would have pulled their son aside at the first sign of anything untoward and told Hud in no uncertain terms that the race was his goal, not romance. But Hudson hadn't so much as looked with interest at a woman in two years so Vivian had a different agenda. Testing the waters, she pulled Hud back to her and whispered in his ear, "Be careful. This one's a handful."

Frowning, Hud straightened.

"Here's your speech," Rosie said, blushing as she handed it to Hud.

Stu's eyes bulged. "But I haven't read it yet."

"Good. I like an unbiased opinion." Hud grinned and slapped Stu on the back hard enough that his coffee almost sloshed onto the carpet. "Where are we sitting?"

"Over there." Rosie pointed, stepping out of someone's way until she almost bumped into Hud, then quickly stepping back again as if touching him was taboo.

Hud and Stu headed toward the front of the room.

"Can you tell Hud I'll catch up to him later at the office?" Rosie's cheeks were in full bloom, confirming her attraction to Vivian's son. "I've got a lot to do."

"Are you free for lunch today, dear?" Vivian moved ever so slightly in Rosie's path. "You mentioned there were other things I could do to help the campaign and I'd love to discuss them, but now isn't the time." Hands outstretched in front of her, Vivian smiled reassuringly. She hadn't spent years with political consultants by her side without learning something about nonverbal communication. Then again, she hadn't spent years raising two boys to miss interest for the opposite sex in her son's eyes. That alone was worth pursuing this race and allowing Rosie to fiddle with the McCloud image.

Rosie's gaze was assessing, trying to figure out what Vivian knew or wanted, but in the end she agreed. After all, no one refused Vivian McCloud.

"MOTHER, DID YOU PULL a McCloud on Rosie?" Hud stared at a stiff-backed Rosie retreating through the crowd. He'd decided last night as he spent hours staring at his ceiling that Rosie was right. His workaholic, guarded lifestyle didn't let anyone know who he was. Rosie was the first person he'd let into his life in a long time. He had fun with her. Why not test the public waters by dating someone like Rosie? Not just any someone. He wanted Rosie.

"I'm not trying to get rid of her, dear. In fact, we're having lunch together today." His mother fiddled with his tie. "You know how busy it is at the beginning of a campaign. She said she has a lot to do back at the office. Why don't you go over your speech?"

Hud scanned it quickly. There were hints about what happened to him in the Senate, but essentially, the speech was politicalese. It didn't seem honest enough. But it was exactly within the parameters of his directive to Rosie.

"Everyone please be seated." The announcement came over the loudspeaker.

Hudson took his place at the head table, listening to the meeting notes being read with a sinking feeling in his gut. When he was finally introduced, Hudson stood and duti-fully read from Rosie's pages. After his speech, Hudson walked out with the general membership, leaving his mother and Stu to schmooze the board for donations.

"What was that first part of his speech all about?" someone in front of him asked. "He talked in circles about what happened in the Senate."

"Who knows. We'll donate anyway. You know how the board is," answered another. "They love Vivian McCloud."

Hudson's stomach churned as he veered out a side exit and walked purposefully toward the Folsom office, dis-gusted with himself and half truths. He was going to tell Rosie everything.

CHAPTER NINE

"WHAT'S WITH THE TIGHT LIPS? Are you afraid to tell us what's bothering you?" Selena took a sip of her espresso, her hands splattered with teal paint today. She'd come into Margo's Bistro shortly after Rosie arrived. Rosie wasn't going to point out that it looked as if Axel had chewed the cuff of one leg on Selena's overalls.

"I just needed time away from the office," Rosie said, cradling a cup of coffee as she wondered what she was going to do. A chocolate pecan muffin sat untouched in front of her. The McClouds were boxing her in.

"It's him, isn't it?" Margo asked, joining them while Bailey, recently back from her honeymoon with Derrick, one of the Thursday night coffee group, manned the counter. "Hudson?"

"Yes and no," Rosie admitted. It was one thing to keep a secret when no one in her life was affected by it. But it was another thing entirely to work with those she was hiding the truth from.

"How did you know?" Selena ignored Rosie.

Margo gave a sly look. "He showed up here last night and was asking about her."

Rosie waved off the idea. "I told him he had to become a regular."

"He wanted to know if you were seeing anyone." Margo beamed. "It took him nearly twenty minutes to get around to asking."

"I told you he had potential," Selena said. "Gorgeous. Sexy. Single. Where's the problem?"

Where indeed. "I'm having lunch with his mother."

"I love Mrs. McCloud." Margo's smile was a bit dreamy. "She always looks so perfect and seems so gracious, like nothing can phase her." Once upon a time in high school, Margo had lived such a life—blond, popular—before reality and kids came along. Now on her second marriage, she was living the dream once more.

"You're still the queen bee, Margo. You have nothing to envy Mrs. McCloud for." Rosie patted Margo's hand, and then leaned toward the center of the table and lowered her voice. "Hudson asked me out."

"I take it that's a bad thing," Margo said.

Rosie rolled her eyes. "I can't go out with him. We work together and…that's enough of a hurdle to get past. Besides, he sort of blurted it out by accident."

"I went out with Robert while he helped me with the café," Margo added. "And now we're happily married."

"No offense, but my next job depends on my reputation, not just whether or not my candidate wins." Rosie was a realist. She was due for a loss. But a loss combined with sleeping with her candidate wouldn't look so hot on her resume. And it certainly wouldn't get her any recommendations for the presidential campaign.

"Back up. I don't get it. Why would having lunch with Mrs. McCloud be a problem?" Selena sipped her espresso and waited.

Rosie blew out a breath and confessed, "I think she noticed the tension between us."

"So there is an attraction," Selena murmured, eyes sparkling.

Much as she'd like to, Rosie couldn't deny it.

"What does Hudson say about it?" Margo asked. "Can you just be friends until this is over?"

"Have you seen Hudson McCloud?" Selena laughed. "All that sex appeal and power tied up in one yummy package."

"Okay, I see your point." Margo stared thoughtfully out the window. "Dating California royalty wouldn't exactly be an easy or discreet event. Your entire life would be dissected by the press, not to mention his mother. Is he worth it?"

"Honestly, no man I've met has ever come close to the way Hudson makes me feel. He's nothing like I expected. He's got a strong set of values." Nothing like Samuel described. "He challenges my intellect and it's like my body has a mind of its own when he's around." Rosie put her head in her hands as she realized the truth. "Even if I wasn't working with him, I couldn't date him." Because of the lies it would require to shelter Casey from the media circus.

"Hold on. Are you saying his mother would never approve of you?" Selena was offended.

"Or that Hudson thinks you're not marriage material?" Margo demanded.

"It has nothing to do with how the McClouds feel about me." Rosie squared her shoulders. She had to tell someone. She had to find out if what she'd done was right or wrong. "What if I told you Casey is Samuel McCloud's son?"

Selena reached over and felt Rosie's forehead. "She's not running a fever, but I think she's delusional."

"No. She's serious. The only thing she's ever admitted about Casey's father is that he's dead. Not a name. Not a history. Nothing," Margo said quietly. She fiddled with a lock of blond hair while she studied Rosie. Then her eyes got as big as saucers. "Oh, my God. Do you know what this means?"

"That my son's face is going to grace the cover of every tabloid across America if anyone finds out?"

Margo shook her head. "All those times you struggled to make ends meet, all those nights you worried about how to save for Casey's college education, that's all behind you."

Rosie looked down at her hands. "No, it isn't. I can't tell the McClouds about Casey."

"Why wouldn't you tell them about the little whipper-snapper?" Selena asked.

"Do you remember the media coverage after Samuel died?" Rosie asked, then continued without waiting for their answer. "The press followed Hudson and Vivian McCloud everywhere."

"That was nothing new. They follow them everywhere now."

"Yeah, but the press has never followed me. I don't pretend to have been in love with Samuel. We were young, we met and fell into deep infatuation. During our time together, Samuel told me that it was hard growing up in the McCloud fishbowl. The pressure to be good was just too much for him."

"Come on. That boy was born to be bad." Selena didn't look as if bad was a bad thing.

Margo shushed her.

"By the time I realized I was pregnant, Samuel was dead. I tried to contact the McClouds, but I couldn't get through the layers of security and administrative assistants. And then as I watched strangers hold vigil outside

Mrs. McCloud's home and the paparazzi camped out practically on their doorstep I realized I didn't want that for my child." Rosie looked at her two friends in turn. "Can you imagine Casey's reaction to seeing himself on television with a black eye? Or how the kids would pick on him if some reporter spun their own version of how he got that black eye?"

"I wouldn't want Drew to go through that," Selena allowed.

"Or Peter." Margo gave Rosie's shoulder a supportive squeeze. "Unfortunately, that doesn't mean that Samuel's family doesn't deserve to know about Casey."

Rosie hung her head. "I knew it. I'm such a failure when it comes to my personal life. Casey will hold this against me forever. If I'd told the McClouds when he was born, maybe they would have respected my request for privacy, but now…"

"You're not a failure," Selena said, gently rubbing Rosie's shoulder.

"Selena's right. You're not a failure, but sometimes, you can't ignore what's right," Margo added. "And maybe, deep down, you've known this all along."

"They'll hate me. He'll hate me. And my career will be over." Walter, with his strong ties to the McClouds, wouldn't support her after this.

"Maybe," Margo allowed. "But you didn't keep Casey away from them with malicious intent so I don't think so."

"I've got to pull myself together." Rosie lifted her coffee cup and then set it down untouched. "Hud's going to be done with his speech soon and then I have lunch with Vivian. I don't know who I should tell first or how I should tell them."

"Don't tell them today," Selena advised. Margo sputtered.

But Selena didn't give in. "What? You want Rosie to just blurt it all out to the McClouds without thinking about the best way to break the news? Look at her. It drained her just to tell us."

In the end, Margo agreed with Selena. And Rosie? Rosie was just happy to put it off another day.

"YOU LEFT ME at the Rotary Club," Hud told Rosie as he closed her office door behind him.

The thirty-minute walk had left him resigned to the task before him. Rosie was going to hate him for not telling the entire truth, but he'd do everything in his power to keep her from leaving the campaign.

"We got some more volunteers today," Rosie said without looking up, emitting a clear "stay away from me" signal. She had a coffee cup from Margo's and a partially eaten muffin on her desk.

What had happened to upset her between the time he'd seen her at the Rotary Club and now? She'd weathered a run-in with Stu and his mother, so it had to be...

"I guess you heard about my speech." Hud slumped farther into the chair. "They looked at me as if I was reading them calculus equations."

Rosie looked surprised, which threw him. "I'm sorry," she said.

That was it? That couldn't be all she was going to say. "I know what you're thinking. Just say it," Hudson prompted, bracing himself. She was going to say "I told you so." "Don't make it pretty just for me."

But she didn't gloat. In fact, she looked down and moped some more. "The party conducted a small poll last night to gauge reaction to your candidacy. Your numbers went *down* from a week ago." All doom and gloom, she tossed him a sheet of paper. "This changes everything I planned."

At first, Hud was relieved that her low spirits weren't about his Rotary Club speech. But then he perused the percentages and realized they had a lot to be morose about. He needed to do something drastic. And he needed Rosie more than ever to win the race.

"I'm going to have to make a change," Hud began, placing the poll results on the corner of her desk.

"Yes." Only she didn't get up and dance like he'd seen her do at Casey's day care. If anything, she looked more depressed. A lock of hair hung limply over her cheek.

"Okay. Well. Yes," Hud stalled, not ready to see the respect Rosie had for him turn to contempt. Finally, he just sighed and told her, "You might want to write some of this down." It was going to get ugly.

"I don't think we need to do anything that formal. I was expecting it, so I've already packed my things."

"Packed your... What do you think is going on?"

"You're firing me. You've decided to go with someone more traditional for your campaign, someone who doesn't rock your boat."

"I'm—I'm what?" He liked the way she rocked his boat.

Her smile was washed out, defeated, and her eyes full of regret. "Don't feel bad. This actually makes my life easier."

"Wait a minute." Nobody quit this soon. There had to be some other reason Rosie was giving up on him. "Is Walter behind this?"

"No."

"Then unpack your things, damn it. I have something to say."

"I think it's for the best if I—"

Hud rocketed to his feet and pounded his fist on the top of her desk. "McCloud Inc. was using child labor overseas."

That shut Rosie up, giving Hud the floor. Coward that he was, he chose to sink back into the chair.

"I found out when I confronted our CEO after the rumors started. I couldn't allow the practice to continue and when I lost my influence in the Senate, I had two choices—stick things out and save my career, or make things right."

The good news was Rosie didn't walk out right away. "Why are you telling me this now?"

"You mean why didn't I tell you the complete truth before?" Hud forced himself to look at her. "I hoped I wouldn't have to. I hoped the fact that I'd retooled the company to operating within the law meant that no one, not even you, would care about the past, not when I was focusing on the future." This was where Rosie would go ballistic and bail.

But Rosie stayed glued where she was, sitting stock-still as if Hud's news was too much of a shock to take any other way than sitting down. "That still doesn't explain why you're telling me this today."

"You were honest with me about my chances if I didn't explain the past, but you did as I asked and created a speech that danced around the issues." If Hud had been right, Rosie's speech would have worked. "The speech you wrote bombed. And it hit me that without my father's name and my mother's influence, I wouldn't stand a chance. If I'm serious about a career in politics, I have to be honest and I have to be honest starting with you."

Rosie didn't say anything for a long time, but there was

a crease in her brow. "I made a decision this morning. I have something to tell you, too…. Something about my past. You won't want me to work for you when you hear it."

A decision this morning? Not work for him? That could only mean one thing. "About last night—"

"There's so much more to discuss here than last night. If I tell you…" Rosie paused, a bit of color creeping up her cheeks again. "*When* I tell you—"

"You're upset because I asked you out. I don't care what happened in your past. If it was something serious, the party wouldn't have hired you."

"Please, let me explain."

And then have her leave the campaign? Disappear from his life? No way. "Look, whatever it is that's been bugging you, I don't want to know." He'd been inside her home, seen her high school yearbook and played chess with her son. Hud knew what kind of person Rosie was—the kind of person he'd trust his future with.

"But—"

"I want you running my campaign." That came out louder than he'd planned, but he was desperate.

Rosie flinched. "But—"

"Look, you've built a solid career and raised a wonderful kid. That says a lot about a person. I don't need to know more than that." When Rosie opened her mouth to protest once more, Hud quickly created a compromise. "If you feel the need to tell me, write me a letter, seal it up in an envelope and give it to me. That way, if I get the overwhelming urge to know this deep, dark secret, I'll read it. But I can tell you right now that I'm not going to open it up until the day after the election."

"You'd do that?" There was a hint of wonder in her voice.

He'd do so much more if it meant she'd stick by him. Hud held up three fingers. "Scout's honor."

"And we'd keep our relationship professional. No more home visits." She eyed him shrewdly until he nodded, then Rosie reverted to business mode. "When you come forward with the truth it's not going to be pretty, at least not at first."

"We'll get through it together. Deal?" Hud stood and held out his hand. He'd gotten the important concession by having her stay on the campaign. The rest—the dating, that kiss—would come. Somewhere between his pushing the spark between them and getting to know her better, Hud realized he could fall in love with her.

"Deal." Rosie shook his hand briefly.

"Let's start with a working lunch," Hud proposed, glancing at his watch. "You can postpone lunch with my mother so we can work out the details of my speech."

"How did you..." Rosie eyed Hud speculatively. "Never mind. This is a bad idea."

"Working lunches mean you don't have to stay late," Hud pointed out. "Besides, bad ideas sometimes lead to good things, like heartfelt speeches. I'll be on my best behavior, I promise."

"Your definition of good behavior is different than mine." But Rosie smiled. "I'm so going to regret this."

"No, you won't."

"I MISSED YOU THIS EVENING."

Rosie glanced at the clock. Ten-thirty. Of course, it would be Hudson calling her cell phone. No one else knew she'd be up this late. Rosie moved from her make-shift desk at the kitchen table to the couch, settling into the overstuffed cushions. She'd been trying to compose the letter Hudson had requested knowing that someday the truth would be told and she'd accept the consequences. However, the best she'd been able to come up with for the letter was short and sweet—*Casey is Samuel's son.*

"Hello? Someone answered the phone," Hudson said, when she stayed silent. "Maybe I should come over to check and see if you're okay."

Since Hudson had told her everything this morning, he'd become more comfortable with her about other things, including his attraction to Rosie. She'd quickly learned her protests fell on deaf ears. She could have told Hudson her secret at anytime and that would have ended everything, but Rosie was a wimp. She enjoyed working on his campaign. She enjoyed being with him. And yes, she even enjoyed his flirtatious advances. Proving once again that Hudson was more honorable than she'd ever thought he could be.

"No home visits," Rosie said, trying not to imagine him calling her as he sat propped up in bed. "You know it's for the best."

Hudson chuckled. "The best for who?"

Wisely, Rosie steered the conversation to more neutral waters. "How did the appearances go tonight?"

"The PTA speech went smooth, and the radio interview was pretty good. They had tough questions about policy specifics that we haven't yet designed programs for."

She'd hoped the questions wouldn't be so intense this early in the campaign. As far as she was concerned, they were still searching for Hudson's silver bullet, that one thing that voters responded to.

"Then I played some basketball with the guys at the Washington Community Center and I think I threw out my back."

"You didn't." Sitting up, Rosie was already rescheduling Hudson's meetings and appearances for tomorrow when he started to laugh.

"No. But I did have to sit in the hot tub to work out the kinks because I don't have my own personal masseuse."

It was a hint, but Rosie wasn't taking it. "What a hardship."

"A man can try." Hudson sighed. "I thought of Casey when I was playing ball tonight. We could go to the park this weekend and shoot some hoops."

Standing, Rosie objected. Casey was already too attached to the man. She couldn't allow that when she couldn't trust Hudson's reaction to the truth. What if he didn't believe her and shunned Casey? Her baby would be crushed.

"I could have offered to bring over my boxing gloves." Hudson sounded hurt. "My dad made Samuel and I learn how to defend ourselves, but I figured teaching Casey basketball might help him fit in better."

"He fits in as well as I did in high school." And Hudson knew how well she'd done that. Criminy.

"I'm sure he does, but a little man-surance would be good in either case."

She smiled, but couldn't allow him to continue unchecked. "Please don't make up words or the only appearance I'll be able to arrange for you is on *The Man Show*."

"So we're on for this weekend?"

Tempting, but so was cheesecake and she hadn't had any in months. "It's a lovely gesture—"

"Why do I sense a but here? I did the same for Samuel and look how social he was."

"I admit, you must have done something right." With effort, Rosie used her serious voice. "Samuel fit in everywhere. He wanted to see the world and make friends wherever he went, while you wanted to conquer it."

"Ouch. We may have been different, but you don't have to say you liked one of us better than the other."

"Is everything a competition to you?"

"Reading. Reading isn't a competition. But just about everything else, yes."

"We're back to that killer instinct of yours." Which would destroy his campaign if she didn't curb it.

"Which, by the way, was carefully hidden from public view until you became my campaign manager."

Sometimes Rosie forgot the sacrifices he'd made. Ninety percent of the time, Hudson appeared so cocky that she forgot how wounded and honorable he was beneath the surface.

Hudson cleared his throat. "Would you like to go out to dinner this weekend?"

Holy smokes. "No." But a part of her was pleased.

"Uh, perhaps you shouldn't turn me down so quickly. It's a bit tough on a guy's ego…unless there's someone else."

Something simultaneously dreadful and exciting made Rosie tremble. She'd never wanted to be with a man as much as she wanted to be with Hudson. She paced around the living room before finally managing to say, "I don't date."

There was an equally long pause from Hudson's end of the line. "Because you're still in love with Casey's father?"

"No…I told you I don't have time to date."

"You did say that dating the right person would win me votes. The press would love you."

"I don't want that kind of vote." Not to mention the press would pick her apart, dissecting everything from her hair to what she wore. This was exactly what she'd been trying to shield Casey from.

"Okay, not a date then. A dinner between friends. We'll bring Casey along for pizza on Friday."

Rosie really wanted to say yes. "Your timing is all off."

"We can work on that." His tone suggested something more intimate than asking her out.

"Hudson." She stopped in front of a curio cabinet filled with pictures of Casey, friends and family. And in the back, one small picture of her and Samuel in front of the Eiffel Tower.

"I'd be true. You know I'd apply my two-handed handshake only to you."

Despite herself, Rosie grinned. Besides, Hudson couldn't see her. "No."

"I can tell you're smiling." She could tell he was, too. What had she gotten herself into?

"We'll talk about this another time. Good night, Rosie."

CHAPTER TEN

HUD LOADED UP his briefcase Wednesday night before heading to a late dinner with a city councilman and his wife. He paused before slipping the letter-sized envelope Rosie had given him earlier into his briefcase. When she'd put it in his hand, she'd been reluctant to let it go.

Hud tapped the envelope against his fingers. What could she possibly need to tell him that she thought he'd disapprove of? The contents of the envelope were very thin, perhaps containing only one page, not nearly enough to confess anything of consequence…right?

He'd promised Rosie he wouldn't open the letter until after the election was over.

"Good night," someone called from the front of the office.

Hud automatically returned the greeting, but no one else did. It was a slow night. He was alone. With her confession.

Someone honked outside and Hud waved, still holding the envelope.

"I can't believe I'm doing this," he mumbled.

And then Hud did what he should have done the moment Rosie handed the envelope to him.

IT TURNS OUT Ms. Phan was right," Rosie said, cradling her coffee mug as she curled up in the corner of the couch in the annex of Margo's Bistro. "My being late and working so hard has made Casey too needy. As soon as kids start being picked up in the afternoon he sits in front of the clock waiting for me. Every night he comes up with excuses not to go to bed on time. This morning when I dropped him off at school he wouldn't let go of me."

"It's just a phase," Nora said from the other end of the couch. She had a five-year-old boy, too.

"Nothing serious," Derrick seconded. He had two girls several years older than Casey. "Trust me, when he gets to the sixth grade and doesn't want to be seen with you, you'll look back fondly on this."

"I've read all about separation anxiety, but wasn't that supposed to happen years ago?" Rosie scanned the room.

It was Thursday night, the regular meeting time for Rosie's small group of friends. Margo, Derrick, Selena, Rosie, Nora and her twin, Suzanne, were all seated in the annex. At one time the friends had referred to each other as the Singles with Kids, but that was before Margo had married Robert, and Derrick had married Bailey. The only singles left were Selena and Rosie. Suzanne hadn't been one of the original group, but came occasionally with Nora now that she was planning Nora's wedding to Erik. Based on the distracted expression on Nora's face, things weren't going as smoothly as she'd like.

"Kids are tougher than you think." Suzanne loaded her plate with a second helping of Margo's homemade dessert. Considering Suzanne could barely care for herself, Rosie didn't take her comment seriously. "Tougher than a certain mom-to-be I know."

"Suzanne!" Nora looked horrified. "You promised not to tell."

"What's everyone going to think of your wedding

planner when you don't fit into the wedding dress?" Suzanne sniffed.

No one spoke. Everyone looked at Nora.

"We decided to try for a baby right away since Erik is pushing forty. Only, surprise," Nora said, smiling weakly. "We got pregnant right out of the gate."

"That's wonderful news." Rosie stood along with everyone else to give Nora a hug.

"I'm so happy for you," Selena said.

"No wonder you asked for decaf," Margo added.

Derrick looked uncomfortable. "You're not going to give us the play-by-play, are you?" Being a former college football star and now a successful lawyer, it had always been a bit of a challenge to Derrick's ego to hang out with four women.

"No details." Nora blushed. "It's still so early. I'm just a few weeks along."

The conversation moved to other things and all too soon it was time to go home. Rosie and Selena stayed to help Margo clean up.

"How could you not tell Hudson?" Margo asked, taking two coffee mugs from Rosie and dropping them gently in the hot soapy water filling the kitchen sink. "You knew you'd have to tell him when you left here on Tuesday morning."

"Really, Margo, she's kept quiet for more than five years. You can't expect her to spit out the truth just like that." Selena set a stack of dirty dessert plates on the stainless steel counter.

"I tried to tell him," Rosie said. "I was fully expecting to get fired when I told him about Casey and I said so."

"You told Hudson you were going to tell him something that would get you fired?" Margo rolled up her sleeves. "If anyone can get him elected, you can. Of course he wouldn't want to hear anything you had to say. That's the way it works. Don't ask, don't tell."

"It wasn't like that. We made a deal. I wrote him a letter and he promised to open it the day after the election." She shook out a folded dish towel.

"And you believed him?" Margo shut the water off and began washing.

"Isn't that like leaving a child alone with a stack of Christmas presents?" Selena asked. "You know, they peek."

The peace Rosie had felt the past two days deflated. "Hudson wouldn't do that."

"This is the same man who's been saying he covered up what happened to him two years ago?" Margo shook her head.

"He was trying to do the right thing," Rosie protested. "I trust him."

Selena, who was usually on Rosie's side, beat Margo to the punch. "But should you?"

"WE HAVEN'T BEEN ABLE to lure the right speechwriter to the team yet," Rosie told Hud with a toss of her beautiful hair. "While I work on the speech for the community center opening, can you write the speech for the yacht club?"

It had been more than a week since she'd given Hud that troublesome letter and every day Rosie greeted him the same way—anxiously, as if he'd discovered her secret and was about to fire her. And forget telling her it didn't matter. Rosie was as tense as a mouse in a roomful of hungry cats.

"Speechwriting isn't my strength," Hud admitted slowly. He'd stayed away from Rosie's apartment and he was starting to feel as edgy as the greeting she gave him every morning. "Isn't that something Martin could tackle?"

The purple-haired, multi-pierced college student was proving to be a valuable asset. He practiced interviewing Hud and he'd even written variations of Hud's "come clean" speech, none of which seemed to be doing anything for Hud's poll figures. In Rosie's opinion, they'd missed their opportunity.

Rosie frowned. "This is a speech we're talking about. You must have had a skill for it when you ran for the Senate."

"Well…"

"Oh, come on. It's the same thing. Start with broad statements, go a little more in-depth and close strong."

"I can't. I never…" Hud's father, a tremendously talented speechwriter, had told Hud many times he wasn't good at the subtleties and that he had to leave the speech-writing to professionals.

Rosie stared at him. "What do you mean you can't?"

Men weren't supposed to squirm, but Hud did. "I can't because I never wrote my speeches. Not even in high school. Stu wrote everything."

There had only been a few times in Hud's life when he'd made a statement that was met with a jaw-dropping reaction. He reached over and gently lifted Rosie's chin. She swatted his hand away.

"I can't believe this." She rose to her feet. "Did you ever do anything, *think* about anything, for yourself?"

"What did you expect me to do?"

Rosie looked at him with disappointment in her eyes.

"Do you think it was easy for me? Nothing I ever did was good enough for my father." Or his mother. Or Samuel. And now, apparently, Rosie.

Eyes wide, Rosie backed away. "Excuse me."

Hud sank into the nearest chair. Things weren't working out as he'd envisioned.

"WHAT HAVE I DONE?" Rosie escaped toward Market Street. She couldn't figure Hudson out. Was he the honorable man she'd thought he was? She couldn't go for coffee because Margo had been right. Hudson had her letter admitting Casey was Samuel's and she had no faith that he'd keep it sealed as he'd promised.

Did he know already? Was he toying with her? She didn't want to believe it, but she couldn't stop wondering....

Rosie's cell phone interrupted her panic attack a block from headquarters.

"Ms. DeWitt? This is Bonnie, the nurse at Casey's school."

Rosie latched onto her cell phone.

"Casey is complaining of a stomachache, but he doesn't have a fever and he hasn't thrown up."

"Oh." Rosie's mind raced. It was only eleven o'clock. Would she be a bad mother if she made him finish the remainder of the day? And then sent him on to day care after school? Yes, she would.

"He wants to talk to you."

"Mommy." Casey's voice was a thin wail. "I feel sick." He sounded horrible.

"You do?" Rosie mentally reviewed the afternoon's schedule. Her postponed lunch with Vivian was today, plus a visit with Hudson to the local children's cancer ward, a planning meeting with the team, and a conference call to a national magazine that wanted to include Hudson as one of the most eligible bachelors in the United States.

Rosie could move most things to other days, but not the lunch.

"I feel sick. I need to go home."

"Are you sure you can't finish out the day?" It would be good to get away from Hudson, hide out at home with Casey and pretend her world wasn't about to crash around her.

"No-o-o, Mommy."

"I won't be able to come get you until almost one o'clock." Casey went to full-day kindergarten. Normally, he didn't finish until three. Why did he always seem to get sick when she was desperately trying to make things happen? Immediately, Rosie was consumed with remorse at the thought.

"Hurry."

"Let me talk to the nurse." Rosie explained her situation to the nurse, trying as hard as she could to keep the guilt out of her voice. Her son was sick, yet she wasn't coming to get him right away. Her hard work would pay off in the long run, but that didn't mean she wasn't failing her son today.

"I could send Casey back to class or let him lay here in my office." The nurse seemed awfully understanding.

"Could you let him stay with you?" Rosie hoped she didn't sound too desperate. It would be hard to make good to a teacher if Casey threw up in her classroom. She explained that she had a meeting she couldn't miss and asked the nurse to call her on the off chance that Casey felt better before she picked him up. "Do you think he'll be okay for two hours?" *Please, please, please...*

The nurse lowered her voice. "He seems fine. Sometimes all they need is a day with mom or dad to make them all better."

The nurse's comment tweaked Rosie's guilt even more.

Once she was off the phone, Rosie had a decision to make—work the rest of the day from home or bring Casey to work. She could pick him up and bring him to the office, except that meant watching Hudson charm her son. Not an option. Unless…she sent Hudson out for the entire afternoon. She'd been wanting to have him shake hands with the people of the city and test the waters to find an issue or cause that would make him shine.

Rosie scrolled through her contact list and started making calls.

"I'M SORRY I'M LATE." Rosie slid into a chair opposite Vivian at the exclusive Gary Denko restaurant. "Everything's been happening so fast that I wasn't able to include you in some of our initial agenda discussions or talk to you about the role I want you to play in the campaign."

Over the past week Vivian had come to terms with that fact that Hud was going to reshape the family image in the way that would most benefit him. Her *prudish* way of looking at things, shaped by Mama McCloud and Vivian's own desire to fit in, wouldn't matter in the long term. Vivian had become more interested in hearing what Rosie had to say, but she also had her own agenda in mind—to discover what was going on between her son and Rosie. She'd seen nothing more between them than what was appropriate for colleagues, but every once in a while Vivian caught Hud looking at Rosie with a grin Rosie tried hard to ignore. And that was all a wannabe grandmother needed.

"The more united we are, the smoother this will be for Hudson and the harder it will be for our opposition." Rosie slid off her shoulder bag with a weary sigh.

"I agree that Hud should be the priority." Along with her plan for grandkids.

For the first time Vivian noticed the bags under Rosie's eyes. Her smile tended to outshine her deficits, like those puffy eyes and the stress lines around her mouth. If her son's campaign manager wasn't careful, politics would age her before her time, which was a shame since she had a natural beauty.

"Would it be possible for your secretary to copy me on your calendar? We have a lot of challenges ahead and I'll need as much of your time as you can spare."

"For fund-raising, of course." Vivian waved off the waiter. She wanted more time alone before they got distracted by food.

Rosie shook her head. "Not just fund-raising. The McClouds are a beloved family in the city. I'm comfortable with you making appearances on your own, with Stu if you'd like."

Vivian almost fainted at the possibility, at the freedom. Hamilton had only wanted her at his side watching his back and working a room to raise money. She'd been his silent partner when it came to weighing in on political issues. No one needed silent partners.

"You're more than a body standing behind Hudson. You're a force unto your own."

Vivian was so pleased she couldn't do more than nod her head in agreement.

"This campaign is about making a connection with the voters. You're the heart of the McCloud family. Who better to embody the compassion that will make San Francisco families stronger?"

"Yes." Here was a woman who understood Vivian's potential. Her mind spun in new, exciting directions. There was so much to do. She'd need a new ensemble or two, something classic yet warm and approachable. Appearances were important, but causes more so. Should she propose…? "Do you think…the campaign could incorporate programs for low income at-risk children? I've donated to certain charities for years, but it would feel so good to make a real difference."

"What a wonderful idea. If you could make a list of your interests, I'll have someone put together some ideas and run them by Hudson. There's also a possibility of speaking at San Francisco State next week. They had someone in their speaker series cancel and are looking to fill a slot." Rosie jotted something down in a small notebook unaware that she was giving Vivian a gift she hadn't dared ask for. Vivian only wished she'd do the same for Hud. "Now, I know you want to talk about the office—"

"As far as I'm concerned, the office is totally inappropriate." Vivian watched disappointment weigh Rosie's expression. The woman needed to learn to hide her feelings better. "However, Walter thinks it's brilliant and Hud finds it useful, so I suppose we can continue with it for now."

"Thank you, Vivian. I'm trying not to let it become a circus."

"I know you are." Vivian drew upon her most gracious smile. There'd be plenty of time later to grill Rosie about any romantic attachment she might have to her son. "Unfortunately, that's often what these races become."

"CAN WE GO TO THE PARK?" Casey asked as he pushed a couple of Hot Wheels cars across the carpet in campaign headquarters, all trace of stomach upset gone.

"No." Rosie had to write a speech and the words

weren't coming. Casey's constant interruptions weren't helping, either. She reached for her coffee cup, but it was empty.

He watched her toss the cup into the trash and stood with a hopeful smile. "Can we go to Margo's?"

"No. I can't go anywhere until I finish this."

"Hello, Rosie." Vivian appeared in the doorway to Rosie's office, her features softening when she saw Casey. "Who's your new assistant?"

Rosie's heart was pounding as she said, "This is my son, Casey." *Your grandson.* "Casey, this is Mrs. McCloud, Hudson's mother."

Having been exposed to the office environment in the past, Casey exhibited good manners, standing up tall and offering his hand to his grandmother. "It's nice to meet you."

Rosie gasped as they shook hands. Did she know? Would Vivian see any of Samuel in Casey?

Vivian seemed overjoyed to meet Casey, but for no other reason than a natural affinity with kids. "The pleasure is all mine. Am I mistaken or should you be in school today?"

As serious as any candidate under scrutiny, Casey said, "I had a stomachache and I told the nurse I couldn't make it to the end of the day."

"I see." Vivian smiled and exchanged a knowing glance with Rosie and whispered, "A child's version of a personal day."

Weak-kneed with relief, Rosie mouthed, "He's fine." Good at concocting a scheme to get his way. He didn't realize the consequences of his innocent deception. What a mess. Rosie forced herself to meet Vivian's gaze. "Can I help you?"

Someone paused outside the window to look in. After a moment of stiff shock, Vivian nodded at the man.

"I was excited by our lunch discussion and I wanted to pass a few of my thoughts on to you."

"I'm surprised you made a list so quickly." Rosie glanced at the clock. It had only been two hours since their lunch.

Vivian appeared oddly nervous. "You do want them, don't you?"

"Yes. I wish everyone worked so fast." Including Rosie herself. She glanced at her mostly blank computer screen.

"Now that Mrs. McCloud is here, we can go to the park," Casey announced. "You said the reason you had to work so hard was because you didn't have enough workers."

"Sorry, Case," Rosie said firmly. "I need to talk with Vivian."

"You always have to talk to somebody. I'm bored, Mommy." Casey's manners were quickly evaporating, sending Rosie's deodorant into overdrive beneath her wool suit jacket.

She didn't dare look at Hudson's mother. "Why don't I see if the conference room is open. You can watch TV." When Casey was safely ensconced in front of the conference room television, Rosie hurried back to her office and closed the door behind her. "I'm sorry about that."

"I understand completely. Your son is charming." Vivian withdrew a sheet of paper from her conservative designer bag but hesitated handing it over.

"Why do you keep looking at me as if you think I've changed my mind?" Rosie laughed, buoyed by the good impression Casey made on his grandmother. It was easier than fretting over what would soon turn awkward. "This is a tremendous help. I'll want you to spend some time with Martin, our interim speechwriter." Rosie hoped

Vivian wouldn't freak out over Martin's punked-out appearance, because the college student had talent.

"I thought Stu would write something for me once we agreed to the list."

"I have no problem with any of these, but Stu's talents are a bit…" Rosie paused. "Dated. Martin has a strong pulse on the voters today."

"I'm more comfortable with Stu," Mrs. McCloud said staunchly.

Some days, getting the McClouds to see things her way was like pulling teeth. "Let's compromise. The three of you can work on your speeches together." Rosie was betting Martin was tough enough to corral Stu and Mrs. McCloud, because if she lost Martin, she'd be in deep doo-doo.

Martin poked his purple head of hair into Rosie's office. "That reporter is here again."

Surprisingly, Vivian took in Martin's spiky hair and eyebrow piercing in stride when Rosie introduced them. Rosie's respect for Hudson's mother increased.

"Tell her our man isn't here," Rosie instructed.

Martin looked pained. "She wants to talk to Mrs. McCloud. I think she saw her through the window."

Not sure if that was a good or a bad thing, Rosie pasted a smile on her face and shifted into crisis mode. "Are you up to this? We can put them off if you like."

Vivian looked a little shell-shocked. "What would I talk about?"

"You have this." Rosie held up her list of charitable interests. "And you can also announce that you'll be speaking at the university next Monday."

"About what?" Vivian's eyes widened.

"About whatever you like. You so rarely speak that I

think you could talk about the weather and people would want to listen. Besides, all the proceeds will go to one of your charities." Rosie knew one coffee shop owner who'd be first in line for tickets. "Unless you're having second thoughts."

Vivian seemed to ponder this for a moment, then smiled gamely. "I want to do this."

CHAPTER ELEVEN

"I REALIZE YOU'RE PRESSED for time, Mrs. McCloud. Thank you for speaking with me." The reporter, that Amy Furokawa woman, sounded sincere and Rosie had reassured Vivian that this would be a quick sound bite. Still, Vivian's heart pounded.

"Thank you for helping to spread the word." This was becoming a boring mutual admiration society. Vivian hurried on. "I'd like to announce An Evening of Caring, a benefit for Children's Charities of America to be held this Monday at the University of San Francisco."

"What's your involvement in this event?"

"I'm one of the coordinators and the featured speaker."

Amy nodded, her eyes glazed as if from boredom. Rosie stood out of camera range, making an encouraging hand gesture for Vivian to keep talking.

Vivian glanced down at the condensed notes Rosie had scribbled off moments before. "I'll be sharing some of the McCloud history and answering questions from attendees. One hundred percent of the proceeds will be going directly to Children's Charities of America."

"Will Hudson be attending?" Amy's eyes sharpened.

"He will be busy campaigning elsewhere that night, but he's supportive of me and this event." Vivian sounded as stiff and stilted as she felt.

Amy turned to the camera. "You heard it first live and on the streets from Amy Furokawa, Action News." Amy spun on Rosie. "This isn't the kind of coverage we envisioned. That was free air time and nothing more."

Vivian stood silently like a third appendage as the impertinent reporter continued with her disparaging remarks. Rosie's little boy must have felt the same way, because he was standing at the glass window frowning and making streaks with his fingers. Vivian smiled. It wouldn't be so bad to have a ready-made grandchild.

Rosie closed in on Amy and lowered her voice. "You're the first person to get an interview with Mrs. McCloud in over a year. Let's hash out topics for a more in-depth interview later."

Amy's expression perked up. "When?"

"When?" Rosie glanced at Vivian, who gave a small shrug. "Perhaps next week."

Amy frowned again. "I'll need something sooner. There isn't enough on the campaign so far to generate much air time."

"We'll be in touch." Rosie took Vivian gently by the arm. Once the glass door closed behind the reporter, Rosie pulled Casey away from the window and said, "You did a good job on short notice. You should have told me you have stage fright."

She'd noticed? "I have nerves of steel." Oh, she was such a liar. Vivian pointed to the reporter on her cell phone outside. "She's a horrid person."

"Reporters are just like people." Rosie smiled. "Some you love and others make you cringe, but we try to make the best of it."

"I think that's been my motto for quite some time."

ROSIE SHOULDN'T have been surprised to open the door to Hudson shortly after six-thirty on Thursday night. He'd managed to stay away from her apartment for more than a week, seemingly satisfied with their late-night phone calls. As had become her usual habit, she studied his face to see if he'd read her letter, but nothing in his expression indicated he had.

Wearing jeans and a deep blue designer sweater that set off his dark hair, Hudson somehow managed to look energetic and put-together after a full day's work, while Rosie felt drained and frumpy in her clearance-rack duds.

Sporting an easygoing grin, Hudson held up bags of food. "Soup, salad and French bread? How did it go with my mother?"

"Your mother was wonderful. If I had to guess, I'd say she's been yearning to get out there in front of people for years and no one's ever given her a chance." Rosie didn't budge. She wasn't going to let him in.

Hudson's smile warmed Rosie to her toes. "Kudos to you."

Holding on to the door, Rosie switched to a different topic, hoping that Casey would stay in the bathroom a few more minutes. "How did the appearances go?"

"The cancer ward was agonizing. I felt so helpless." His gaze fell to the floor and Rosie knew exactly what he was feeling. Meeting frail children fighting for their lives was heartbreaking. "I needed a breather between that and my next stop. So Graham and I went to Margo's. She introduced me to the icy pleasure of a strawberry frappucino."

"If that didn't pick you up, nothing would." Rosie allowed herself a smile, just enough to let Hudson know she understood, but not enough to encourage him.

His gaze burned into hers. "I've missed you and Casey. Where is the little chess prodigy? Can I come in?"

"You see me every day." She'd come to appreciate evenings away from him without the pressure of moral dilemmas.

Hudson leaned against the doorframe, drinking her in as if he hadn't seen her just this morning. "Do you know what I do every night?"

"Fall asleep?"

His smile was gentle. "My cook prepares my dinner. I come home and eat alone. Read. Catch a little bit of ESPN. And then, yes, I fall asleep."

Rosie imagined Hudson's life had changed drastically after he ended his senatorial career. But this? "That sounds rather—"

"Boring," Hud said, at the same time that Rosie finished with, "Domesticated."

"You can see why coming over here is the highlight of my day. It's life-in-the-fast-lane stuff."

"I'd rather you didn't admit your evening routine in any of your interviews," Rosie said, mirroring his position as she leaned against the door. "It doesn't sound very intriguing."

"I've been thinking about that. What if I mentioned I was dating my campaign manager? That sends a very specific impression."

"We're not dating." And they never would be dating, not with Casey's secret between them. Although that didn't stop Rosie from stealing a look at his lips.

"Is that the mayor?" Casey ran over to the door. "What did you bring us to eat? Tomorrow is pizza day."

Knowing when she'd been defeated, Rosie reluctantly let Hudson inside. He leaned over and planted a kiss on top of her head as he came in, sending a jolt of awareness throughout her system. A few minutes ago she'd been tired. And now? *Zing.*

"You can't stay long," Rosie found herself babbling. "I'm meeting friends at Margo's."

"The mayor's a friend," Casey said, sitting on his knees in a kitchen chair as he watched Hudson unpack the food. "He can play chess with me while you talk to your friends. Would you like that?"

"That sounds like a lot of fun," Hudson replied, staring at Rosie as if he wanted to sweep her into his arms and kiss her senseless.

The depressing thing was that Rosie was disappointed when he didn't.

"Isn't that sweet?" Margo said when she saw Hudson sit on the floor next to the children's table.

"Who would have known Hudson was so good with kids?" Nora commented. "I haven't liked him since that scandal a few years back, but he's nothing like I expected."

Among her friends, Rosie wasn't just the straight-laced political aide or a mother. With this small group, she was a person with many facets, someone who could laugh and cry about the joys of parenting, or talk about personal dreams, loneliness or chances missed. Tonight, she couldn't be anything but Hudson's campaign manager.

"And he knows football," Derrick said, pulling Bailey closer and kissing her temple. Since they'd returned from their honeymoon their tans had faded but they were still noticeably relaxed. "I didn't think guys like him cared about the game, but he remembered me."

"It's a shame he's perfect," Selena said with a remorseful glance Rosie's way.

Margo stopped drawing the ginger-colored curtains

over the windows long enough to reassure Rosie. "Everything will be all right."

Gripping her bright orange mug topped with whipped cream that—she had to face it—was going right past that nonfat milk to her thighs, Rosie looked around at her friends, momentarily aware of how lucky she'd been to have found them. They were a steady force in her suddenly tumultuous world.

"The party's launching another poll tonight," Rosie admitted. "I have yet to move Hudson's numbers in the right direction."

"They wouldn't fire you. Would they?" Selena set her espresso down untouched.

Derrick frowned. "That hardly seems fair. You've never lost before."

Margo came around the table and hugged Rosie tight. "You'll think of something. You always do."

"It's complicated," Rosie admitted. "He needs something to define him with the voters, something he'll stand for that they care about. I've tried to get him to loosen up. I've looked at every angle of his interests, voting record and charitable causes, but nothing clicks."

"Come on," Derrick prompted. "I'm sure Hudson helps old ladies to cross the street or saves homeless animals or something."

"Of course he does. But Hudson keeps people at a distance. He let his guard down tonight and charmed you all." As she watched him ruffle Casey's hair, Rosie wrestled with what Hudson's campaign needed and how she could give it to him. "He's got to be more relaxed and spontaneous, but turn a camera on him and he delivers lines like a B movie actor. If I can't find a way to loosen him up, someone else will."

"I HAD FUN WITH your coffee group last night. Thanks for inviting me." Hud handed Rosie a container of live violets in a pink ceramic pot. He'd added a small card beneath the white ribbon. The flowers and the message in the card were meant to take her mind off that damn letter.

Hud gestured to Margo to bring him a cup of coffee and sat next to Rosie, who blushed furiously because everyone was looking at them. Let them look. Rosie was the most beautiful, dynamic woman in the room. This morning she had her hair pulled back in a loose ponytail at the base of her neck and was wearing a dark, feminine pantsuit that didn't look like the uncomfortable full body armor some women chose for business attire.

"You can't give me flowers. Walter is due here any minute." Without even reading the card, Rosie handed the plant to Margo as she delivered Hud's coffee. "Put these somewhere, will you?"

Hud raised a hand toward the bouquet as Margo carried it past. "But you didn't even see—"

"Flowers for your campaign manager? Do I smell romance?" Amy Furokawa sidled up to their table.

"No. Hud was just…" Rosie sent Hudson a pleading look.

"Congratulating Rosie on a strong start for my campaign," Hud filled in with a meager smile. Yes, the campaign was important, but Hud was starting to believe he'd found something just as important with Rosie. "Can we talk later, Amy? We're expecting others for a meeting."

"Certainly. We're live during the next hour if you'll have time for me." At Hud's nod, Amy spoke directly to Rosie. "We'll have to arrange an interview. I just realized that we haven't gotten any film of you."

"I don't do on-camera interviews. I have a little boy and—"

"We'd love to put him on air, as well, the working mother angle is appealing to our viewers." Amy's tone sounded off. "I'll call you later to set that up. Oh, we can get your husband on camera, too, right?" With a wave, Amy left to place a coffee order at the counter.

"I'm not married," Rosie called out, then gave up with a toss of her hands. "I hope Walter brought your numbers."

"I did." The chairman shook their hands and sat down. He'd flown up from Los Angeles for their early-morning meeting and looked uncommonly rumpled. "Granted, it's early, but we're not gaining any momentum."

Hud's spirits sank. He reached over and gently held Rosie's hand. She was driving herself into the ground over the campaign, determined to find the right note to resonate with voters. "This is all my fault. I still haven't gotten the tone Rosie wants from my practice media interviews."

Rosie stared at Hud's hand on hers and then extricated herself, cradling her coffee mug with both hands. Hud wished that she would have read the card on the flowers.

"The clock is ticking now," Walter continued. "The city council will announce today that an election for mayor will be held in mid-March."

"It's taken us a bit longer to get off the ground without a speechwriter on staff." Rosie was on the defensive, her keen gaze trained on Walter. "We've got more public appearances coming up next week for both Hudson and Vivian. And we're going to be trying some new angles."

"Fund-raising won't kick up his popularity points," Walter pointed out.

Hud felt the need to defend his mother. "Mother is

doing a live interview with Action News and a special charity event where she's telling stories about the McClouds and answering audience questions."

Walter's white eyebrows shot up. "Viv's speaking?"

"She's very excited about it," Rosie said, her words deceptively casual. There was a crease in her brow and Rosie's grip on the coffee mug was rigid, as if very little was keeping her from falling apart.

Hud wanted to soothe her apprehension and kiss her worries away. Yes, there was a lot at stake in this race, but when it was over Hud would still have these feelings for Rosie.

"She doesn't…she gets…she's a very private person." Hud couldn't tell from Walter's faltering speech if the older man was angry or concerned. "Viv didn't tell me about this. In fact—" Walter glared at Rosie "—no one told me."

"I sent you an e-mail update last night." Rosie seemed wound up tight enough to burst. "Didn't you open the attachment?"

Walter dug his BlackBerry out of his pocket. "I can't open attachments. I can barely open e-mail on this thing, much less read the small print. I thought technology was supposed to make my life easier."

Chuckling, Hud reached for Walter's BlackBerry. "Let me help you." Hud increased the font size on the handheld e-mail device and showed Walter how to open an attached file.

"I won't remember how to do this tomorrow," Walter said, pocketing his BlackBerry without reading the attachment. "And by the way, we've got a chance at the presidential endorsement if we can bring your numbers up. He's coming through town next week. It could mean big things."

Walter patted Rosie's shoulder with a significant look, then turned to Hud. "Can you get me a coffee? Black."

WALTER LOWERED HIS VOICE so that only Rosie could hear when Hudson left to get his coffee. "I'm relying on you to keep things on an even keel until the president is out of town. No scandals, no upsets. Understood?"

No coming clean about secrets, like long-lost nephews. Rosie understood far too well. "I'll do my best," was all Rosie managed to say. She'd cross her fingers that Hudson wouldn't read her letter, continue to keep him at arm's length and swallow the guilt for a few more days. No problem at all.

"We need to talk," Rosie said to Hudson after Walter left with his coffee.

This morning Rosie wore sensible flats. This morning, nothing Hudson said would send her equilibrium rocking. Even if Rosie loved how Hudson hadn't been so cliché as to give her roses.

Instead of reminding him that home visits weren't allowed—he'd already broken that rule last night—Rosie shuffled her feet slowly across the linoleum and found herself admiring how handsome Hudson looked when he smiled at her. She shouldn't want him to gather her close and ask her what was wrong.

"I never thanked you for bringing food over last night," Rosie blurted.

"I'll bring over Italian tonight. It's pizza night, right?"

"That's not such a good idea." Rosie had to tell Hudson to stay away, regardless of how she felt about him. Two more months until the election seemed like an eternity with this secret hanging over her head. "Aren't there any models in town to keep you busy?"

"Models lost their appeal a few years ago when I realized women weren't interested in me." Hudson frowned. "Well, they're interested in the idea of me—the only McCloud heir and a man in his thirties who will obviously want to settle down and start a family right away."

"Clearly, they're missing out on your good points." Rosie was going to miss him. She couldn't wait two months. She'd tell him after the president came. She'd have to quit first. All of these thoughts were very depressing.

"My good points? Such as?"

She'd stepped right into that one. Somehow she kept the mood light. "Well, let's see. You never interrupt, you're incredibly patient and never challenge someone else's opinion unless you do so with respect to their feelings." Rosie couldn't resist ribbing Hudson because she'd finally found someone who was interested in her that understood politics, someone who didn't kowtow to her every wish, but someone who understood how important it was to step up and make a difference at any level. Rosie didn't want any of this to end. She tried to smile. "Need I go on?"

"No. Those sound like good qualifications for mayor." His smile was killer, sending heat down to her toes.

"Now that your meeting's over…" Amy Furokawa closed in with her camera crew. "Can we get a live interview for the morning show?"

Hudson nodded toward the cameras and put on what Rosie recognized as his public, whitewashed persona. She wished she'd been able to break him of that habit, to get him to talk to the press as he talked to her, his personality shining through flaws and all. "Of course. Would you like Margo to make you a coffee?"

"No. We need to hurry because the Republicans are announcing their candidate at city hall at nine." Holding a microphone, Amy moved closer to Hudson, sending Rosie's jealousy meter up several notches as one of her crew counted down. "We're here live with the Democratic candidate for mayor, Hudson McCloud. Do you want to know who you're running against?"

"Roger Bartholomew," Hudson said.

Amy's smile wavered but the camera didn't catch her reaction as the cameraman leaned in for an extreme close-up of Hudson.

"He's a good man," Hudson continued. "I'm looking forward to hearing what he has to say."

"Worried?"

"It's no secret that San Francisco has both conservative and liberal constituents, but I had no idea Bartholemew had switched to the Republican party."

Amy's off-camera expression was withdrawn. Her lips wound slowly upward as she turned to the camera. "There you have it, Dave. Hudson McCloud's early morning strategy sessions at a little-known café in SOMA—Margo's Bistro. Looks like the race for mayor is shaping up to be a good one."

"And…we're off," said a man standing behind the cameraman.

"We'll see you around." Amy gave Hudson a little wave before hustling her crew out the door and into the rain.

Rosie watched the crew load up their double-parked van while Amy stood beneath Margo's canopy making a phone call. Several times Amy glanced back at Rosie and Hudson. "That woman is up to no good."

"If she's looking for dirt, she's not going to find it," Hudson said.

Rosie wasn't so sure. She couldn't avoid it any longer. She'd try to keep the peace as Walter wanted by not divulging that Casey was Samuel's son, but she couldn't work like this. Rosie squared her shoulders and dropped her gaze to her coffee. "I've been thinking—"

"That's a bad habit."

"And I'm going to resign from your campaign next week." There. She'd said it. Now she just needed to brace herself for Hudson's arguments against her resignation.

Only he didn't say a word. He just left her sitting there.

This couldn't be happening. "Margo, you have a back room here, don't you?" Hud asked, trying to stay cool.

"Our kitchen is that way." Margo gestured with a nod to a closed door behind her as she prepared someone's coffee and Em, her day-shift assistant, took orders.

When he returned to their table, Hud flipped open his phone and put it to his ear as if taking a call. He took Rosie by the arm and nodded to Amy, who had once more turned to check on them.

"What are we doing?" With a glance out the window, Rosie followed. "Didn't you hear what I said?"

Hud ignored her. At the door of the kitchen Hud paused and gestured as if Rosie needed to hear what was being said on the phone. Through the corner of his eye, he saw Amy, no longer even pretending nonchalant interest, peering into the glass front windows.

"Work with me on this," Hud said.

Rosie glanced over her shoulder and spotted the camera crew. "And you said you weren't an actor."

Hud pressed a finger to his ear as if he couldn't hear. He ushered Rosie into the kitchen, waved his thanks to Margo and closed the door behind them.

"What's this all about?" Rosie's cheeks were a tender shade of pink. She backed against a stainless steel counter.

"You can't quit." Hud's heart pounded as he moved closer to her. "You didn't even read the card that went with the flowers."

"I don't want to talk about the flowers. I need to talk to you about my letter."

"You should have read the card. In it I said that I'd thrown your letter away. Unread."

"Oh." Her breathy reaction made him grin.

"If anyone should be asking for forgiveness, it's me. I've made my share of mistakes in the past." He was close enough now to reach out and stroke her cheek, to brush a curl behind her ear. "I told you that first day in my office that I wanted to look to the future and I think you should, too. Stop worrying about the past. Don't quit. You give me hope for the future." Hud put a hand on the counter on either side of her. "I haven't felt this way in a long time."

"What way? Annoyed? Irritable?"

"Ecstatic and frustrated. Tense and wanting. Sound familiar?"

Her gaze slid away as another curl worked its way loose. "You're in the middle of an important campaign. I'll see you through the presidential visit, but there are other circumstances that—"

Hud pressed two fingers against Rosie's lips. "I want to be with you all the time. I want to share what I'm feeling with you. I've told myself to hold off. I've tried to respect your boundaries at work and at home, but I can't."

Unable to wait any longer, Hud bent to kiss her temple, breathing in her scent accented by a lightly floral perfume. He bent farther to kiss her cheek, then angled his head to kiss her lips, his mouth hovering, almost touching hers, waiting for her signal that she wanted him, too.

Nothing happened.

Had he read her wrong?

And then Rosie closed the millimeter between them and pressed her lips to his.

KISSING HUDSON was like a roller-coaster ride that started at the top, sent you into a corkscrew and flipped you upside down and right side up again. Rosie barely dared to breathe as she wound her arms around Hudson's neck, speared her fingers into his thick, short hair and pulled him closer, because if she didn't hang on, her knees would buckle when the ride ended.

Someone opened the door. "Excuse me." Em's horrified voice. The door slammed shut.

Rosie stumbled back against the counter even as Hudson tried to steady her. Steam must have been rising off their bodies because every inch of Rosie's throbbed with heat. Hudson's hands roved along either side of her rib cage, his thumbs brushing over the curve of her breasts as his whiskey-colored eyes seemed to strip her clothes right off. All Rosie wanted to do was kiss Hudson again.

Kiss. Hudson. Again.

Rosie tilted toward a second ride.

This time, there was a knock. "Rosie?" Margo's voice. "We need milk from the refrigerator."

And suddenly, Rosie was very cold. "What did you do that for?" She brushed away Hudson's hands and escaped to the refrigerator. Finding a carton of milk, she darted for the door.

Hudson was quicker. "Oh, no, you don't." He blocked her path.

"Are you out of your mind? You don't want to be kissing me. Kissing me will only lead to trouble for both of us." She shoved at Hudson's shoulder with one hand, but since he was nearly twice her size, he didn't budge.

"That kiss was…" Hudson paused, searching for a word even as he reached for her with one hand.

"Don't start." Rosie danced out of reach. She wanted him, but the only way she could let Hudson touch her again was if he knew he was Casey's uncle. Of course, if he knew the truth he wouldn't want Rosie. Why on earth had he thrown the letter away?

"Hot. Combustible." His grin was huge and annoying. "Don't even think about denying it."

"I won't deny a thing." She'd carry that feeling to her grave. Her body trembled as it attempted to recover from that earth-shattering kiss. "But it's not going to happen again."

"Rosie?" Margo pounded on the door this time.

"There's probably someone outside desperate for a latte. The least you can do is hand this to her." *And look as discombobulated as she felt.* Rosie thrust the carton into Hudson's chest.

"You can't run from this." Hudson opened the door, one eye on Rosie as he handed Margo the milk.

Rosie peeked around his shoulder. Amy Furokawa was at the counter staring back at her. "You wanna bet?" If only the truth wouldn't make Casey's life miserable. If only the truth wouldn't ruin her professional life. If only she'd met Hudson all those years ago instead of Samuel.

"I don't care and neither should you."

"We both know you can't afford that attitude in politics. We've got a reporter hovering outside and we've got to increase your numbers in time for the president's visit." Heaven only knew how Rosie was going to do that in just a few days.

This time, when Rosie reached for the doorknob, Hudson let her escape.

CHAPTER TWELVE

"THERE SHE IS, Graham, at that light." Hud pointed over the front seat. He'd been slow to follow because Rosie's words had hit home. She'd pointed out the rational reasons why they couldn't be together. She had no way of knowing that Hud was falling in love with her.

As big fat raindrops started to fall, Graham slowed and pulled Hud's Lincoln up to the curb.

Hud opened the back door. Rosie wasn't walking out on him. "Get in!"

"No, thanks!" Damn if she didn't shut the door and walk on.

Hud scrambled out of the car and into the rain. Someone honked as Hud ran after her. For someone with such short legs, Rosie could certainly cover distance quickly when she wanted to. He snagged her arm before she crossed another block.

"Don't be stupid, Rosie. Whatever's bothering you, we can work out."

"So now I'm stupid because I'm trying to do the right thing and save your career?" Beneath the weight of the rain, her hair was starting to droop into her eyes. Her raincoat lacked a hood and she was once more without an umbrella. "With Amy Furokawa watching your every move a sex scandal is the last thing you need."

"When we make *love*, I'll worry about it," Hud said through gritted teeth. Was it only a few minutes ago that he'd held her in his arms and fantasized about exploring every inch of her body? "You are the most frustrating woman."

"Considering the source, I'll take that as a compliment."

It started to pour. There was a break in traffic and Graham pulled the car up beside them. Rosie and Hud remained locked in a stare down.

Rosie was the first to give in. "This is just stupid." She ran for the car. "Look, here's that car you promised would be at my disposal," she said, climbing in. "Can you take me home, please, Graham?"

Rosie's hair and face were drenched, but she still managed to look as if she could do Hud harm even as she reached for her phone. At great risk to himself, Hud reached across to fasten her seat belt and then confiscated her cell phone before she could dial.

"Drop Hudson off at the office, Graham."

"Don't stop at the office, Graham."

Both of their cell phones rang at the same time, a reminder that they were busy people and this was a workday. Hud glanced at the caller ID screens.

"Yours is Walter. Mine is Martin. I'm letting them roll to voice mail. We have more important things to discuss." Hud reached for Rosie's hand. It was cold as ice. "How can you kiss me like that one minute and tell me you're quitting the next? You bolted as if I were a serial killer."

"I'm going to resign," she said flatly, practically giving him a heart attack.

"Don't talk like that." Hud captured her other hand. "Together, no one can beat us."

"You're going to be my first...my worst failure." Rosie sniffed.

"You're quitting because of the campaign?" And here he thought it was all because of him. "Were you depressed by Walter's figures? It's a miracle we're holding steady. It's a triumph."

"I'll transition with whoever Walter recommends. They'll know what to do," Rosie continued as if she hadn't heard him. She looked at him, her dark gaze unsteady. "And this idea you have about us isn't going to work. You would have known that if you read my letter."

Hud felt as if they were walking uphill on a sand dune. They just kept slipping back to the same spot while Hud was desperate to scale that dune. "There's only one reason why what's between us won't work."

She eyed her phone, fingers twitching. "There are so many obstacles—"

Hud placed a hand over hers. "You have to be brave enough to let there be an us."

"Hudson—"

"I've told you before I'd rather you called me Hud." He handed her the phone as Graham pulled in front of Chin-Chin's. "Look, we can argue for another twenty minutes in the car or go inside, get you in dry clothes and talk this through. But I promise you one thing." Hud waited until she looked at him again. She was beautifully fragile soaking wet and in the midst of her breakdown. "No matter what was in that letter, I'll understand."

Rosie opened her mouth to reply, then closed it, and searched his expression until she gave a tight nod. With that small, hard-won victory, Hud didn't dare smile, didn't dare do anything but escort her upstairs.

THEY TOOK OFF their raincoats and shoes in the silence of Rosie's apartment. After all Hudson's talk in the car, he was now letting her set the pace.

"I don't know what to say," Rosie admitted. She excelled at telling it like it is with her candidates, but this was different. Walter had forbidden her to cause the McClouds distress until after the president came. If Rosie had any hope of salvaging her career once the news came out, she'd need to hold on to her secret for a few more days. And then they needed to stop writing notes like school kids and tell each other the truth. Well. Mostly Rosie had to tell the truth. It didn't matter that his kiss still burned her lips. She had no right to make love with Hudson when Casey's identity was still a secret. But that didn't stop her from wishing.

"Well, I know what to say." Hud took both her hands in his. "The McCloud men choose strong, stubborn women. But right now, I'm thinking a woman who doesn't argue would be a better choice for me. I've told you the past doesn't matter. I'll wait until you're ready to tell me whatever it is you need to say, whether that's today or a year from now."

Rosie's heart thudded and she sank into a chair, but Hudson didn't relinquish his hold on her. Nothing Hudson could say would convince her to invite him into her bed and into her heart without telling him the truth, but this unconditional acceptance came darn close. Rosie tried to focus on Casey's baby picture on the wall to remind herself that he'd hate her afterward if she followed her heart when she shouldn't.

"How hard would it be to agree with me? Just once? We argue over the words you choose to use in my speeches. We spar over my suggestions for Casey. They're just suggestions. You have a great kid yet you worry all the time if you're being a good mom. Let me tell you, great kids rarely get raised by lunatic, loser parents." He gave her hands a gentle shake.

"I know this isn't the right time to explore whatever is happening between us. I can't predict how it will affect my chances or your career. And I know something's bothering you." Hudson's gaze brimmed with longing that arced right to Rosie's core. "I'm not willing to let this chance slip by. I'll swallow my pride and be whatever you want me to be—candidate, friend—for however long you want me to wait. But know this…"

At some point, he'd accepted her for who she was— a stressed-out, driven mess of a woman. At some point, he'd dropped to his knees, closing the gap between them by running his hands up her arms to cradle her face and draw her close. At some point, she realized that she loved him, despite his pride and impatience, despite all the reasons she shouldn't cross the divide between candidate and campaign manager.

"Someday, Rosie, when you say the word, I'll take you to my bed and I'll make you sorry you waited so long to say yes."

Rosie's breath hitched in her throat. She'd been wrong. She had no defense, no chance of refusing to take Hud into her heart when he opened up his. She touched the cleft in his chin lovingly with one finger, knowing that loving him wouldn't be easy, that loving him was selfish, but loving him in this moment was what she had to do.

Rosie's hands slid around his neck and she found herself surrendering on a word. "Yes."

HUD WAS RIGHT WHERE he wanted to be—laying in Rosie's four-poster bed, his body momentarily stripped of need, his arms wrapped around her. Making love with Rosie had been everything their explosive chemistry promised. She wanted a say in how he pleased her, in the way she pleased him and in how they rocketed to the ultimate pleasure together. Life with Rosie wasn't going to be boring in or out of bed.

Her cell phone rang. Hud was amazed it hadn't disturbed them before. Tossing the worn quilt aside, Rosie ran naked across the room to answer it. Hud propped his head on his hand and watched her, not bothering to cover himself and the rising need he had for her again.

Rosie pushed her hair out of her face. "I'm finishing up a meeting. I'll be there in an hour."

A glance at her bedside clock revealed eleven o'clock was approaching. He wanted to spend the rest of the day in bed with her.

"I've got to go." Rosie began pulling undergarments out of a dresser stenciled with flowers. "You should probably get back, too. You have a full afternoon planned."

"Come back to bed." Hud didn't care about schedules and appearances and work.

"This is exactly what I'm talking about. You've lost focus." Rosie slid her arms into her bra straps and arched her spine to hook it in the back.

"I'm extremely focused." On her. On regaining that feeling that he'd found what he'd been looking for, which was odd considering he hadn't realized he'd been missing anything. "Come back to bed."

Wearing only her panties and bra, Rosie caught sight of herself in the mirror. She fluffed her hair. "I'm a wreck." With clothes in hand, Rosie retreated into the bathroom and locked the door behind her.

"Hey," Hud called, but the blow dryer had already

started and there was no way Rosie could hear him. Which was probably exactly how she wanted it.

"WHEN WERE YOU GOING to tell me about this question-and-answer charity event you're doing?" Walter charged into Vivian's home office and loomed over her desk.

"I… The next time we spoke?" Vivian set aside the edited draft Stu had given her. She'd put off calling Walter because she wanted to feel put together when they spoke. Walter was her crutch and it had become important to Vivian to do this without him.

And yet, no matter how hard Vivian tried to revise what she wanted to say, the words sounded formal and stilted. Maybe Rosie was right. Maybe Vivian needed more skill than Stu could provide. Martin was supposed to be available to help her anytime today.

"If you're not comfortable with this, I'll speak with Rosie and it'll all vanish." Walter pulled a chair next to hers and sat down. He took her hands in his with a surprisingly gentle touch. He studied her features, all bluster and masculine affront gone.

Vivian found herself staring into his green eyes longer than was appropriate.

"You seem a little shell-shocked," Walter noted.

"I am." The idea of speaking in front of hundreds of strangers wasn't so daunting. It was the thought of them asking questions she wasn't sure she was ready for. And then there was the unsettling way Walter's touch had changed from friend to beau since they'd embarked upon Hud's campaign. She missed having a man in her life, but Vivian wasn't about to risk her friendship with Walter just because she was lonely.

"You don't have to do this. Politics was always something you endured."

How had he known that? "This is different. By opening up, by speaking out, I can make a difference without holding office." She squeezed his hands. "And maybe if I toughen up, if I can get to a place where I can talk about my losses, I can effect change."

"I like you the way you are—proud, courageous, a woman of mystery."

"You have to say that. You're my friend." Vivian pulled her hands away from his. "I'm a coward. I hide behind the McCloud name in this huge, empty house and I pretend that all I have to do is protect this iconic legacy that's gone on for generations. I want to be more than Hamilton's widow or Samuel's grieving mother. Maybe this isn't exactly what I need to do, but if I don't do something meaningful soon, I'll be a lonely old crone." Drat. That hadn't come out right.

Walter frowned and seemed about to refute her statement, but Vivian didn't want to talk about herself anymore. "Now, why are you here? I'm sure you have a full calendar. You shouldn't be wasting your time with me."

"Viv, you aren't—"

"Look at the time." She stood and smoothed her skirt, not brave enough to hear what Walter had to say. "I've got to be downtown for a meeting in less than an hour."

"Viv—"

"We'll do dinner soon," Vivian promised as she walked away, impatient to embark upon this new adventure even if it was scaring the girdle off her.

"I'm in town tonight. I thought we'd have dinner at Girabaldi's."

Vivian paused in the doorway. "You've been spending far too much time with me. I'm sure your family misses you, or perhaps a woman…" She trailed off even as she lost her nerve and stopped looking at him. The trouble with thinking about Walter as more than a friend was that Vivian couldn't risk losing him as a friend. "I really have to go."

"I'M READY." Rosie emerged from the bathroom already full of regrets. She'd braided her long, wet hair but a few untamable tendrils still clung to her face, much as Hud's scent clung to her body. "I could really use a cup of coffee." And a time machine to turn back the clock and erase the last hour and a half of her life. It was going to be harder to keep Hud away now that she'd succumbed to his touch. And he was no longer Hudson in her mind, but Hud. Amazingly giving Hud.

Forget that his hair had finally betrayed his perfection when they made love by sticking every way her fingers coaxed. Hud had put his dark gray suit back on and looked composed enough to give a speech. She, on the other hand, could barely string a sentence together.

He put his hands on her waist and leaned over to kiss her, but Rosie turned her head at the last minute so his lips landed on her cheek. She could rationalize falling into bed with him once as foolishness, but twice? Unforgivable.

"Duty calls." Rosie went to stand by the bedroom door, the heat in her cheeks increasing as she realized that Graham probably knew what they'd been doing all this time. She had to transition back to work mode. Distance. She needed distance. Particularly from the bed.

"All you have to do is tell me you need time to get used to the idea of us and I'll understand," Hud said as if reading her mind. He captured her hand and led the way back to the front of the apartment. "But until then keep your past to yourself."

Impossible. Come Tuesday, she was determined to bring Vivian and Hudson together to show them Casey's birth certificate and ask for understanding.

"Have I ever told you that I have the best coffee machine on the planet at my house?"

"Is that a bribe?" Rosie was woefully happy to let him distract her.

Hud shook his head. "It's a perk…if you can figure out how to make it work."

"Please tell me you're joking. You know how to brew coffee, right?" Rosie tried not to remember how those same hands had skimmed across her body as he learned what pleased her.

"I was raised with a cook. I employ a full-time cook. I don't know the first thing about cooking." His words were a reminder of how differently he lived, of the possibilities and challenges Casey would face if the McClouds accepted him.

Rosie wanted a normal life for her son, but she had to admit that in their own way the McClouds had created a family as normal as possible while living in the spotlight. "I should have noticed this major character flaw of yours before. Making coffee isn't cooking. It's a necessity of life."

"That's why there are Starbucks on every corner." Hud gave her a teasing smile. "Technically, I don't think what you drink is coffee. There's so much milk in there it's almost white. And three packets of sugar substitute? All topped off with whipped cream? There's no way you can taste the coffee."

"It still has caffeine, doesn't it?" And given the few hours of sleep she survived on, it kept her going. She'd need a lot of coffee over the next few days since she was anticipating a few sleepless nights. "It makes me wonder if you know how to do other necessities, like drive or—"

"Make love? I think I've already proven that I can do all sorts of things. Just call me Mr. Necessity."

Shaking her head, Rosie laughed, her attempts to detach herself emotionally from what had happened thwarted by Hud. "It's amazing you got elected the first time."

He paused at the front door, an apologetic expression on his face. "We both know I rode the coattails of my family's name into office. I don't think I can do that twice."

Rosie studied him a moment. He was an amazing man full of surprises. If the voters only knew... "That kind of honesty will help get you into office on your own name." But he'd have to do it without her.

"MOMMY, I DON'T FEEL GOOD."

Rosie stepped out of the conference room almost an hour later and tucked a stray lock of hair behind her ear. "Honey, you just came home sick last week." It seemed awfully soon for Casey to be taking another sick day from school.

"We didn't go home. You took me to work."

Guilty as charged. Rosie sighed. "Let me talk to the nurse."

"He doesn't have a fever," the nurse said. "What would you like me to do?"

"Rosie, can you approve this?" Martin handed her something as he passed her in the hallway. "Are you coming to the public relations meeting?"

"Yes, I…"

"Ms. DeWitt?" The nurse interrupted Rosie's brain freeze. "I can send him back to class or you can come pick him up."

"Rosie, I've got the *Chronicle* on the phone," someone called over the wall of a cubicle.

She'd already lost the morning to one of the most beautiful mistakes of her life. Common sense told Rosie to let Casey finish out his day at school, but in her heart Rosie knew she wanted Casey to realize she'd always be there for him…even if he was faking. Besides, Hud was going to be out all afternoon and Rosie needed Casey to remind her why the morning's lovemaking was going to be her last with Hud. "I'll come get him during lunch."

"I COULD LISTEN TO YOU all day, Mrs. McCloud."

Vivian didn't quite believe the purple-haired volunteer she'd been talking to for the past hour, but it was nice to hear. "Do you understand what I'm trying to say? I can't seem to get it right."

"Me, neither," Stu admitted, obviously taken with the stud in Martin's eyebrow. "Did that hurt?"

The experienced campaigner was fascinated with the lifestyles and opinions of Hud's youthful staff. Had Rosie figured that out, too?

"Not as much as when I got my ear pierced," Martin replied good-naturedly. "Don't worry. I'll write up something that will bring the crowd from tears to laughter based on what you told me. You read through it this weekend and if we need to change it Monday, that's not a problem."

Vivian thanked him.

"Do you do that—" Stu twiddled his finger in front of his hair "—yourself?"

Martin grinned. He didn't seem to mind Stu's questions. "No, my girlfriend does it. You should see her hair. She has orange streaks that go down to her waist."

A small head bobbed into the window in the conference

room door. Vivian lost track of the conversation as she smiled at Rosie's son. He must have pretended to be sick again. Samuel had done that quite a bit when he was in elementary school.

Vivian excused herself and opened the door slowly, so as not to startle the boy. "Are you here again? We need volunteers to make phone calls."

"Mommy won't let me talk on the phone, but I can write speeches." His dark hair was curly and wild and in need of a trim, but it complemented his mischievous eyes.

"We need a lot of help in that department as well." She took his hand. "Shall we find you a piece of paper and pencil?"

"I write on a computer," he said solemnly.

"There you are." Rosie rounded the corner, her smile full of apology.

Vivian assumed she was sorry that Casey was underfoot again. "He's not a problem."

"That's good to hear." Rosie's smile was still regretful. "But I wasn't looking for him. I was looking for you. Somehow we got our dates mixed up. I know we said next week, but the television reporter is here for your interview now."

Vivian wasn't going to let her desire for privacy overpower her need to be doing something more important with her life. She swallowed her fear and dug in her purse for some lipstick. "Well, we make the best of it, don't we?"

"I'LL PUT MORE SUPPORT behind special needs retirement centers on my to-do list." Hud shook hands with the director of the Mission District Center, but his attention was elsewhere, tangled with memories of Rosie's satisfied smile and long damp curls brushing over his bare skin, and counting the hours until he could be with her again.

"Do you think your mother could come out to visit?" The retirement center director didn't let go of Hud's hand. "We have a lot of residents who remember your father. It would mean a lot to them."

Hud nodded toward his college assistant, who was taking notes, and extricated himself from the director's grip. "We'll check her schedule."

"Tuesdays would be best."

Hud waved to a blue-haired woman in a wheelchair as he headed toward the door. In no time, Hud was relaxing into the deep leather upholstery of his waiting car. "Where to now, Graham?"

"I'm taking you to the YMCA, sir. There's an after-school program that Ms. DeWitt wants you to see."

Rosie had him shaking hands—one-handed—and listening to the concerns of city residents. Rosie called it an opportunity tour, but she wasn't here with him, getting depressed by the poor conditions and hopeless situations of those living beneath the poverty line. Instead, she'd sent along another in her league of college students, this one so intimidated by Hud that he barely spoke.

"It's getting close to four." Hud glanced at the paper on the seat with his schedule. "What's this 'bus' notation?"

"Ms. DeWitt says you need to take the bus back downtown," the college student said.

"You're kidding?"

"She left you a bus schedule, too." He handed Hud the colorful, folded bus map.

Hud had never in his life ridden the bus and he wasn't about to start now.

"I know what you're thinking," Graham said, smiling

into the rearview mirror. "Ms. DeWitt won't like it if you don't take the bus."

"So that means you won't be waiting for me when I get out of the Y?" Hud drummed his fingers on the armrest.

"That's exactly what that means." Graham pulled to the curb. "I'm dropping Danny at the campus for his night class and then I'm taking the night off."

Danny had the decency to look uncomfortable.

"You'll need coin to ride the bus," Graham pointed out.

"For the love of…" Hud rarely paid cash for anything. He didn't have any coins on him. He didn't jingle when he walked. With a clenched jaw, Hud managed to say, "I don't suppose you have change for a five."

CHAPTER THIRTEEN

"WE'RE HERE WITH ONE of San Francisco's most beloved matriarchs, Vivian McCloud." Amy Furokawa's perky smile was for the camera. When she turned her back to the lens, there was a glint in her eye that made Vivian uncomfortable. "Your son, Hudson, is running for mayor. Why do you think he'd make a good mayor?"

From where she stood, Vivian could see Rosie standing, her arm wrapped around Casey's shoulders as she held him lovingly close. She could remember those days when her heart had been filled with love and hope for her sons and their futures. "As his mother, I am a bit biased to answer that question. What parent wouldn't think their son was the best choice for the job?"

A few of those in the office had come out to watch. There was a smattering of laughter at her remark that bolstered Vivian's confidence.

The reporter frowned.

"But if you were to ask me as a resident of the city, I'd have to say that he understands the character of San Francisco and has a strong vision for how to improve it." Vivian caught Rosie's approving nod before smiling directly into the camera.

Her interviewer still had that anticipatory look in her eye, as if Amy had something up her sleeve, which was so unattractive. Here was a woman who would go for the jugular of her own young if it meant her career would be advanced.

"This is one of the first interviews you've granted in more than five years. First you suffered the devastating loss of your son, Samuel. Then Hudson gave up his senatorial seat amidst rumors of conflict of interest, which must have been so disappointing. How are you doing?"

"My dear." Vivian struggled to keep her smile in place. She couldn't do this. "Let me clarify one thing. I have never been disappointed in Hudson. I'm not here to talk about my loss. Many mothers have suffered the same fate in this war and previous wars."

"But—"

"If those are all your questions, I'll wish you a good day."

THE NOISE in the YMCA was deafening. Kids darted in and out of hallways, preteens clustered about computers in a room to one side of the lobby, balls were bouncing somewhere down the hall. Hud's brain was on information overload. He'd seen too many new faces today. These field trips of Rosie's were a challenge because he felt as if he had to discover why she'd sent him to each place. The hospice visit was eye opening. They needed a stronger link to other service agencies, which would cut a lot of the red tape they currently dealt with. The retirement center visit had been about affordable assisted living options for seniors. And the Y?

"Ain't no ties allowed in here." The cocky young voice came from behind the check-in counter to Hud's right.

Hud smiled at a plump little girl with pigtails wearing a YMCA T-shirt. "I'm just visiting."

"That don't matter. We collect all ties right here." She extended a small hand across the counter, curling her fingers to encourage him. Her other hand wielded a pair of scissors. "Hurry up. I don't have all day."

A slender woman with long frizzy hair and a purple paisley skirt swirling about her ankles came to Hud's rescue. "Elizé, give Mr. McCloud a moment. He's never been here before." She set her clipboard down on the counter. "I'm Wendy Allen, the facility director. We're so pleased to have you visit."

Hud returned the sentiment as he shook Ms. Allen's hand, then gestured to the rooms full of activity behind her. "You have a full house today. That's quite an accomplishment."

"We have a full house everyday. Now, Ms. DeWitt wanted me to give you a tour, but I'm afraid Elizé is right. I'll need your tie."

Hud had heard of checking in do-rags and other gang paraphernalia at neighborhood centers, but his tie?

"It helps equalize the status here. No ties, no briefcases, no looking down upon others," Ms. Allen explained.

Recalling how Rosie had him loosen his tie and roll up his shirt sleeves, Hudson quickly removed his tie and even handed over his jacket to Elizé. "I get those back when I leave, right?"

"Ain't nobody gonna want your stuff, mister," she said, rolling her beautiful brown eyes.

Ms. Allen led him down the hallway. "Elizé is a bit overzealous in her duties, but she means well and she's safe here. I can't say as much when she goes home at night."

Hud looked back at the front counter in time to catch Elizé haranguing someone else. "Don't you bring that skateboard in here. You can check it behind the desk or check your butt back outside." She may have been small, but she was a pistol.

"How old is she?"

"She's ten and living with her grandmother a few blocks over. Her brother lives with them, too, when he's out of prison." She stopped in front of the gym doorway. Two small courts were filled with basketball shooters of all shapes, sizes and colors. "As you can see, we've got a large number of children interested in basketball. When school's out, the court is full of kids."

A ball rolled into his foot. Hud bent to pick it up, dribbled onto the court and put up a beautiful three-point shot that hit the rim and rebounded back to him. Hudson handed the ball to a wiry boy wearing a wrinkled, tattered T-shirt. "My game's rusty."

"That's what happens when you get old." Not exactly Shaquille O'Neal himself, the boy dribbled off with unorthodox form.

"How late do they stay?" Hud studied the court and counted the available balls. Twenty balls and no noticeable holes in the gym floor. A glance to the ceiling showed no stains from a leaky roof.

"Some go home when we close up at nine." Shock must have shown on Hud's face because Ms. Allen quickly added, "This is a tough neighborhood for kids and adults alike. I'd keep them here twenty-four hours a day if the city would let me." Ms. Allen moved briskly back down the hall. "If you're interested in helping us, it would be nice to have funds for some new computers. I'd even take old computers. We never have enough to go around." She gestured into the room with the preteens. The computers looked to be at least five years old, if not older.

Hud breathed a sigh of relief. "I might be able to help you with that."

Her smile was weary as if she'd been disappointed in the past and was afraid to put much stock in his offer. "And over here we've got our Che-Che Club." She led him to a quieter room. About ten teenage girls were clustered around a gray-haired woman who sat in a chair. Everyone in the room had a crochet hook and a ball of yarn and was busy making something. "A local store donates yarn to us every month. The girls love to make scarves. We've been selling them at local festivals to raise money."

"What a great endeavor."

"Our homework helpers are in this room." Ms. Allen led him even farther back to a large classroom. "We've got a large group of kids classified as English as a second language. It helps them tremendously to come here every day."

"You have every right to be proud of your center, Ms. Allen." They'd come full circle back to the front desk. "Out of curiosity, what did Rosie want me to see today?" Hud was betting on the computers. It was an easy fix. McCloud Inc. was in the process of upgrading their computers. Hud had recommended they donate the old ones to various charities. He'd add the YMCA to their list.

Ms. Allen's laughter was self-conscious. "Elizé, can you ask Ms. Dominguez to join us out here?"

"You'll keep watch on the desk while I'm gone?" Elizé waited until Ms. Allen agreed before she hopped down and trotted off on short legs.

"Elizé," Ms. Allen lowered her voice. "She wanted you to meet Elizé."

"THIS IS NOT THE KIND of access we were promised," Amy complained to Rosie as they squared off on the sidewalk.

"I told you beforehand what the parameters of the interview were." Rosie pretended she didn't have a five-year-old pulling her arm behind her. "You're the one who decided to overstep those bounds."

"I never agree to limit questions." Leaning her head to one side so that she could see Casey, Amy's glance was superior, as if were she to have kids they'd be well-behaved in all situations every day. "It would impinge upon my integrity as a reporter."

Rosie cocked an eyebrow at the younger woman.

"I have nothing for this evening's news segment." Amy glared at everyone in the vicinity, including Rosie and her crew.

Rosie didn't care how big of a tantrum Amy threw. "Your choices are to catch up with our man—"

"Oooh, I like the way you say that."

"Or apologize to Mrs. McCloud and start over."

"I'll apologize." Amy gritted her teeth. "But I'll need some kind of human interest story this weekend. Perhaps you and your son?" She gestured at Casey.

Rosie's hand gripped Casey's so tight he whined. After taking a deep breath, Rosie said emphatically, "My son is not a part of this campaign."

"How about *our man?* Is Hudson willing to share—" Amy looked Rosie up and down "—this weekend with me?"

Rosie forced a smile on her face, knowing Amy had already noticed she'd upset her. "I think he's stopping by the youth basketball program tomorrow about nine." Rosie referred to the address on her clipboard.

"Great. Maybe I'll get to see what a good athlete he is."

"I'll go get Mrs. McCloud." Rosie used the momentum of Casey dragging her back into the office to suppress the urge to wallop the reporter with her clipboard and warn her that Hud was off-limits. She hurried to find Vivian, stopping only to put Casey into the conference room with the television and make a quick phone call.

"Hank, can you assign a different reporter to our coverage. Amy is a bit—"

"Overly ambitious? Yeah, I know. She treats everyone around here as if we're pond scum, but management likes her and until she steps over the line we're stuck with her."

"We've given her an all-access pass to our campaign and she's not respectful of the McClouds." This was strictly a professional complaint. Jealousy had nothing to do with it.

"I feel for you. If you discover a way to manage Amy, you let me know," Hank said before he hung up.

When Rosie found Hud's mother, she was straightening up Hudson's desk. "Sorry about that. I've had a talk with her and she'd like to continue the interview."

"I don't think I do." Vivian didn't look up as she organized Hud's pens.

Taking a stab at what was bothering Vivian, Rosie said, "I met Samuel in college and even though I don't claim to have known him that well, I miss him. A lot of people feel the same way. I think he was the kind of man you saw and felt an immediate affinity to."

Vivian's blue eyes were filled with sadness. "Thank you." She drew a deep breath. "I knew this was a mistake. They only ask me about my losses, as if they have the right to know how I mourned and if I still grieve."

Rosie realized how lucky she'd been to offer Vivian an important role in the campaign. "Perhaps that's because you don't grant too many interviews. Reporters and the public don't know much about you." But when Vivian spoke it was heartfelt and more spontaneous than Hud had ever achieved.

Vivian flinched when someone tapped on the glass behind her. Rosie waved and came to put her arm around Vivian. "Maybe that's why they speculate. Maybe that's why they ask the most painful questions first. Have you ever heard it takes one hundred tellings?"

Vivian shook her head.

"They preach it at Hospice. Don't hold in your grief. It takes one hundred tellings to heal. I figure you've got another ninety or so to go. But it's up to you."

"If only it wasn't telling with someone as heartless as that woman." Vivian sighed, then added under her breath, "I can do this."

Rosie wasn't sure if she was saying it to Rosie or to herself.

Later, when the interview was over, Rosie escorted Vivian and Casey inside her office, complimenting Vivian on the fabulous job she'd done.

"There's a wonderful park close by." Vivian surprised both Casey and Rosie by saying. "Why don't we take Casey over there?"

"Are you sure?"

"I don't usually offer twice," Vivian said.

"Put on your jacket, Case." Not needing to be asked again, Rosie grabbed her own coat and stuffed a notebook into her large purse. In no time they had escaped the phones and computers and reporters.

"He's a beautiful boy." Vivian sat next to Rosie on a park bench near the carousel at Yerba Buena Gardens.

"I'm partial to him." Rosie waved at Casey as he sat

waiting for the carousel to start. "But we didn't come here for you to watch him. You wanted to talk to me?"

"I wanted to thank you for goading me to go out and speak about the difficult things."

"You can thank me after your speech on Monday."

The carousel started up and Casey kicked his legs as if urging his horse to go faster.

"We've never come here, but it's a beautiful place." Hugging her jacket tighter about her, Rosie wished it was a warm, sunny day. So much had happened today, she was finding it hard to believe just this morning she'd been in bed with Hud.

"That carousel is nearly one hundred years old. It used to be outdoors at that children's park on the west side until the seventies when the city bought it for this park." People were turning to look at Vivian. Vivian nodded to a few, then waved at Casey as he sailed past. "They did a beautiful job with the restoration."

"You're amazing."

"What do you mean?"

"I've seen politicians and celebrities in public before. They posture and pretend to be better than everyone else. You're very gracious."

Her smile was gentle even as they watched a photographer approach. "San Francisco is my city. I started out no better than anyone else, a foolish young girl who fell in love with a handsome man before I realized how important his family was."

"I can't believe I'm here sitting with you."

"We'll be doing this more often, won't we?"

Rosie froze. "What do you mean?"

"I haven't seen my son in such a state since...well, I

don't know when." Vivian tucked her purse more firmly into her lap.

"He's excited about the campaign." Rosie tried to keep her words casual. Did she have *Hud made love to me* stamped across her forehead?

"I may be old, but I've been around the block a time or two." Vivian chuckled. "I have a lot of respect for you. No one else ever figured out Hud or that I wanted to be heard."

Rosie chose to ignore any reference to Hud. "Figuring people out isn't rocket science. You're intelligent with strong opinions yet you rarely express them publicly." Rosie shrugged. "It just seemed out of character for you."

Vivian turned to look at Rosie. "I've been involved in a lot of campaigns and I've never been let loose like this. It's liberating. I feel as if I could conquer anything, as if the sky's the limit."

There was a glow to Vivian's face that had been missing before and considering all that had happened to Rosie lately, she had to ask, "Are you…" Rosie chickened out like the coward Hud accused her of being. This was Vivian McCloud, after all, not her high school girlfriend.

"Go ahead," Vivian encouraged her. "I'll answer any question you have."

Trapped, Rosie tilted her head nervously. "I was going to ask if you were seeing someone. You look more relaxed than you did the first day I met you." She prepared for Vivian's set down.

Three shades of pink passed over Vivian's cheeks.

"It's okay to have a life." Rosie stood as the carousel slowed to a stop. "Just don't get carried away. I don't want to have to explain to Hud why you suddenly took off to Las Vegas."

"I won't do something so drastic. Or maybe I could.

There is a man….” Vivian blushed furiously. “I didn’t come here for a girl talk. I was intrigued by what you said about Samuel earlier. I wanted to ask you what was so special about him that everyone asks me about him. Doesn’t anyone have respect for personal boundaries anymore?”

“You should feel flattered that the public cares so much about you and Samuel that they want to know more. He enjoyed life, as if he knew he wasn’t going to be around a long time and he wanted to live it right.” Her knees didn’t seem to want to hold her up. Rosie found herself back on the bench. Vivian reached over to rub her arm consolingly. It took Rosie a moment more to push words past her tight throat. “Share what you’re comfortable sharing on Monday. Honestly, I don’t envy you that, but you did a great job with Amy today.”

“After a false start.”

“At least Amy gave us a second chance. You really are a huge prize for her to have snagged. Let’s not lose sight of that. A strong finish is what people remember.”

Casey ran up to Vivian and gave her one of his bear hugs. “This is my best sick day ever.”

Rosie’s heart must have stopped beating because her ears buzzed and she didn’t hear what Vivian said in reply. Whatever it was, it must have been good, because both grandmother and grandson were laughing when Rosie’s ears started working again.

“HEY, AREN’T YOU…” A man in a stained blue mechanics shirt leaned against the bus stop pole and pointed at Hud.

Trying not to grimace, Hud gave a brief nod. He wasn’t enjoying himself standing at the bus stop in what Ms. Allen had referred to as an unsafe neighborhood. And now he was being recognized. Next thing you knew, he'd be mugged. And you could bet they wouldn't take his bus token money. Rosie's little field trip would backfire when the story hit the news.

"He's one of those Kennedys," said an ancient woman, who was missing her front teeth, as she squinted at him through thick lenses. "What in the world are you doing out here on our coast?"

"Nah, he's not a Kennedy." The mechanic looked Hud over again. "He's that actor. What's his name? Don't tell me." He held out a grease-stained hand. "I know—Tom Cruise!"

A tall black man in an army jacket had walked up to the bus stop. Despite a slight limp, his solid build and almost cocky demeanor put Hud on guard.

"You're crazy. He's Ronald Reagan's son," proclaimed a woman in a maid's uniform. "He's too old to be Tom Cruise and those Kennedys haven't set foot in this city since I don't know when."

"He's Hamilton McCloud's boy," said the man in the army jacket.

Hud scowled. He hadn't been called a boy in years.

"Nah!" Scoffed the woman with no teeth. "Nah, he ain't. He's too tall."

"Go ahead, tell them who you are and get it over with," said the man who'd identified him with an attitude that Hud didn't like. "Maybe they'll ask for your autograph."

Hud gritted his teeth. "You're right. I'm Tom Cruise."

The group repeated the movie star's name reverently with boisterous chuckles and a few slaps on Hud's back.

The man in the army jacket studied him for a moment before grinning. "I thought so. I liked your dad a lot. You, I'm not so impressed with."

"Really?"

"Really." The man glanced around as if looking for Hud's entourage. "What are you doing down here? Waiting for a taxi?"

Hud glanced up at the bus sign. "It's a bus stop, isn't it?"

"You ain't ridin no bus."

"I am." Although Hud couldn't figure out why. He checked out the times printed on the tiny grid again and then looked at his watch. Maybe he'd read the schedule wrong.

"The buses are always late. Takes me an hour to go across town this time of day. I know some that walk it in thirty minutes. With my bum leg, I ain't walkin'."

"Always late?" Was this why Rosie had sent him out here? She had a nose for trouble spots and an apparent penchant for having him experience problems firsthand.

"Ain't no way these buses can get through on time with so many cars crowding the street." He shrugged deeper into his jacket as the wind whipped past. "Our last mayor was good with social issues, but he wasn't much for improving San Francisco's infrastructure."

"Would you vote for someone who was for improving infrastructure?" Hud asked.

"Vote for him? Hell, I'd probably go door to door to get him elected."

A bus made a slow turn, then rumbled down the street toward the stop.

"Good. I'll see you at my campaign headquarters on Folsom. Bring a list of ideas and we'll see if we can't put them into our agenda."

The man shook his head. "I don't know. I'm no joiner."

"Me, neither. But I am against late buses and grid-locked traffic." There was more in the city that needed fixing than Hud had ever imagined. He'd need a lot of help if he was elected to effect change, but with the help of people who cared, like the man in the army jacket, it just might be possible.

CHAPTER FOURTEEN

"YOU SENT ME on a scavenger hunt today." Hud greeted Rosie with a pizza box and a bottle of wine.

She'd known he'd be showing up tonight. She'd even anticipated how his gaze would envelope her and bring back the feeling of him moving inside her. What Rosie hadn't acknowledged was the way she wanted to have him kiss away the uncertainty and reassure her everything would be all right.

And so Hud made it past Rosie's weak defenses into the apartment. "I learned a few things about the city. Is there going to be a test later?" he asked with a glint in his eye. Hud took off his raincoat, then his jacket and hung them on a hook by the door as if he belonged there. He wasn't wearing a tie.

"I see you met Elizé." Had he discovered that Elizé and her grandmother were in hiding from Elizé's abusive father?

Scuttling up to the table, Casey asked, "Did you like Elizé? Mom says she's a pip. I didn't know what a pip was until I met Elizé."

"She made me take off my tie," Hud admitted, stroking his exposed throat.

"She didn't cut your tie off, did she?" Casey seemed a bit too excited at the prospect. Rosie brushed the curls out of his eyes. "I've always wanted to see her cut someone's tie off."

"I surrendered willingly." Hud grinned at Rosie, as if to say he'd do the same for her.

Rosie allowed that image to play out for less than a second before common sense prevailed. He was the only man who'd been able to get her out of her shell since Casey was born. They had so much in common. And yet, Rosie wasn't good enough for someone like Hud, who strove to be on the up-and-up in everything he did. She was a hypocrite, encouraging Hud to explain his actions to the world when she wasn't willing to share her secrets with him. Sure, she could hide behind Walter's wishes and her own desire to protect Casey, but why did that give her the right to keep Casey's identity a secret from his uncle and grandmother?

Casey needed his mother to be less of an emotional wreck. His clock-watching, the fight with Jeremy, calling her from school claiming to be sick had all occurred after Walter had asked her to work on Hud's campaign. Quitting was best for all involved. Rosie sat abruptly, attracting Hud's attention when all she wanted was to sink in the floor and disappear.

"That's a bummer." Casey heaved a sigh.

Hud laughed. "Not for me. I'm glad my tie survived."

"I hope I never have to wear one. I'll get the chess set."

"You can still see his shiner," Hud pulled out a chair and sat next to her. "Has he had any more problems at school?"

"Yes and no. This campaign…the stress I've been under…it's shaken his confidence." Rosie made sure Casey was down the hall. "Hud, I need you to leave."

"Come on. I'm good for the little guy. I'm good for you, too." Hud stroked her arm, creating a stubborn physical ache at war with her common sense. "I thought everything was okay."

Gripping the edge of the table, Rosie shook her head in an effort to fend off Hud's effect on her hormones. "You said I could ask for space and I am."

"That sounds suspiciously like part of the 'let's be friends' speech."

"I thought I could do this, but I can't." She wasn't ready to subject Casey to a fishbowl existence. Wimp that she was, Rosie was going to take a day to formulate her resignation letter, let Hud cool off and then tell him the truth. She couldn't give him and the job up and turn around and tell him about Casey.

"I've spent the day thinking about you, about us…." He swallowed and looked away from her. When he spoke again, something bitter tinged his words. "I guess I'll see you at the office. You will be coming to the office on Monday, won't you?"

Casey, who'd been setting up the chess board in the living room, looked up.

Rosie had chosen her path. "I'm sorry…."

Hud's face fell. He stood up without any of his usual grace. "I'll go."

"That would be best." Safer for her heart, which pounded uncontrollably as it started to break.

"You can't go. We didn't play yet." Casey's fists were at his sides. He took a step forward.

"I'm intruding. I'm sorry." Hud didn't speak to Casey as he gathered his things. He seemed barely able to look at Rosie.

"Mommy," Casey pleaded.

Hud was putting on his raincoat. "I've got to go. We'll play another time. Don't blame your mom."

In spite of Hud's words, Casey would blame her, yet Rosie couldn't ask Hud to stay.

"WHAT ARE YOU DOING HERE?"

"It's always nice to be welcomed home, Mother." Hud already had a gin and tonic in hand. The prospect of going to his empty house had been too depressing. Nine hours of happiness from the time they'd made love until Rosie had ended it. Hud wasn't kidding himself into believing time alone would solve whatever was bothering Rosie. He should have read what was in the damn envelope. At least then he'd know what he was dealing with. "Can I fix you a drink?"

"Make it a double." His mother glided into the room in khaki slacks, a sweater and pearls. Instead of perching on the formal, uncomfortable sofa, she slouched uncharacteristically into the brocade cushions and said testily, "Why aren't you out wooing voters...or Rosie?"

"I guess I don't have to ask you about your day." Hudson busied himself with mixing her drink.

"I'm going to be on the late news. I stopped by your campaign office to work on my speech for Monday and barely had time to put on lipstick before this woman with a camera crew began asking all sorts of impertinent questions."

"I'm sure you did fine."

"According to Rosie, yes. But it was a painful process that I'm afraid I may have to repeat about ninety times," she mumbled as she accepted her drink.

"Rosie sent me on a field trip this afternoon." Just saying her name was painful. Hud gripped his tumbler. "I read to a hospice patient, had tea with some seniors, had my tie taken away by a ten-year-old and was not recognized by most people I rode the bus home with."

"You rode the bus?" His mother looked appalled, then sighed. "You really do want to get elected, don't you?"

"Did you know you could walk faster across town than

it takes the bus to drive the same route during rush hour? I know traffic is snarled in the city but that's no way to live." Hudson propped his feet up on the coffee table.

"As for rush hour, I try not to be out between the hours of four and seven." She took a sip of her drink.

"That's not the answer to the problem." Hud couldn't get a handle on his mother's mood. "I also met a little girl today named Elizé whose mother is dead and whose father is abusive. She and her grandmother moved here from Oakland. The grandmother is scared to file a restraining order because she'll have to list her address and she's deathly afraid he'll find them somehow if she does."

"My goodness, what will they do?"

"Go on, I suppose. If only they had an advocate in their neighborhood to explain things and help them manage the problem. Instead, they just live in fear." At least, the grandmother did. Elizé, bless her heart, refused to cower. He'd have to make some phone calls and get them some help. "I knew people needed help, but I didn't know how much." Hud hoped he was elected so he could improve things for people like Elizé and the group of bus riders he'd met. He paused before asking, "Did Dad ever have to choose between you and office?"

"Are you having trouble with Walter's protégé?" His mother's gaze was far too knowing.

"I find her incredibly…bewildering." Hud took a drink, lingering over the feel of the alcohol going down before admitting. "And for some reason, despite a mutual attraction, she doesn't want to be with me."

"Rejected, huh? That girl is full of surprises." His mother had closed her eyes and put her glass on her forehead when Hud had been expecting her to jump down his throat for jeopardizing his reputation. "Romance and politics don't mix."

"They mix well and you know it firsthand. There's something about Rosie and her situation that I'm missing." His ego had taken a direct hit when he'd been thrown out of Rosie's apartment. He was afraid she'd call Walter over the weekend and quit. Maybe she had already and Walter had yet to tell Hud. "Did you see Walter today?"

Looking older than she had in a long time, his mother rested her head against the pillows. "Good grief. Why the interrogation? So what if I saw Walter today? He and I are friends. It's not as if I'm having dinner with him every night."

Whoa. What set her off? "I'm sorry. I'm worried about Rosie quitting."

"You bumbled it with her, didn't you?" His mother shook her head. "Well, don't you worry. You'll wear her down. We McClouds may not be very good at dating, but persistence is a family trait."

"I'm going to need a lot more than persistence." But where Rosie was concerned, persistence was a good start.

"WHY DO YOU CHASE people away?"

In the midst of tucking Casey's covers tightly around him, Rosie paused. "I don't chase people away." Sometimes she ran. "Hud is my boss. It's not right that he comes to the house."

"The only friends we have are from school and Margo's." Casey sucked his face into an unhappy pout.

"And the park. And from Chin-Chin's. And the YMCA. And—"

"But he could have been my daddy. You never make

friends with someone who's a daddy." His voice softened. "It's lonely when it's only us."

Not knowing what to say, Rosie bid Casey good-night and wandered back out to the kitchen table and her laptop. But she couldn't sit down to work. She ended up by the window, staring out at the wisps of fog blanketing the street and fighting a feeling of despair.

She wasn't providing enough love or attention or something to her son. The truth was, as long as she was in politics, she couldn't be everything he needed, not when her job took so much out of her. She had to face some harsh realities. The truth was she couldn't work on a presidential campaign as a single mom. So what did it matter if she lost the respect of the McClouds when she told them about Casey? She'd be working on local campaigns until Casey entered college.

Reality sucked. Tonight, she really needed Hud's gentle teasing and sound perspective. But at eleven-thirty, it became clear that she'd finally got her point across.

Hud wasn't going to call.

"DID YOU SEE THAT MOVE, Mommy?" Casey leaned in between Rosie's jean-clad legs while she sat on a cold bench in Golden Gate Park. "Mr. Stephanopolis is good, isn't he? Some day I'm going to be that good at chess."

It was a rare sunny winter morning and Rosie had capitulated when Casey asked to play chess at the park. They'd bundled up in their winter jackets and taken the bus. Rosie was trying not to think about the campaign or Hud and since she'd run out of coffee at home she hadn't had a drop of caffeine this morning. Her brain was as foggy as the City by the Bay usually was—very conducive for not thinking about how much she missed talking to Hud last night.

"Did you see that move?" Casey jumped up and ran for a closer look.

"I thought I might find you here." Hud's deep voice tumbled into Rosie's system like a jolt of espresso. He handed her a coffee cup from Margo's. "Actually, Margo thought you might be here."

Rosie attempted a joke when what she really wanted to do was scoot closer to him. "I hope you didn't skimp on the whipped cream."

"I may not know much, but I know what you like." Hud grinned as he gazed at the chess players. He was trying so hard to make this work and Rosie desperately wished he'd be that determined and sympathetic when he knew about Casey. But she'd been reluctant to give up on her belief in Santa Claus, too.

She took a sip of her coffee and turned to explain what she should have years ago. "There's something you should know about—"

"Mister Mayor!" Casey's grin glowed as he ran into Hud's arms. After giving him a big squeeze, Casey said, "You owe me a game of chess." Casey had no one to play with until the older men finished their more competitive games, which could take hours.

So close. Rosie's heart pounded.

"Do you want to play now?" Hud asked.

"I'll set up the game, okay?" Without waiting for an answer, Casey grabbed his box of chess pieces and ran for one of the tables. "Mr. Stephanopolis, I'm gonna play a game with…" Casey turned back toward Hud. "The mayor!"

Hud chuckled. "That kid's got attitude."

Rosie bowed her head over her coffee cup. She'd let Hud and Casey have one last game.

"But that hat's gotta go. Definitely not the kind of hat that makes a boy fit in. Where did you get it? A *Gilligan's Island* trade show? No wonder Casey has no friends."

Rosie realized he'd only said that to lighten the moment, but he'd unintentionally struck a nerve. "There is such a thing as melanoma and sun damage that can happen as early as age two." She slid farther down the bench away from him unwillingly registering how his dark hair glinted in the sunlight and how relaxed he looked in blue jeans and a black leather bomber jacket, despite the circles under his eyes that matched her own.

"Put sunscreen on the poor kid's ears and buy him a baseball cap."

Of all the— "Do you have parenting experience? Some qualification that makes you an expert in child rearing?"

"I know you've noticed I'm a man." His fingertips made small circles on her shoulder, and Rosie wanted to pull away, she really did. "I had eighteen years experience growing up as a boy and I had lots of friends."

She snorted. "Beer-drinking, class-skipping aristocrats."

"Well, we're going to need those votes, so don't knock them now."

"Come on, Mister Mayor," Casey called.

"You don't think he's a hopeless geek, do you?" Rosie caught Hud's fingers as he stood. "I went through high school as a square peg and it wasn't an experience I want for him."

Cupping her chin in his palm, Hud leaned close. "Maybe if you didn't try so hard to be so buttoned up and perfect all the time he'd loosen up and be a regular kid. Maybe if you delegated more, you'd get more sleep and spend more time with Casey and with me." After a moment, he released her and went to join Casey.

Spreading her hand over her eyes, Rosie rubbed her temples. The trouble with admitting she was flawed was that she'd lose the man who was perfect for her.

"DO YOU LIKE MY MOM?" Casey asked, squinting up at Hud.

"Yes." Hud went back pretending to study the chessboard while sneaking sideways glances at Rosie.

"Do you want to marry her?" Casey grinned, his adult teeth looking too large for his young face. Samuel's teeth had looked like that until he was about ten and grew into those prominent incisors. Hud's teeth had always been perfect.

"Marriage is a serious thing." Now Hud knew why he didn't date women with children. Most people had a line of questioning they wouldn't cross, while a kid had no knowledge such a line existed. "You don't rush into something like that." But if Hud did, it would be with Rosie.

"Have you ever been married?"

"No." Hud moved his knight into play.

"Me, either. I'm not going to get married. Ever." Sitting up on his knees, Casey scanned the board from above.

"Why not?"

"If my wife dies, I'll be sad. My kids will be sad." As if unaware of the depth of his statement, Casey moved his queen into position to take Hud's knight and grinned at Hud. "Your move."

Hud glanced over at Rosie sitting alone on the park bench. She waved, then tossed her long curls over one shoulder. He wanted to be with Rosie, but how badly? What if the kid got attached to him and things didn't work out like they weren't working out now? There were more consequences to a relationship with Rosie than simply who keeps which friends when things went sour.

"HE'S A CHARMER, isn't he? Babies, kids and old ladies love Hudson McCloud." Amy Furokawa slid onto the bench next to Rosie. "Get a couple of shots of the chess match, Bobby."

Stopping herself from doing a double take, Rosie watched Amy's cameraman approach Hud and Casey. "I don't want my son to be on camera."

"It's just a few seconds of film. You're not hiding him from someone, are you?"

"No," Rosie said too quickly. "What are you doing out and about on a Saturday, Amy?"

"Following a story," Amy said cryptically.

Had Amy followed Hud to the park? That was creepy, more like tabloid surveillance than respectable news reporting. "As long as we understand each other about my son."

Amy waved off Rosie's concerns. "Is he a child prodigy? You don't see many young chess players nowadays." Amy's smile was the one she used for the camera.

"He's just an average kid." Alarms went off in Rosie's head. "Does Hud know you're here?"

Amy's smile brightened. "He does now."

"Are you following Bartholemew at all?" *Following* being a word Rosie was beginning to equate with stalking when used in context with Amy Furokawa.

"He's not the story." Amy rocked side to side on the bench. "The story's right here."

"SATURDAY AT THE ZOO." Hud barely held his smile in place. "I haven't done this in years." More like decades. If it wasn't for Casey's enthusiasm, Hud would have lost his patience with the camera crew and the crowd of parents with strollers long ago. Rosie didn't look as if she liked the attention, either.

"Are seals always so quiet? They make noise in movies.

Selena says if you bark at them like this—ork-ork!—they'll do it, too." Casey continued to bark and added a clapping motion, but the seals lay poolside, quietly unenthusiastic. "Come on," he encouraged Hudson and Rosie to join him.

With a significant glance at the camera trained on them and raised brows that dared him to follow along, Rosie did a horrible imitation of a seal.

"Is that the best you can do?" Casey asked with a dramatic eye roll that ended with an expectant look at Hud.

A red light on the news crew's camera blinked on and Amy lifted her microphone. Babies reclining in strollers gummed graham crackers while their mothers watched expectantly.

"We're here at the San Francisco zoo with Hudson McCloud, candidate for mayor, and Rosie DeWitt, his campaign manager," Amy announced.

Rosie began her horrid noise again with a scene-stealing urgency that cut Amy off. A few of the chubby-cheeked audience giggled.

"This is my rendition of the male seal's mating call." Hud proceeded to make a fool of himself, moving his arms stiffly, clapping loudly and sounding more like a wounded moose than an amorous seal.

More stroller occupants guffawed, joined by their parents. Hud took pity on his audience and stopped, surprised by the smattering of applause he received.

"Mommy, I gotta go," Casey said, his limbs squirming awkwardly.

"Show's over." Rosie stepped between Casey and the camera. "Hud, can you take him?"

Assuming Amy and the cameras weren't going to follow him into the men's room, Hudson readily agreed.

"I'll be over there." Rosie gestured toward the women's restroom.

"I like coming in the boys' room," Casey skipped ahead. "Mommy always makes me go in the girls' side."

Hud and Casey went in and took care of their business. Hud enjoyed the relative quiet, actually considering hiding out there for a while as he leisurely rinsed the soap from his hands. The only reason to leave the safety of the men's room was the fact that Rosie was talking to him again.

"You take a long time to wash up. Are you singing 'Happy Birthday'?" Casey bounced up and down.

"I'm not singing." Nothing about this day was going as planned. He'd imagined sitting and talking with Rosie on a park bench while Casey played in the park, not being hounded by a reporter interested in his every move.

"Ms. Phan says you should sing 'Happy Birthday' while you wash your hands to get them really clean, but I sing it fast so I sing it twice."

Hud chuckled and took Casey by the hand, but his steps were slow.

"What's that noise?" Casey tugged him outside where pandemonium was breaking loose.

"The monkeys escaped!"

"Somebody let the monkeys out!

"Hurry. Let's go see!"

There was a stampede of people running to see the monkeys, who had probably already disappeared. Before Hud knew what was happening, Casey neatly twisted out of his grip and put his gangly legs into motion.

"Oh, no, you don't." Rosie appeared out of the crowd and snagged Casey's arm. Then she turned and grabbed Hud's hand, sending his heart thudding in his chest. "Come on."

"But I want to see the monkeys," Casey whined, dragging his feet.

"We saw the monkeys in their cages," Rosie countered, pulling them upstream against the flow of zoo visitors. "They're still in their cages."

Casey started to cry. "I want to see the monkeys."

With effort, Rosie swung her son into her arms, his spindly legs dangling on either side of her hips, his feet at her knees, his expression hidden beneath the goofy brim of his hat. "Casey, I promise you those monkeys are still in their cages. If we leave now, we can go to the Rainforest Café. But if I have to take you to see the monkeys, we'll go right home after this."

Casey sniffed with a longing look back toward the monkeys. "Okay."

"How do you know the monkeys are still in their cages?" Hud asked as a group of zoo employees ran past.

"You wanted to lose Amy, didn't you?" Rosie's lopsided grin was as good as a confession. "All I ask in exchange is a ride to lunch."

"Let's go buy Casey a decent hat before we eat." Hud couldn't stop grinning as they hurried toward the exit gates. And to think one of his first impressions of Rosie had been that she was no fun.

CHAPTER FIFTEEN

"I CAN SEE FOREVER UP HERE," Casey announced from his perch on top of Hud's shoulders. He scanned the sidewalk ahead of them from beneath the brim of his new San Francisco Giants baseball cap.

Tilting her head, Rosie smiled up at her son as she squeezed his foot. The back of her fingers brushed against Hud's hand. "For the most part, the crowd Mr. Mayor drew at the zoo was smaller than I expected and very well-behaved."

"According to some polls, I'm not as popular as I once was." Hud glanced her way, his grin just as relaxed as hers felt. "But I can still attract attention."

"The cameras were fun, Mommy. Are we going to be on TV?"

"I hope not. I think we experienced a slice of the McCloud life." After sharing the scrutiny of the cameras all morning with Hud and being conscious of every look, every word and every gesture he made toward her, Rosie felt justified in trying to protect Casey as long as she had. "One wrong move and—"

"There it is!" Casey bobbled excitedly on Hud's shoulders as if he rode on his uncle's shoulders every day.

Once seated, Casey wandered around looking at the mechanical jungle creatures, only scampering back when they started their animatronics show. A few heads turned when they recognized Hud, but most families seemed to be tourists and were too busy keeping their children occupied to pay much attention to him.

"How many kids did you bribe to start the monkey madness at the zoo?" Hud's hand slipped under the table, his fingers wrapping around hers, as if aware that what they shared should be private.

"I gave four teenagers a twenty to make a little noise, that's all," she admitted, a brief pang of guilt tweaking her conscience. "You don't think anyone got hurt, do you?"

"No. We would have heard the ambulance sirens." He leaned closer so that those around them couldn't hear what he said. "That was brilliant."

"We'd suffered enough and it didn't seem like Amy was going anywhere." Rosie sighed and stroked her thumb across the back of Hud's hand. The need to finish what she'd started this morning was strong, but she couldn't drop the bomb in such a public place. "Did you see Amy at basketball this morning?"

"Yes." Hud frowned, sitting back in his chair. "She followed me?"

"Yes. She said you were the story." But Rosie couldn't help but wonder if Amy thought Casey was the story.

Casey ran up and threw his arms around Rosie's neck, pressing a kiss to her cheek and then plopping into his chair. "When's our food coming?" His elbows landed on the table and he covered his flushed cheeks with his palms. "Are you coming home with us?" Casey asked Hud. "We can play another game of chess."

Hud smiled tentatively. "I'd like that."

With a stiff nod and a sinking heart, Rosie gave her assent, knowing Hud wasn't going to like this at all.

WHILE ROSIE TUCKED Casey into bed, Hudson wandered around her living room, trying to get a better sense of who this woman he'd fallen for was and what might be giving her reservations.

A macramé plant-hanger hung in one corner with viney tendrils dangling toward the carpet. A copper Buddha like the ones sold in Chinatown held incense in his belly on the windowsill. She had one of those floor-to-ceiling corner CD shelf units. Her tastes varied from eighties pop to classical to some interesting alternative rock from bands he'd never heard of before. Hudson had to assume the Barney CDs were Casey's.

A curio cabinet with a lace runner held a collection of framed pictures, many of Casey as a baby. It was hard to mistake that gummy grin for anyone else. He leaned closer to get a better look at the photos in the back. Was that…? It couldn't be.

Hudson opened the door and carefully withdrew a picture tucked into the back corner. Standing in front of the Eiffel Tower, Rosie wore a short skirt and halter top, her curls piled high on her head. The man next to her had his arm draped across her shoulders. In shorts and a polo, his dark hair and cleft chin were as familiar to Hudson as his own features. Samuel.

She'd met him in Paris. Something bitter—a lot like jealousy—flamed to life as he stared at the picture.

"He's asleep," Rosie whispered, hesitating in the hallway. "What's that?"

"A picture of you and Samuel." He turned it toward her. "When was it taken?"

Rosie took the photo from him with trembling fingers. "After I got my graduate degree." She returned the picture to its place at the back of the curio cabinet.

"He looked happy." Hud sank onto the couch as several things clicked into place.

"He seemed happy," Rosie allowed.

"When I see pictures of Samuel like that, I resent what he had." Hud confessed, staring at his hands.

Rosie perched on the other edge of the couch.

"I don't think I've ever been as content as he looks for longer than an hour or two," Hud continued. "And I probably never will be."

Rosie frowned. "Hud, let me—"

"All my life I've been looking ahead to the next hurdle. When I won the Senate seat, I couldn't help but dream about the presidency. After I stepped down, I couldn't stop thinking about what I'd lost and wondering how to get it back. Samuel never lost sight of what was important." Hudson pushed past his resentment for his brother because if anyone could help him get past it and be a better person, it was Rosie. "My brother lived every moment like he should. He was comfortable with his life. If he had any setbacks, he just shrugged them off. He didn't carry them on his shoulders and withdraw from the world." Hud didn't have to reach for her hand. Rosie already held his.

"Maybe finding you was what I needed. With you guiding my campaign, I actually feel as if I can open up and help people, real people, not just numbers on a page. It's gratifying that you believe in me." Hud was a different man with Rosie in his life. "Because I don't think I've ever met anyone with moral standards as high as yours."

Rosie stared at their clasped hands with a surprised expression. Slowly, she pulled her hand back.

"Not that you're perfect or boring. I still can't believe you created a distraction so we could escape from the zoo." When

Rosie didn't look at him, Hud started grasping at straws. "You're worried that I'm going to screw up this campaign. I'm not going soft on you." Well, he was in fact, very soft on her. Just looking at her made him want to write speeches and do good work. This must be how great artists felt when inspired to create, or how athletes dedicated a competition to someone who'd touched them. This must be…love.

Hud examined Rosie's face with new admiration. The full curve of her cheek, the intensity of her dark eyes, the natural vulnerability in her expression that hid the intelligence he'd come to appreciate. His lips lifted in a smile. Come hell or high water, he was going to spend the rest of his life with Rosie.

"I'm not worried about you screwing up," she said.

But Hud didn't believe her, not with a crease sitting between her brows.

Rosie would be extremely worried if he told her what was going through his mind—Rosie in his bed wearing nothing but a smile, political arguments in front of the fireplace over a cup of coffee, converting rooms in his house for Casey and a new baby. How did one go about taking a romance to the next step? Hud didn't know. And this was too important to screw up.

"I should go." Hud stood, fully intending to leave without planting a kiss on Rosie's lips. Instead, his arms pulled her close and he cradled her head to his chest as if she were the most precious thing in his life. "But I don't want to. I want to hold on to this feeling forever."

Then Hudson bent his head and kissed Rosie as if his life depended upon tasting her.

HUD WAS ALL around her—his arms, his scent, his taste. Rosie couldn't escape even as she told herself to break away from his strength, separate herself from his warmth, keep her hands from the tantalizing feel of him. It should have been easy when he attributed her with such high morals. But then he'd gone and ruined it by saying forever. And wrecked it some more by wrapping his arms around her. And kissing her.

Hud deepened the kiss on her sigh, bringing them closer together by tightening his embrace. She should have been struggling for breath, but the oxygen she was breathing was Hud and her blood beat a rhythm of wanting that only he could fulfill.

Somehow they'd become entangled on her too short couch. Rosie was stretched across Hud's torso, his hand splayed across her back after having released her bra hook. But his hand was moving and part of Rosie didn't care that soon he'd be cupping her breast. She shifted her weight to allow him easier access.

Something bumped into the wall down the hall and Rosie sprang to her feet. Hud hadn't heard a thing. She could tell by the way his hand reached for her. Casey could have come out at any time and discovered his mother racing for second base. The thought of discovery was mortifying. She sucked in air as if she'd been deprived of it for hours and listened for her son's footsteps in the hallway.

Nothing.

It was probably just Casey bumping his arm against the wall as he turned in his sleep.

Hud had risen and was nibbling his way down her neck, tugging at the high collar of her T-shirt. "Does your bedroom door have a lock?"

"Yes." But sanity had returned and Rosie didn't think she'd need that lock tonight. "But we need to talk first."

"Let's talk later." Hud's hand slid beneath her shirt,

beneath her bra. He cupped her breast with a circular motion that had her sinking back against him. "I want to see you," Hud whispered in her ear. "I want to taste you." His tongue traced the shell of her ear.

A shaft of heat shuddered through her body as Hud's hand and mouth continued to drive her to the brink.

Tell him in the morning.

She wanted to protect Hud from the critics, from his past, from reporters who wouldn't let him alone even on a Saturday. She wanted to stand by his side and hold his hand through good times and bad.

If only Hud would let her after he learned the truth.

A DOOR SLAMMED. Her front door? Not possible. Casey knew better than to open it. She must have heard the Halburts' door close across the hall.

Rosie rolled over and breathed deeply, then sniffed again. Drat. She'd forgotten to load and program the coffee machine. But there was a different smell in the air this morning and her body ached in the most luxurious way as if she…

Rosie dragged herself into a sitting position, clutching the sheet to her bare chest, searching for Hud.

Casey burst into the room. "Good morning, Mommy."

She glanced around but there was no sign of Hud. Had she dreamed the entire evening?

No. The pillow next to her had an imprint and the sheet was tossed back from the other side of the bed.

He'd left her? Of all the low—

"The mayor had to take his mom somewhere," Casey explained.

Oh, my. "You saw Hud?" Rosie gripped the sheet tighter. What kind of role model was she?

"Yes, he made me waffles. He put them in the toaster quietly so we wouldn't wake you. I was on TV again. Hud said he came over early just so you could sleep longer."

She glanced at the clock. Nearly ten? The morning was practically gone and Rosie hadn't gotten any work done yesterday. She had a gazillion things to do since she planned to transition Hud's campaign to someone else in just a few days. Why had Hud let her sleep? Had he left on purpose, knowing she wanted to talk to him?

Collapsing onto the foot of the bed, Casey began his interrogation. "Is the mayor coming back? Can we go to the park and play chess with him again today?"

"He might be back later."

"You like him, don't you?"

The light of day, the absence of Hud's hypnotizing touch and Casey's optimism combined to create a knot of apprehension in Rosie's belly. What had she done…again? "Hud's a busy man."

Casey frowned. "But Mommy—"

"I've got to get moving, Case. Let's talk about this later when I've had a cup of coffee." And washed Hud's scent off her skin.

"GOOD MORNING," Hud kissed his mother's cheek before sliding into the seat next to her at the Ritz-Carlton's Terrace restaurant. He'd barely had time to go home, shower and change before meeting his mother for Sunday brunch.

"You're in good spirits."

"It's not so bad being me this morning." Not when he'd spent a miraculous night with Rosie. As long as she saw the good in him, as long as they had a future together, nothing could faze him, not even the sight of Roger Bartholomew across the room with a city councilman.

"Hudson, I can't see how it would be anything but good to be you. You've managed to turn the business around and return to politics in two years." His mother waved over the waiter with a tray of mimosas.

Hud may as well admit it. He'd thought about it all night as he held Rosie while she slept. "I'll never be able to replace Samuel." Hud was incredibly lucky that Rosie found enough good in him to let him love her. He hadn't yet told her he loved her, but there was always tonight.

His mother froze with the hand holding the champagne flute hanging midair as if ready to toast. After a moment, she set down the glass untouched. "Have I ever complained about the choices you've made or compared you to Samuel?"

"No, but you loved him more. And Dad was your life."

"Oh, for heaven's sake." With a shake of her head, his mother sighed. "Samuel was all I had. Despite my protests, your father was grooming you for politics from the day you were born. I didn't love Samuel more. I just spoiled Samuel more than I was ever allowed to spoil you."

Hud couldn't think of a thing to say.

"If you're returning to public life to make me happy, drop out of the race now. I may not have been very happy these past few years but none of my funk was because I was stuck with you. I'm blessed to have such a close relationship with you."

"I...uh..."

"How long has this been bothering you?" Hud hadn't heard that disparaging tone of voice from his mother in years.

"A long time," he admitted. "I've always envied Samuel his ability to enjoy life and the opportunities he had to share those moments with you." And with Rosie. But that was going to change. Samuel hadn't known what he'd had with Rosie so their time together had been brief. Hud recognized her for the gem she was.

"And Samuel envied your time with your father." His mother tapped the table with her forefinger. "The political arena is not soft on children and those who raise them. If you don't know that after that reporter hounded you and Casey yesterday, you're not as sharp as I thought."

No wonder Rosie continuously requested to be out of the spotlight. "All I've ever wanted to do is live up to the McCloud name, but if I pursue a career in politics I might not ever have personal happiness." The love of the one woman who understood who he was.

"It's not a yes-or-no question." His mother gripped his hand fiercely. "Love is about compromise and supporting the dreams of the ones you care for. Because I loved your father, my aspirations had to take a backseat."

"But not anymore. You're free to do as you please."

"Something like that, yes." His mother's gaze drifted away from their table. "Even now I can't pursue all my dreams."

"I don't see why not. You deserve some selfish pursuits. And who's to stand in your way? Nobody refuses Vivian McCloud. Men would fall at your feet."

His mother laughed.

"What's so funny?"

"Something Rosie said to me the other day suddenly made a lot of sense when you spoke just now."

"And…"

"It had to do with Las Vegas." But his mother refused to elaborate.

"YOU SEEM TENSE," Hud said from where he reclined on Rosie's couch Sunday night. "Come here and let me work those kinks out of your shoulders."

Having just put Casey to bed after spending the evening waiting for this chance alone, Rosie didn't want Hud's touch to distract her. She perched in a chair just out of his reach. "I have something to say first."

Hud sat up stiffly. "You're not asking me to leave again, are you?"

"No. I have something to say," Rosie repeated carefully. She just needed the courage to say it, because there was no easy way to pad the truth. "Casey is Samuel's son." She watched Hud closely, not daring to miss his reaction.

Hud's eyes widened in shock and then his jaw tensed. "You do realize what you're saying to me."

"Yes. You're Casey's uncle."

"And Casey—he's ours."

"He's not a possession."

"He's a McCloud. The party will be so pleased. So much for me wondering what Walter offered you to work with me. You had a bigger card up your sleeve," Hud said darkly. He stood, backed away, and lowered his voice. "He doesn't look anything like Samuel."

"No, he doesn't. But I'm sure that he's still, as you say, a McCloud." Despite his reaction, Rosie held on to the slim hope that Hud would forgive her.

Hud paced her small apartment. "When you said you dated him, I thought it was just one night. Sometimes his encounters lasted less than an afternoon."

Rosie knew what Hud was asking her, but it was hard

to tell one lover about your affair with another, especially when they were brothers. "I met him in Paris. We spent a few days together."

"That implies you weren't too choosy about who you slept with."

"I was young. I'd lived in the dorm at college but my parents taught on campus. I'd never been away from my parents before and I'd just discovered that I was…" She didn't want to say it. Not when he already seemed to think of her as a whore, but Hud glared at her until she explained. "You saw me in high school. Boys weren't interested in me. And then in college I participated in a study about self-esteem. My group went to the beauty parlor and put on makeup and had fashion counseling."

"That's a useful kind of intervention," he snapped.

She pleaded with him to understand. "It was the first time in my life I felt beautiful on the outside."

"So you went to Paris and took a lover. Did you bother with protection?"

"Yes. Condoms fail, you know." Rosie forced herself to sit still instead of shouting at him to forgive her. Maybe she'd misread how he felt about her. Maybe Hud was more like Samuel than she'd thought.

"Did Samuel know about the…about Casey?"

"No. I never heard from him once he returned to the States and shortly after…well, you know the rest." And now, Rosie did, too.

HUD BARRELED DOWN the hallway and into Casey's room with Rosie on his heels. By the dim glow of the night light, he stared at Casey. The kid—his nephew—was cuddled beneath a worn, well-loved Shrek blanket. Hudson inspected his little face for any indication that Casey was his brother's son. But other than the lanky body, Casey seemed to take after Rosie with his dark eyes and wild curly locks.

"Hud—"

"Don't." Hudson held up a hand.

She frowned, not with annoyance, but with pain as she looked from Hud to Casey. And then he got it. She hadn't told Casey, either. He followed Rosie back to the living room.

"You've surrounded yourself with lies. And yet you didn't come to us for help."

"Would you have given it?" Anger flashed in Rosie's eyes. "You told me about all those women who wear their time with Samuel like a badge of honor. I heard the resentment in your voice. Don't lie to me and tell me you would have welcomed me into the family."

"We would have." But Hud wouldn't look at her. Instead, he stared at the picture of Rosie and Casey at the beach.

"You would have tossed me to the tabloids to protect that McCloud honor of yours. My career would have been ruined." Her anger swelled while his abated.

"I can't...I can't go back in time and predict what I would have done." Hud punched his arms into his jacket.

"I was hoping you'd take this differently," Rosie whispered, looking drained, as if that last burst of anger had taken the fight out of her.

"This will kill my mother." Hud strode the few steps to where Rosie stood and grabbed her by the shoulders. "If I get hit by a bus before the truth comes out, you will tell my mother." Hud's gaze moved down to her belly. "Especially, if lightning decides to strike twice and condoms fail again."

Rosie's hand drifted to her belly and her face drained of color as Hud walked out the door.

CHAPTER SIXTEEN

"I THOUGHT YOU'D never get here," Margo said, handing Rosie her order before she'd even paid.

"Casey's always hard to roll out the door on Monday." Rosie handed over a five and drank deeply from a mug that said, Wake Up and Smell the Coffee. Why couldn't she have had that advice Friday morning before she'd given her heart to Hud only to have him break it?

"Hud's been over in the corner pretending to be working, but I know he's just waiting for you." With a devilish glint in her eye, Margo handed Rosie her change. "I hate to disappoint you, but my kitchen is off-limits."

"Your kitchen is safe from me," Rosie said, but her cheeks felt hot as she turned toward Hud.

"I haven't told anyone about Casey yet." Hud's words were spoken softly, but the accusation behind them was powerful enough to wound. He pulled out a chair for Rosie, his body so close she could smell his subtle after-shave, the same scent that had clung to her sheets Sunday morning. "I'd appreciate the chance to tell my mother my way, after she speaks tonight."

Rosie pulled her dignity around her like a cloak. "I'd prefer we—"

"We?"

"—didn't make any kind of announcement until after

the election, but I don't think we have the luxury of time."

"Why not?" His gaze became guarded.

"Amy knows something about me she's not letting on. She hinted as much on Saturday." Rosie held onto her coffee cup as if it were a lifeline. "Much as it pains me to admit, I don't know what will happen to your popularity numbers if Amy gets wind of anything beyond a business relationship between us. Making an announcement about Casey will be more positive and control the sensationalism that's sure to follow." Although it was exactly what she'd been trying to avoid.

"I don't think—"

"You should." Rosie cut him off.

The angle of his jaw telegraphed his dissatisfaction with the situation.

"Excuse me, Rosie?" It was Martin, college student and volunteer extraordinaire, to Rosie's rescue. "I've got this weekend's poll numbers."

At first, Rosie didn't reach for them. What if their Saturday in the park diluted Hud's numbers?

Martin grinned and leaned down to whisper. "Up fifteen points."

Rosie hadn't realized she'd been holding her breath. "All interviewing took place Sunday?" A day after Amy's story, complete with seal imitations and monkey stampedes, aired?

A vigorous nod from Martin confirmed it. "Congratulations."

Congratulations? For what? Letting Hud play with his nephew? Although she hadn't manipulated the situation, Rosie couldn't quite revel in it.

"Oh, and Walter O'Connell called to say the president

will be attending Mrs. McCloud's event this evening," Martin said. "And the president wants to congratulate you on Hud's poll numbers." He pointed at Rosie with a huge grin. "I'm so grateful you let me volunteer, because I'm going to meet the president of the United States tonight. Me." He thumbed himself in the chest.

On one level, everything she'd worked years to achieve was all coming into place. Rosie thought it would feel different. She'd assumed she'd be more enthusiastic, like Martin, or at least triumphant. But sitting next to Hud and knowing what she'd lost and that she was about to lose more took all the joy from the moment.

"I've met the president. Nice guy. Could use breath mints." Hud returned to perusing his poll report with a closed expression on his face.

"WHY DID YOU CANCEL my dinner plans?" Hud stood in the doorway of Rosie's office, trying not to think that she'd kept Samuel's child away from his family all this time, which was easier to stomach than to think about what she'd done to his heart. "I was looking forward to dining with the vice mayor and his wife." Not.

The afternoon was closing in on five o'clock and Hudson had just received a revised schedule. Someone honked outside and Hudson waved without looking up. The gesture was getting so automatic he did it on the street, probably when people weren't honking at him.

"I thought you might want to take in your mother's engagement tonight. She's very nervous, what with the president showing up and all." Rosie didn't bother looking up. That was the way they'd dealt with each other all day—by never looking directly into each other's eyes.

"I'll go if you go." Would Rosie remember the way he'd touched her when their gazes connected and he was inside of her a month from now?

As if reading his thoughts, her gaze slid away and there might have been more color to her cheeks. "I can't. There's no way I could get a sitter on such short notice."

"Bring him along."

Rosie laughed, but it lacked energy. "Bring a five-year-old to an hour-long event? I think not."

Hud had to step around a box on the floor filled with her things to touch the violets on her credenza. "Bring Casey tonight."

"I—"

"I don't care. The both of you are coming. End of story." Hudson walked out the door, then leaned back in. "It will mean a lot to Casey's *grandmother.*"

Rosie's gaze bounced off his before she gave a curt nod.

"YOU LOOK NERVOUS." Walter's gravelly voice cut into Vivian's perusal of the speech Martin had written with her and Stu.

As nervous as she was, Vivian couldn't make heads or tails of it. She clutched the arm of Walter's jacket and pulled him farther away from the stage. "Can you tell?"

Walter's faded green eyes took her measure. "I was just kidding before. You look ready to win them over. And all the pressure's off now that the president got called away to some emergency summit meeting."

"Thank heavens." Vivian glanced at the paper, but the words were blurring. "Can you read this? I can't read this." She thrust the speech at Walter.

He squinted at it, then produced a pair of reading glasses. "Wow. It reads as if you were talking to me."

"Let me see those." Vivian held out her hand.

"My glasses aren't exactly your style."

With their thick, black frames, Vivian couldn't agree more. But if she was going to make heads or tails out of the speech, she needed something.

"Don't you have reading glasses of your own?"

"Only old people need reading glasses," Vivian scoffed, pushing the glasses up her nose. Thankfully, the words came into focus.

Walter chuckled, then leaned in to kiss her cheek. "You're as young as you feel, but there are a lot of products out there that help me feel a lot younger."

"Behave," she warned. When he turned away, she caught his arm again. "What if someone asks me about Samuel and I break down? What if I fall flat on my face? Everyone will hate me."

For the second time in as many minutes, Walter looked surprised. "Everyone loves you, Viv. How could they not?"

"Well, just look at me." She held out her hands. "For years, I've stood two steps behind the podium and nodded like a puppet as my men talked about their ideas. I don't belong up there at the podium."

His brows drew low. "Don't bullshit a bullshitter. You chose to walk two steps behind when you could have walked side-by-side with Hamilton. You knew he wanted to be the star in the family. Now it's your turn."

His words confused her. "It's Hud's turn."

Walter took both her hands in his. "I want to hear what the beautiful and gracious Vivian McCloud has to say about the world. And I want the rest of the world to know that beneath all these designer clothes beats the heart of a caring, intelligent woman." He kissed the back of each of her hands, sending delightful sensations across her skin. "And when you've done that, I'll be here in the wings, waiting to stand side-by-side." Walter pressed his lips briefly to hers, too briefly. "Because it just so happens that I love you. I'm tired of letting you push me away. It's you I want, not some young woman who doesn't remember President Kennedy's inaugural address."

Walter released her hands, which fell uselessly to Vivian's side. The speech fluttered to the floor, perhaps a precursor of what awaited her after Walter's surprising declaration. Her knees were as sturdy as San Francisco during an earthquake.

"Wh-wh-what?" Her cheeks were hotter than an oven.

"They're introducing you." Walter bent to pick up her speech and pressed it into her hands. He took her by the shoulders and gently turned her toward the stage. His lips hovered near her ear. "Give them what they want, then we'll talk about what you and I want."

"I can't go out there now." Not after what he'd said. What Walter said was preposterous. She must have misunderstood him. Or maybe she was dreaming because she'd been thinking too much about Walter of late.

There was thunderous applause and the woman who'd read lines of introduction turned to Vivian with an expectant look on her face.

Hamilton would have told her to go out there and garner some votes for Hud. The applause kept going. Was that really for her?

With a gentle shove, Walter jump-started Vivian's frozen legs toward the podium. The applause got louder as soon as she came into view, causing her steps to falter. They were clapping for *her*, not her father-in-law or her husband or her son. Vivian's steps gained strength. She was holding

Walter's thick-rimmed glasses in one hand and her crumpled speech in the other as she took the podium and thanked the emcee for the introduction she hadn't heard a word of.

Slipping on the glasses to the chorus of shutter clicks in the audience—wasn't she a picture for *Glamour don'ts*—Vivian drew a deep breath and started reading.

"AND THAT'S THE MOMENT I knew I was going to marry Hamilton McCloud."

The applause thundered through the hall. Sitting next to Margo with Casey in her lap, Rosie couldn't help but feel proud. Vivian McCloud was a natural speaker.

"She's great, isn't she?" Margo asked in hushed tones as Vivian took a drink of water and prepared to continue. "Can we really go backstage to meet her afterward?"

"Yes. But the president is a no-show." As was Hud. At the last minute, he'd claimed his mother had to do this on her own without the crutch of a McCloud man at her side. Not that this was a reprieve. Unlike Rosie, Hud wouldn't put off telling his mother the truth for long.

Rosie rocked Casey gently from side to side with a heavy sigh. At least there was one McCloud supporting Vivian in the audience.

Margo spared Rosie a sympathetic look as Rosie kissed the wild curls on her son's head and tried to think of something besides her predicament. Somehow she had to get Martin on the paid staff before she left. The college student was brilliant. Rosie had to believe things would shake out for the best, but it was too soon for easy smiles masking lost dreams.

ROSIE WAS AWAKENED by the urgent thundering of footsteps on the stairs followed by insistent pounding on her door. Throwing on a robe, she ran barefoot out to the living room.

"Set up the camera so we can get a shot of him as we open the door." Amy Furokawa's voice.

Retreating to her bedroom, Rosie grabbed her cell phone and called Hud. "Pick up, pick up, pick up."

He didn't and she passed through to voice mail. "Hud, time's run out. Your favorite reporter is at my door." And based on the pounding, it didn't seem as if she was going to go away.

Casey wandered into her bedroom and flopped on the bed. "Why aren't you answering the door?"

"We know you're in there," Amy called with that ingratiating voice Rosie had come to hate.

"It's that funny news lady, and I don't want her to see me in my pajamas." As soon as Rosie said it, she knew what to do. It only took her a few minutes to get dressed and make herself presentable for the cameras. Jeans, minimal makeup and her hair in a ponytail. It was a tougher task to get Casey to stay hidden in his bedroom.

"I want to be on TV again," he whined with his Spider-Man pajamas askew and his hair looking like a wild squirrel inhabited his head.

"You will be. I promise. But this one time, Mommy has to be on TV alone."

"Promise?" Casey looked tentative.

"I promise." Rosie crossed her heart. As soon as the news about Casey got out, there'd be no escaping the cameras.

"All right, but only if I can have McDonalds' later." He shuffled back toward his bedroom.

"Anything you want, Case. Just don't come out until I tell you it's okay."

Casey paused in the hallway to pick up his blanket. "It's nice to have a daddy around."

"He's not your daddy." She crouched in front of him. "I told you last night. He's your uncle. He's your dad's brother."

Casey launched himself into Rosie's arms. "That's almost better than a daddy. It's family."

Maybe so, but it was a family that wasn't going to include Rosie.

Less than a minute later, Rosie had to take a few deep breaths before she opened the door to Amy and her bright lights. "Can I help you, Amy?"

"We're live at the apartment of Hudson McCloud's campaign manager and apparent girlfriend with a breaking story. I've obtained a copy of a birth certificate that proves Samuel McCloud is the father of your little boy. All of San Francisco is holding their breath this morning waiting to find out the details of your affair with the deceased playboy." Amy shoved her microphone in Rosie's face.

They wanted sordid details about her past? Rosie's spine stiffened, her knuckles were white on the doorknob. This was not at all what she'd been expecting.

"Ms. DeWitt," Amy prompted.

"No comment." Rosie sent the door slamming into Amy's face.

But the pounding only started up again.

"ARE YOU SITTING DOWN?" Hud asked on the other end of the phone.

"Of course, I'm having my morning coffee and paper." Vivian tugged her silk robe tighter together and risked a glance at Walter. She could tell he was awake by the way his hand stroked her bare thigh. She was feeling marvelous; better than she had in years. "Is there an earth-quake?"

"No."

"Then call me back later."

Hud ignored her request. "Do you remember how Samuel used to date a variety of girls?"

Vivian did not want to think about Samuel now, not with the warmth of Walter's hand seeping into her skin. But Hud was no mind reader. He just kept on talking.

"Well, he dated Rosie."

That caught Vivian off guard. "Our Rosie."

"My *campaign manager.*"

Oh, dear. That explained a lot. Why Hud seemed distant when Vivian brought up Rosie's name yesterday. Why Rosie appeared heartbroken. "I'll call her up later and see if she's free for lunch."

"Oh, no, you won't," Walter said.

"Is someone there with you?" Hud asked.

"I'm having my morning coffee and paper, Hud. Of course, I'm alone." She put her hand over Walter's mouth. A mistake, since he immediately started outlining circles on her palm with his tongue. "I really must go." Go reclaim her womanhood one more time before lunch.

"Casey is Samuel's child."

"What?" Vivian sat up in bed. Casey? Rosie? Oh, dear heavens above, poor Samuel.

"I know. She lied about the whole thing." Hud sounded hurt.

"We'll sort this out." Quietly, in a civilized manner at a civilized hour.

"This is not something you sort out, Mother. She was probably never going to tell us Casey existed."

"What's happening?" Walter sat up and wrapped his

arms around her. She appreciated the way Walter acknowledged her strength, but knew when she needed his.

"Someone is there with you. Mother, what's going on?" The irritation in Hud's voice escalated to anger.

"I'll get dressed as soon as I can and be right over." She threw her covers onto Walter and hurried to the bathroom.

"No. Not here. The press has gotten wind of this. I'll come to you."

The press…

Breaking the connection, Vivian glanced back at Walter. If the press were involved, they'd be at her house next. "You've got to get out of here."

"Not until you tell me what's happened." He stood, naked and proud of himself at seventy, while she hid in a nightgown.

"Rosie's little boy is Samuel's. I have a grandchild." The admission was life-altering. A grandmother. She was old and yet she didn't care. A little bit of Samuel existed in her world. "The press will be here any minute and you can't be seen coming out of my house in the same clothes you entered with."

"That's perfect. Just what we need to send Hud's polls over the top."

It took Vivian a moment to process what Walter was saying. "You will not use my grandchild as a promotional tool."

"Why not? Hamilton used you and your children in every election."

"He's just a baby." A refreshing breath of fresh air. She'd rather he stay that way—precocious yet solemn, exuberant yet thoughtful.

"Oh, come on, Viv. You want Hud elected just as much as I do and using this grandchild of yours practically guarantees the race."

Wasn't this a fine kettle of fish? Their first fight after becoming lovers. "He won't want to win that way. I don't want him to win that way."

"I wouldn't think twice if it was my grandchild. He'll thank you for it in thirty years when he's elected to higher office."

"Well, he's not your grandchild and the way you're acting he may not have a chance at being your step-grandchild." She'd deal with Walter's misconceptions later. Vivian rushed to her closet, wondering what would be appropriate for a grandmother to wear.

HIS MOTHER HAD BREAKFAST laid out in the dining room by the time Hud arrived, but the bitter taste of betrayal had ruined any appetite he might have had.

"What are you doing here?" Hud asked Walter when the chairman walked into the room a few minutes later.

"Don't let your bad mood spill over onto Walter," his mother said quickly. "He's here to support me. Just don't ask him his opinion on how this affects the race because I'm going to veto whatever he says."

Hud's shoulders stiffened. "This is a family matter, Walter. I'll have to ask you to leave."

"The family gets bigger every day," Stu said, coming in from the kitchen with a cup of coffee.

"I think it affects your career more directly than the family," Walter pointed out.

"How did…" Hud turned to his mother. "You told him?"

Her chin came up. "Yes, I did. He's right. We'll welcome Casey into our family with open arms, but the more immediate question is how this will affect your candidacy."

"I don't care about that now." He didn't have the heart for politics, not today, maybe not ever again.

"Hudson," his mother scolded him as if he was Casey's
ge. "Have you seen that horrid woman's news report?
She's not just talking about Casey, she's hypothesizing
bout Rosie's relationship with Samuel."

Rubbing a hand over his face, Hud tried to accept that
he race was important, only it didn't seem as important
s it should anymore.

"Pull yourself together and attack each problem separ-
tely," Walter advised. "It's not as if it's your child—"

But I wish he was. Hudson clenched his teeth. He'd
never been particularly jealous of his brother's partners,
ut damn it, he felt betrayed on so many levels that he
ouldn't decide what hurt more—Rosie keeping the secret
f Casey's heritage from him or Samuel having been with
er before Hud ever met her.

"We need Rosie here," his mother said. "And Martin."

A cell phone rang. Walter's.

"Excuse me. I have to take this." Walter stepped out into
he hallway.

I'M RESIGNING. Effective immediately." Rosie didn't let
Walter get more than "hello" in before she blurted the
news. She was talking to him on her cell phone while her
partment phone rang insistently. Her cell phone beeped
n her ear announcing another call but she ignored that as
well. The last time she'd picked up the line, it had been a
eporter. Perhaps it hadn't been a good idea to include her
ell number on Hud's press releases.

"Let's not be hasty. I hear you're part of the McCloud
amily."

"How…?" But she knew. Hud. "That doesn't matter.
f I quit now, you can find a replacement by tomorrow and
tart damage control."

"You don't know if your son will help or hurt Hud's chances."

"Ignoring the fact that Casey is *not* an asset to the campaign, I've disappointed Hud in ways I can't begin to explain." At least in that, Hud was right. She was a hypocrite. He deserved someone so much better than she was.

"I thought you were tougher than that. Aren't you the gal who spent years in the background making things happen? Aren't you the one who shored up sagging campaigns and turned things around? Don't back down just because you've been thrust into the spotlight by your own past."

"I don't like the spotlight." At the sound of car doors slamming, Rosie peeked out the window to find another television news crew setting up on the sidewalk downstairs. "I have a child to protect."

"There's a way out of this."

"If there's a way out of this mess, Walter, I just don't see it. I'm sorry."

"I won't accept your resignation without something in writing," he said. "Remember, the presidential campaign is just around the corner and they don't take quitters." The phone clicked as Walter hung up.

Someone pounded on her door. Rosie flinched.

"Aren't you gonna get that, Mommy?" Casey looked up from his cartoons.

"Shhh." She held a finger to her lips. She'd rather hide in her apartment than face the reporters without anything to say.

"Ms. DeWitt, are you home?" The heavy Chinese accent was not that of a television reporter.

"Mrs. Chin?" Rosie hurried to open the door to her landlord.

The diminutive woman stood in the hallway, holding white dishtowels and looking distraught. "My husband downstairs. He not let the reporters in. We go. Now. Out back."

"We don't have a car." They wouldn't get far without one, even by slipping out the back.

"Your friend with wild colors is downstairs in back with car. You go. Now."

"Selena?"

"Yes. Hurry, boy." Mrs. Chin turned to Casey. "Tie your shoes."

Shell-shocked, but ecstatic over the possibility of escape, Rosie helped Casey get ready, grabbed their coats and her laptop. Mrs. Chin led them down the back stairs where Selena waited with her Honda.

CHAPTER SEVENTEEN

HIDDEN SAFELY INSIDE Selena's loft apartment, Rosie watched the news while Casey played with one of Drew's portable video games. Selena had dropped her son off at school on the way to rescue Rosie.

Action News was replaying Rosie's wake-up interview. "We're live at the home of Hudson McCloud's campaign manager and apparent—"

Rosie lunged for the remote control and changed the channel. "I've got to call Hank at the station. Maybe he can do something about this."

"Look at that." Selena shook a hand at the television. "Mrs. Chin just chased away a reporter with a broom."

Too bad it wasn't Amy Furokawa. "Thank heavens I didn't follow your advice and tell her to mind her own business when it comes to Casey's diet."

"When you didn't answer either your cell phone or the home line, I called Chin-Chin's and explained why I was coming over. She suggested I wait in the back with the getaway car."

"Casey will just have to learn to eat squid." Rosie curled into a ball on the couch and tossed Selena the remote.

"Hey." Selena leaned forward after flipping back to Action News. "Isn't that your day care?"

Rosie sunk farther into Selena's couch. "Yes, and here

comes Ms. Phan. She'll probably tell everyone what a bad mother I am. This is the moment she's been waiting for." There was no better way to let Rosie know what Ms. Phan really thought of her than to talk on live television in front of thousands of viewers.

There was a sick feeling in Rosie's stomach as she watched the reporter introduce Ms. Phan. "Put the sound back on. I want to hear this."

"—a wonderful parent and he's a bright, well-behaved boy. That's all I wanted to say. I think it's best for the children if you leave now." Ms. Phan nodded her head graciously and then returned to the safety of Rainbow Day Care.

"She likes me?" When had that happened? Rosie muted the television as the reporter did a recap and another reporter came on in front of Hudson's offices at the Pyramid Center.

"You're too sensitive. Didn't you show me a study once that said women always think the worst? Like when a boss says, 'we need to talk' and a woman always believes she's in trouble?" Selena shook her head.

"Both Ms. Phan and Mrs. Chin rag me constantly about how I'm raising Casey."

"Some people are born advice givers. Maybe they speak up because they care about Casey *and* they care about you." She rubbed Rosie's shoulder. "You've got to regret ever taking on this campaign. I'm so sorry. What are you going to do?"

"I don't know." She'd escaped, for now, but she knew it was only temporary. "I'm going to be on the cover of those grocery store gossip papers along with the women claiming to have had babies spawned by aliens, aren't I?"

Selena had no sympathy. "What about Mrs. McCloud? She must be devastated."

Rosie shied away from the thought. "I suppose selfishly, I was more worried about my baby than Samuel's family. Studies show…" Rosie stopped herself midquote. She suddenly felt the way Hud must have when he admitted he hadn't written any of his speeches. What was right when you were backed into a corner?

Selena scooted closer. "I know facts and figures are your life, but you can't always make a decision based on research. Sometimes you go on gut feel."

"But what if your gut makes things even worse?" She was not going to admit to Selena that she'd slept with Hud. Twice.

"Then you chalk it up as a mistake, learn from it and move on. Haven't you ever had your heart broken before?"

"Not until now," Rosie whispered.

There was a crash from the back of the apartment and Selena leapt up. "That darn dog. Axel! What are you up to?"

Rosie flipped through the channels quickly. She wanted to see where they'd go next. And then she saw Amy Furokawa at the YMCA.

HIS MOTHER'S COOK opened the kitchen door. "Mrs. McCloud, there's more news on." She glanced at Hud apologetically.

They all hurried into the kitchen and stared at the small screen embedded in the refrigerator door. At any other time, Hud would have questioned his mother about the need for a television embedded in her refrigerator, but the sight of Amy Furokawa at the YMCA was enough to freeze all thought.

"On weekends, Rosie DeWitt and her son frequent this YMCA as well as other charitable organizations. Could she be grooming Casey McCloud for bigger things?"

"Elizé," Hud murmured. Ms. Allen had said Elizé was hiding from her father. He glanced at his watch. In another few hours, Elizé was sure to be there. All her father needed to find her was a picture of her on the local news. "When is this crazy reporter going to stop? Don't you know someone at the television station?" Hudson turned to his mother. If Elizé was caught on film and her father saw her...

"I know the owner, but he's probably in ratings heaven over this," his mother pointed out. "Why don't you call Rosie and see if she's all right?"

"She's got those shoes," Stu countered. "Of course, she's all right. We have more important issues to address."

Much as he hated to admit it, Hud agreed with Stu. Rosie was on her own. But... "She's harassing all of Rosie's friends." People Hud cared about, too.

"She's after a story," Walter said. "Whether you give some or all of it to her or Rosie does, probably doesn't matter to her."

Hud didn't know enough to give a complete story, but without something, he suspected Amy Furokawa wouldn't give up.

"MRS. MCCLOUD, please come in. I'm Selena." The woman who ushered Vivian into the loft apartment had long dark hair tied back in an aqua scarf and overalls that bore testament to an artistic bent with paints.

"How is she doing?" Vivian's concern for Rosie had led her first to Margo's Bistro and then here.

"I'm fine," Rosie said, stepping from behind a screen across the room followed by Casey.

"Grandma!" he shouted and pounded across the room toward her followed by a huge, shaggy dog with a lolling tongue.

Selena moved in front of Vivian in a defensive position. "Axel, no jump!" While Rosie chased the hairy beast.

"Oh, dear," Vivian backed up to the door and braced herself in case Selena couldn't stop the brute.

Selena caught Axel by his collar and used his momentum to spin him around in a circle.

Just as Vivian was breathing a sigh of relief, a bundle of joy barreled into her with a fit of giggles.

"Did you think Axel was going to tackle you?" Casey chortled.

"I'll just take him for a walk," Selena said, her face red from the exertion of controlling her dog.

"I told him on the way home last night that you were his grandmother." Rosie led Vivian to a living area by one wall of windows. "Grandmas are like Mommy's dishes, Casey. I don't think Grandma Vivian thought Axel was as funny as you did."

"Grandmas break?" Casey cast a speculative look at Vivian.

"I'm afraid so," Vivian admitted, as she collapsed onto a chair. She held out a hand. "Come here and let me look at you."

Casey half sat in the chair with Vivian, his shoulder against her side. Gently, Vivian took his chin and turned his face to hers. Heartache welled inside her when she couldn't see anything of Samuel in Casey's features, no matter how hard she tried to find him.

"I know this game," Casey said after a moment. He made a face but he continued to stare at Vivian with his mouth in a goofy twist and his eyes wide.

Vivian laughed. There was her Samuel, hidden in Casey's joie de vivre attitude.

"Made you laugh." Casey dissolved into giggles. "Want to play again?"

Vivian didn't think she could draw another breath as

memories of her little Samuel assaulted her—singing as he rode a pony on his birthday, begging her to push him higher on a swing, messy from trying to eat chocolate cake with his tiny hands.

"I'm so sorry," Rosie said to Vivian. "I never meant to hurt you."

"You haven't hurt me, dear." Vivian couldn't tear her eyes from Casey, waiting to see something of Samuel again. "You've given me the most precious gift."

Rosie allowed her to take in the sight of her grandson in silence.

"The men are all in a dither over how this affects Hud's campaign," Vivian said, reluctantly getting down to business. There'd be time to spend with Casey later. "None of them understands the feral drive of that reporter. It doesn't matter what Hud says or what you say on either matter. If you jaywalked and talked your way out of a ticket, she's going to find out about it and report it as news."

"It's not news. *I'm* not news." Rosie pushed her hair away from her face.

"Don't take this the wrong way, dear, but I agree with you wholeheartedly." Vivian tried to be matter of fact, but their situation was grim and likely to go on for a long time. "Unfortunately, if there's one thing I know about the press it's that any story even remotely connected to a famous personality or politician won't die a natural death."

"So you're saying there's nothing we can do. Casey and I should move to Canada?"

"Or wish for a bigger news story. Without both leverage and a good speech, you're at their mercy." Vivian couldn't resist putting her hand on Casey's curls. "As soon as this gets national attention, you'll consider that Amy reporter one of the better ones."

"That's not only depressing, it's creepy. No one at the station would be sorry to see her go, but someone worse..." Rosie shuddered.

Vivian took a last look at Casey, then smiled at Rosie as a plan took shape. "What we need, my dear, is leverage."

THANK YOU FOR OFFERING to do this interview." Smiling triumphantly, Amy Furokawa sat in the television studio across a polished table from Rosie as cameras moved into position.

In a booth across the studio, several people watched in the dark.

As an assistant clipped a microphone onto Rosie's collar, she forced her lips into something she hoped resembled a smile. "What other choice did you leave me?"

Behind Amy, a red light came on.

"I thought if I fished around long enough I'd find a sore spot. You're that goody-two-shoes type that always tries to help others." Amy laughed as Rosie's smile faded. "Who was it that finally got you to call me? The coffee shop owner? The day-care director?" Amy gave Rosie a sly glance. "Perhaps there's another story I should be looking in to."

"And here I thought you were reporting news because you cared about what happened in the city, when in fact you were vindictively looking for a way to get back at Hudson because he didn't want to go out with you."

Amy's smile hardened. "My job isn't to report the news. It's to make a name for myself. Your job isn't so different. You'll do anything to get your candidate elected."

"I only work for politicians I believe in, people whose main concern is not glory for themselves but making their city or their district a better place to live."

"Oh, that sounds so noble. And yet, I hear if Hudson were to be elected, your bonus was to work on the next presidential campaign. How is that any different from me pursuing a story that will get me a promotion?"

"You checked into my background for no reason other than jealousy."

Amy shrugged. "He didn't pick up on the signals I was sending, but I did pick up on yours. And look what I found. You and Samuel both went to grad school at Berkeley at the same time. There's been no record of your marriage or divorce." Amy bent closer. "It made me wonder about your son. And, of course, you were honest enough to put Samuel's name on little Casey's birth certificate."

"At the risk of repeating myself, I want to help make the world a better place. If I do work on a presidential campaign, I'll only receive accolades from my team for doing honest work. I don't expect to become a household name."

"Too late." Amy's plastic smile turned Rosie's stomach. "Are we ready to roll?"

"Oh, you've already been rolling," Rosie said, taking off her microphone, glad that she'd been able to obtain Vivian's leverage.

"But we haven't started."

"I disagree. Talk to your producer. He recorded the entire interview, including your most insightful comments. I'm sure the station manager will be enlightened when he sees this tape." Ignoring her trembling legs, Rosie stood.

"I broke the story. This won't ruin my career," Amy protested.

"No, but it will finish your tenure here." With a nod of thanks to Hank in the shadowy control room, Rosie left

for campaign headquarters, where she had a statement of
another kind to make.

"HUD, WHERE ARE YOU GOING?" his mother asked.

"Not far." Just his mother's office. Rosie wasn't answering her phone. No doubt she was running again, either
to protect her son or to protect someone else dear to her,
like Elizé. Hudson couldn't stand by and do nothing. He
may as well face it. He loved her. When he said he'd
forgive her anything, he'd meant it. It was time to act
upon his own words and leave the past behind.

"Let's not be hasty," Walter cautioned. "Why not let the
dust settle before you make a decision you'll regret later."

"I'm not going to regret this decision," Hud said. He
found a piece of paper in his mother's desk and a gold pen
with a large *M* engraved on it.

"What decision have you made, dear?" His mother
reached for Walter's hand, but Walter put his arm around
her instead.

Hud hesitated, pen over paper. "You two...?" Why
hadn't he seen it before? Because he'd been lost in a fog
of his own problems. "Not that it matters, but I approve."

"It does matter," his mother said.

"It does not. We're old enough to do something crazy
without anyone's consent." Same old Walter. "Are you
going to tell us what you're doing?"

"No." Hud stared at the blank sheet of paper with trepi-
dation. "I'm not sure I know what I'm doing yet."

IGNORING SHOUTED QUESTIONS and microphones thrust
into her face, Rosie pushed through a throng of reporters
to get to the door of campaign headquarters.

"Martin!" Rosie ran toward the back of the office past

gaping volunteers who huddled together in small groups. "Martin, I need you in my office. Now." Rosie threw her purse down on her desk and began searching through file folders.

A sound behind Rosie sent her whirling. Reporters had gathered at the glass behind her. One tapped on the window and shouted a muffled question. "Is it true that you had Samuel McCloud's baby?"

"Scary, isn't it?" Martin said, leaning against the doorframe as if reluctant to enter.

"I'm sorry, Martin. First you don't get to meet the president and now this."

"You must be kidding me. My resume is set for life. No matter how this goes down, I come out ahead." He started to smile, then seemed to think better of it. "No offense."

"None taken." It was funny how her life was crumbling around her ears and others were benefiting from it. She'd have time for wallowing in regrets later—when she made it through the day and moved to Timbuktu.

The reporters increased in volume.

"Where is Hud's schedule for today?"

"Here." Martin handed it to her. "It doesn't matter though."

"If I know Hud, he'll weather this by showing up at his scheduled appearances. And if he does, he'll need his notes and speech, plus a briefing from you." She scanned the schedule. "You can probably catch up to him at the Embarcadero with the business owners association."

"He's not going to that meeting," Martin said with the huffing superiority so like his age group.

"I'm telling you to go," Rosie reiterated.

"Rosie, Hud called first thing this morning. He wanted me to cancel all his appointments for today."

Disappointment speared through her and Rosie sank into her chair. He was quitting. "No." Why hadn't Vivian said anything?

"Yes." Martin grinned. "And then he called thirty minutes ago and asked me to schedule a press conference at city hall at one-thirty."

"No." Just twenty minutes away. Rosie had to get there and stop Hud before he withdrew. She grabbed her purse.

"Look." Martin pointed at the window. "Even the reporters are leaving."

"Of course, they are. They're just getting the news about the press conference." Rosie took Martin by the shoulders and gave him a gentle shaking. "Are you coming with me? I may need help convincing Hud to stay in the race." More likely she'd need a wiry kid breaking a path through the frenzied crowd of reporters that would be surrounding Hud.

Martin grinned. "I'll get us a taxi. My political science class is going to be so envious." He cleared his throat. "No offense."

"As long as you get us that taxi, there'll be none taken."

ROSIE WAS ALWAYS TALKING about honesty and baring souls. Well, Hud was about to do just that, not for the campaign, but for her. And maybe, for himself, too.

He scanned the frenzied crowd of reporters outside city hall on a nippy January afternoon and drew a deep breath. "Thank you all for coming today. Please bear with me and hold all questions until the end." Hud adjusted the microphone, looked down at the speech he'd written and hoped he didn't start to sweat.

"Nearly one hundred and fifty years ago, just after California achieved statehood, my great, great, great grandfather, Harley McCloud, first ran for office. He was a self-made man, a shipping magnate who made his fortune primarily by importing silk from China."

The sun was shining and the crowd was hanging on his every word. It buoyed his spirits enough to continue.

"This was the gold rush years with an influx of workers from China who were being used to build the Central Pacific Railroad. Harley was passionate about protecting these workers, although it was an unpopular stance. One Sunday, a man showed up at Harley's door with a gun, intent upon stopping Harley from voting for Chinese worker's rights. He tried to kill Harley but his bullet struck Harley's wife, Caroline, instead, leaving Harley to raise his two sons alone. Brokenhearted, Harley refused to compromise his beliefs, but he did become a more private, guarded person who shaped generations of McClouds."

Several photographers crept up the steps to get a better picture of Hud. Murmurs were promptly shushed.

"Over the years there have been several who've tried to silence a McCloud. As recently as thirty years ago, someone angered by my father's stance and choice of words on the war and embittered by their own losses, threatened our family. Although no one was hurt, it was a reminder to my father to be careful." Hud's father had become very selective about the words he put in his speeches. And, later, the words Hud was allowed to include in his. "It seemed as if my mother and I hadn't recovered from my father's death when we lost my brother, Samuel, in another war. Instead of opening up about our grief and sharing our sorrows with those around us, we became even more private."

There was a proverbial drum roll in Hud's head. The crowd seemed to be holding their breath.

"I've tried to find a balance between serving our community and holding my family together with dignity. And I've got to tell you, it's not an easy task determining what in my life is public domain and what is personal." Hud came to the end of what he'd written. He hadn't been able to compose a compelling close. It was time to speak from the heart.

Hud met the gazes of several reporters in the front row. "But isn't that the challenge we all face? How much do we share of ourselves with others? We're afraid that if we tell someone our dreams, they'll laugh. Or if we admit we've made a mistake that somehow makes us less of a person. So we keep some things to ourselves. And yet, no one is perfect and no one escapes tragedy. Hopefully, we deal with who we are and what life throws our way with compassion, with strength...and with love." Rosie had dealt with challenges in a way Hud wouldn't have chosen, yet Hud loved her anyway. He hoped she felt the same way about him and that someday soon he'd be standing in front of a similar crowd announcing his intentions toward a certain campaign manager.

Hud cleared his throat as he tried to remain focused. "My brother, Samuel, was a good man who wasn't afraid to laugh and love or to volunteer to protect his country's freedom. Did he make mistakes? Yes, but that doesn't mean I loved him any less."

"What about the boy?" a reporter in front asked.

"Is he your nephew?" someone shouted.

"Was that the boy you accompanied to the park?" a voice from the back yelled.

Hud hesitated. He was proud of the fact that Casey was Samuel's son, but confirming it would change his nephew's life forever.

He could feel the crowd turn from supportive to restless.

"Did you know the boy was your nephew before this morning?"

"Yes, he did." A woman's voice. Rosie's voice.

Hud searched the faces for the last person he expected to see out here. A wave of excitement passed through the crowd as the reporters recognized her. With Martin making way for her, Rosie squeezed between reporters and cameramen until she was at the podium. She looked worn out. Several curls had escaped the clip at her crown and lifted softly in the breeze. He'd never been so happy to see anyone in his life, but Rosie only gave him a cursory nod before she edged him aside and adjusted the microphone so she could be heard.

"My name is Rosie DeWitt. I'm a political consultant with the Democratic Party currently working on Hudson McCloud's campaign." She hesitated, sending a sideways glance in Hud's direction before continuing in a deliberate monotone voice. "My story is not all that uncommon. When I was in college, I met a man. We dated." She drew a deep breath. "He went off to war and was killed as so many tragically are. Later, I discovered I was pregnant and was faced with a choice."

She continued her slow, methodical speech. "I took the path that many women have taken. I took this path alone. In this case, a family who hadn't known me was grieving just as I was. I made another choice—to raise my son out of the spotlight. But I've recently decided that isn't fair to my son or the family that had lost a son of their own."

"I told Hudson when we started this campaign that he couldn't escape his past. And I was right. Secrets in the past hold us back and keep us apart. He told me he wanted to focus on the future. I suppose…in a way…we were both right. Hudson will make a positive difference in this city and in the lives of its citizens. I know he's made a positive difference in mine." Without a backward glance, Rosie slipped back into the crowd, leaving Hud to deal with the reporters.

"My mother and I are overjoyed at the prospect of getting to know Samuel's son. I promise we'll let you know how things go. I ask only this." Hud paused. "Cut the kid some slack. Most kindergartners are challenged reciting the Pledge of Allegiance much less giving a live interview."

There were some chuckles.

"In the past few weeks I've announced my candidacy for mayor and shared my reasons for leaving the Senate. I've spent time with people in shelters, community programs and traveled on the bus during rush hour as I try to understand what the people of this city need. I've already formed several exciting ideas to create jobs, provide affordable day care and medical services, and I'm sure over the next few weeks as I meet more residents more new solutions will arise. I'm not perfect, but I learn from my mistakes and I'm determined to give back to this great city. But to do that, I need your vote come March."

The roar of approval was a long-awaited validation for Hud, but Rosie was gone.

CHAPTER EIGHTEEN

"MOMMY, WHEN CAN I get a job?" Casey stood in the hallway in Spider-Man pajamas that were too short, with hair wet from his evening bath.

Rosie's fingers stopped midword on the keyboard. To avoid reporters, they'd waited at Selena's apartment until nearly ten o'clock before coming home. "What do you need a job for?"

Casey traced a finger along the wall. "Just because."

"Just because, huh?" Rosie saved what little she'd been able to write for her resignation letter and closed the file, opening a new one. "Come here."

Dewey and smelling of soap, Casey climbed into her lap and began poking the laptop's keys. "I can help you, Mommy. I can put the words in."

"Write me a speech." Holding him close, Rosie forced herself to ignore the daunting question that had plagued her since she'd watched Hud give his speech at city hall— what was she going to do now?

With exuberant strokes, Casey typed gibberish. "How does your boss feel about late buses?"

"Hates them."

More pounding on the delicate laptop. "Easy on the keys."

Casey paused. "And crime?"

"Down with it."

Casey hammered the keyboard, each stroke hitting on one of Rosie's taut nerves. She captured his hands as gently as she could. "The keys will break if you abuse them like that."

Thankfully, he didn't get upset. "If I do a good job I could come to work with you, Mommy. Then I wouldn't have to go to Rainbow." Casey leaned into her, accepting a tighter hug. He was such a gentle soul. "Can I come to the office tomorrow?"

"No," she blurted too quickly.

Casey glanced at her over his shoulder, hurt brimming in his eyes and his lower lip thrust out. Shaking off her embrace, he slid to the floor and retreated to the couch.

"I'm sorry, Case. I'm finding a new job." Rosie apologized knowing that it was a lost cause. "Lucky you, you get another day off from school tomorrow."

"What about the mayor? I mean, Uncle Mayor." Casey turned on the television and tried to sink into the couch.

"He'll find someone else." Rosie skittered away from the thought that Hud would find someone else to love and someone else to run his campaign. After his press conference today, Hud was almost untouchable. He'd finally spoken in public from the heart. Roger didn't stand a chance.

"He won't play chess with me," Casey mumbled, lip still thrust out.

"He'll play with you at Grandma Vivian's house. He just won't come over here anymore."

"What good is a family without the mayor to hug me? Who's gonna carry me on his shoulders?"

Rosie didn't have an answer to that.

"WHAT DO YOU MEAN you don't know where Rosie is?" Hud paced campaign headquarters the day after the press conference. "It's after ten. Hasn't anyone seen her?"

Standing in the foyer, Martin had his hands in his pockets. The rest of Hud's campaign staff were huddled and hiding in cubicles as if he was a raving lunatic, not the city's latest golden boy. He had Rosie, Casey and Samuel to thank for his success.

"Rosie didn't come into work today. She doesn't answer her cell phone." Martin fiddled with an earring. "Have you tried calling Walter?"

"Walter and my mother left on a cruise today." Where they would undoubtedly get married and create another feeding frenzy among the press. "I can't believe you lost sight of her in the crowd, Martin."

"She's small and she doesn't stop for anyone."

Hud ran his fingers through his hair. "Rearrange my schedule. Clear everything today."

"But we just cleared your calendar yesterday."

With a look that made it clear there were to be no more questions, Hud headed out the door to find Rosie. First stop? Margo's Bistro.

"I HAVEN'T SEEN HER," Margo said, busy finishing her soup in the kitchen for the lunchtime crowd. "If I hear from her do you want me to give her a message?"

"A message?" Hud tried not to look at the stainless steel counter where he and Rosie had shared a steamy kiss. What he had to say needed to be delivered in person. "No."

Ms. Phan at Casey's day care had heard from Rosie, but only to say that Casey wasn't coming in today. "Check back tomorrow!" She waved cheerfully.

Hud was anything but cheerful. Didn't Rosie have a

campaign to run? There was no way he was letting her resign now. Where was she? He tried Rosie's cell phone again, but this time when she didn't answer the mailbox was full so he couldn't even leave her a message.

"She go very early today," Mrs. Chin told Hud. "You look good on TV."

Although it was nice to be loved by his public and not mistaken for Tom Cruise, Hud needed to make sure that he was loved and forgiven by someone else. Only how could that happen when he couldn't even find Rosie to say he was sorry?

On a long shot, Hud went to Golden Gate Park and interrupted Mr. Stephanoplis's chess game.

"Haven't seen either one of them and don't expect to until Saturday." The retiree moved his castle across the board. "Check. Unless it rains. Then they won't come." Mr. Stephanopolis squinted at Hud through his thick lenses. "Women are often like chess. If you don't think far enough ahead, you're out of the game before you know it."

Thanking Mr. Stephanopolis for his advice, Hud sank down on the bench he'd shared with Rosie just a few days ago and pondered where to go next. The museum seemed a likely choice except that he'd never heard Casey express any interest in it at all. It was getting close to lunchtime, but how likely was it that Rosie and Casey would go to the Rainforest Café again? Which left the zoo. Given Rosie might be wanted at the zoo for starting a near riot, she'd probably be reluctant to visit.

"You think you can fool me," Mr. Stephanopolis clapped his hands and taunted his opponent. "You are pretending to be so carefree with the wind blowing in what's left of your hair when in fact you are setting up the Najdorf defense."

Hud hadn't noticed a breeze. He glanced around. With all the trees, there was barely any wind here in the park, but at the ocean…

The picture so prominently displayed above the dining room table of Casey and Rosie on the beach with the wind blowing in their hair was the only clue Hud had left to go on.

"THAT'S NOT JUST a sand castle, it's a mansion." Hud's voice carried over the brisk ocean breeze and struck a chord in Rosie's aching heart.

"It's Uncle Mayor!" Careful of their construction site, Casey jumped up and ran to meet Hud. "Come see what we're doing."

After one look at Hud's fine wool suit and overcoat, Rosie returned to digging a third system of channels for Casey's sand-castle community without meeting his gaze. She couldn't bear to see the bitterness in his eyes.

"That is an engineering marvel." Hud walked around Rosie, every step coming closer to the edge of the channel the incoming tide had started to fill with water.

Casey pointed out the characteristics of their master-piece. "The dragons live over here. And the army stays over there. And the king lives in the highest castle all by himself. We were going to give him a queen and a prince, but Mommy said no."

Rosie kept digging. It was fitting the king lived alone. Forgiveness was a huge part of love and the king hadn't exhibited any of that at all.

"If you had play clothes on you could help us," Casey said brightly, swinging his pail.

"Hud has to leave. He's got work to do." Rosie didn't know why he was here other than to arrange for some kind of visitation.

"You have work, too," Hud said.

"No, I don't. I e-mailed Walter my resignation this morning."

"In an attachment?"

"Yes." She hoped Hud was getting lots of sand in his shoes.

"Then you haven't resigned. You know Walter can't open attachments on his BlackBerry and even if he could open them, he left his BlackBerry behind." Hud sounded as if he enjoyed her predicament very much.

"Behind?"

"He and Mother have decided they've wasted enough time being friends. They left on a cruise this morning. No cell phones. No BlackBerrys. No computers."

Rosie digested that for a moment.

"So you see, you're still employed. In fact, the place is chaos without you." Yes. Hud was enjoying this too much.

Shading her eyes from the sun, Rosie squinted up at him. "Meaning you created bedlam this morning and I wasn't there to fix it."

"Well…yes. But the anarchy was really all your fault." Hud was swinging Casey's hand. The wind caressed his hair playfully, but it always fell back into place, flawlessly, of course.

Enough of dancing around the issues. Rosie stood. "I lied to you."

"What happened to choices and doing the right thing in that speech of yours yesterday? You came out better in that."

"Yesterday I thought you were quitting the race. I wanted to make sure you couldn't." Rosie wiped a stray strand of hair from her face. "I may have lied by omission, but you have told me some whoppers."

Hud didn't defend himself with the fire she'd come to associate with their arguments. "Rosie, until I met you, I didn't know that I'd been living with half truths for most of my life. All I knew was that I wanted to live without secrets, but I couldn't seem to figure it out until you showed me the way." His gaze was as warm and subtle as a caress. "And what happened yesterday proved that your reasons for keeping Casey a secret were well-founded. It's a feeding frenzy."

Was Hud saying what she thought he was saying? That he'd found a way to forgive her? "That was a nice speech," Rosie said slowly.

"Thank you." Hud didn't stop staring at her. "Most of the time you leave me speechless."

"Most of the time you're better off that way." She couldn't resist.

Hud dropped to one knee. "But I'm not at a loss for words when it comes to saying how much I love you."

Casey plopped onto his bottom next to him. "Cool."

Rosie crossed her arms over her chest. "How much?" He was still too calm and in control. She'd spent the past two days in purgatory.

"How much?"

"Yes. How much do you love me?"

That stubborn cleft chin of his jutted out. "Woman, I'm down on one knee ready to ask you to marry me. And yet you want more?"

"Yes." She took pity on Hud, smiled and offered her hands just so he wouldn't feel as if she were out to humiliate him. "I'm ready."

Hud's eyes blazed, but then he closed them and squeezed her hands ever so gently. "I'm sorry. You were right about everything. About how to turn me—and my campaign—around. About me and what I would have done years ago if you would have told me the truth. But that was before I fell in love with your sharp intellect, the sexy way you fill out a pair of jeans and the way you make everyone fall under your spell." He peeked at her. "Is that enough?"

"I like a man who knows his place." Rosie laughed, helping Hud get to his feet.

Hud held her so tight she didn't think he was going to let her go. "I'll protect you and Casey from the press as much as I can. My only regret is that you won't get a chance to serve on the next presidential campaign, because I plan on expanding this family as soon as possible."

"Oh, I wouldn't worry about that," Rosie traced the cleft on his chin with her finger. She had a feeling she and Hud would be working on a presidential campaign together someday. "Do you think you could learn to make coffee?"

Casey tugged on Hud's jacket and asked, "Are you gonna kiss my mommy?"

Hud grinned. "Yes, why?"

"Because there's a man with a camera ready to take your picture and he's been waiting an awful long time for you to do it." Ever helpful, Casey stood up and yelled, "Hey, mister. They're gonna kiss now."

* * * * *

Only one single parent left in
SINGLES...WITH KIDS!
Be sure to get
BLAME IT ON THE DOG (SR1423)
next month to see who finally gets Selena
to give up her single status!
Turn the page for a sneak peek....

CHAPTER ONE

THE CRASH RATTLED the light fixtures in Selena Milano's loft apartment and made the CD player skip. Earthquake? Twelve-year-old son? Or dog? Betting dog, she turned from the end of the apartment that served as her studio. It wouldn't be the first time she had to recycle the remnants of an Axel accident into one of her pieces.

"Drew! Are you okay?"

The response from the area of the loft partitioned to create her son's sleeping quarters wasn't good. Barking. Laughter. And a scraping noise that sounded as if someone was dragging a barge across the hardwood floor.

"Drew!"

"Chill, Mom, we're okay."

She didn't believe that for a minute.

Fortunately, their oversized apartment in a rehabbed city block in the Mission District had once housed a small garment factory. Delicate it wasn't; which was good because her family of three seemed to require industrial strength.

"I'm almost finished here!" she shouted above the persistent noise. "Why don't you get Axel on his leash? Take him downstairs and wait on the sidewalk, but don't get near Sam's produce." Sam was the greengrocer in one of the storefronts under the apartment, and Axel's nonstop tail always came perilously close to destroying the perfect pyramids of fruit and vegetables Sam erected on his outdoor display counters every morning.

Axel himself, one hundred pounds of sheer canine energy, burst out of Drew's sleeping area and charged the length of the apartment, his leash whipping behind him, clearing the landscape like bulldozers carving a new suburban subdivision. Several feet away from her, he reared up to plant his front paws on her shoulder. Turning her head to avoid his kiss, she smelled the grape jelly before she saw it on his hairy right foot.

Drew appeared seconds later. "Are you ready?"

Longing for the quiet retreat that was Margo's Bistro, Selena pushed Axel toward Drew. "Wash his feet in the work sink. I'll meet you outside after I've tried to rescue this top." Examining the purple smear on her shoulder, she headed for the bathroom. "And don't let go of the leash."

That dog. Rescuing him had seemed like such a good idea when Margo had found him half starved and rummaging in the garbage behind her café. Kindhearted Margo would have taken him in, but she had enough on her plate at the time. So she'd offered him to Selena, who'd been having trouble with Drew and his emerging adolescent angst. Margo thought caring for a pet would help draw the preteen out of his self-involvement. Boy and dog had bonded beautifully. One could call it a growing relationship. The vet had laughed at Selena when she'd brought what she'd thought was a small, but fully grown dog for the necessary shots. Seems Axel was a very large, but emaciated puppy at the time. Now, ten months and several tons of dog food later, he was a gigantic specimen of overgrown-pup exuberance.

Unable to eliminate the jelly stain, Selena changed into

a clean but worn sweatshirt—why did she never seem to be able to keep clothes new and pretty?—threw on a jacket, grabbed an umbrella, then dashed outside to meet her son. Drew kicked a hacky-sack on the crowded sidewalk as Axel, tied by his leash to a bike rack, cavorted about, barking loudly and threatening to overturn the rack and a half dozen bikes. Sam the greengrocer stood outside his shop and eyed both boy and dog uneasily.

"Come on." Untying Axel, Selena urged her son away from the store.

The dog lunged ahead, dragging Selena and narrowly missing a couple heading into the tattoo parlor. Constantly chasing after this mutt, why wasn't she a size two?

Blocks later, the only reason Axel stopped in front of Margo's Bistro was that he knew Margo or Robert or one of their kids would have a biscuit for him if he stood still and looked pathetic.

"Do you want me to get you something?" Selena asked, handing Drew the leash. After one afternoon of busing tables—before the occupants had had a chance to eat the food themselves—Axel was doggie non grata inside Margo's during business hours.

"A ginger-peach smoothie. And, Mom, do you know you have toilet paper stuck to your shoe?"

She looked down at her feet to see a long, white streamer trailing from one heel. Not surprised, but exasperated nonetheless, she bent to remove the offending accessory, then tossed it into the trash receptacle. "Hold on to Axel. I'm going in."

Too late. The café door opened, and a customer came out. The scrabble of claws on the pavement warned Selena that Drew didn't have control of his dog. When did he ever? Before she could sound the alarm, the overgrown mutt knocked the man aside, then burst through the doorway, shedding hair and shaking drool and looking for the biscuit that was his due.

A teenager at the counter screamed. Robert stepped protectively in front of the girl as Margo reached for a broom. Axel took the move as invitation to play, and, grabbing the broom bristles, proceeded to drag Margo for a turn around the café. Selena tried to grab Axel's collar, but the dog, delighted that the adults found this game as much fun as he did, spun around and planted his front paws on Selena's shoulders for the second time today.

"Hey, you two," Robert called out, trying not to laugh. "We're only a café. We don't have a permit for dancing."

Her son managed to pull his dog to a sitting position.

Margo shook her broom at Drew. "Your mother doesn't give you an allowance big enough to buy this monster a leash?"

Drew held up the broken end of the now useless restraint. "The third one this week."

"Oh, no," Selena moaned. "Now how are you going to take him to the park?"

"I'll use my belt."

He might as well. The thing never seemed to hold up his pants.

"And you—" Margo shook her broom at Axel, who now lolled belly-up on the floor at Drew's feet. "I'm not sure you deserve a cookie."

"Aw," Robert said, "can't you see he's wasting away to nothing? Skin and bones." He reached behind the counter, then palmed a biscuit to Drew. "Give it to him in the park. After he's done something he's supposed to, for a change. So what'll you have, kid?"

"I was going to have a smoothie," Drew replied, eyeing

another customer walking through the door, "but I think I'll just grab a Snapple and head out. Mom's paying." Bottle in hand, he shrugged away from Selena's attempted kiss.

As the door clicked behind the pair, warmth and peace descended on the café. Selena desperately needed some quiet time with adults. Ever since she'd walked into Margo's Bistro from an installation she was doing in SOMA, the café had become a touchstone. A safe haven. A place where no one was a stranger for long.

Robert stepped behind the counter, and as Margo put away her broom, she surreptitiously ran her hand down his back. Selena smiled. Robert, an outsourced commercial lender and former flat-out workaholic, had wandered into Margo's Bistro ten months ago to read the want ads over a cup of coffee. He hadn't counted on falling for Margo and being swept up in her definitely noncorporate way of life. But did he ever look happy now. Not even a visit from Axel the Demolition Dog could eradicate the smile marriage to Margo had put on his face.

Selena flopped into one of the two overstuffed armchairs by the front window. When Margo joined her in the chair opposite, Selena asked, "Is it too early for Irish coffee?"

"A wee bit. And every time you ask you seem to conveniently forget we don't have a liquor license."

"You can't blame a girl for suggesting."

"Rough week?"

"No more than usual. You know that controlled chaos call my life? I think I'm losing the controlled part." Glancing around the crowded room, Selena didn't see any of the friends who made up their core circle. "Where is everybody?"

"Well," Margo replied, stretching slowly and luxuriously as if she were the most contented woman in the world, "Rosie and Hud are still on honeymoon. A working honeymoon, some political retreat in D.C. Casey's staying with Bailey and Derrick, who've taken all the kids to Fisherman's Wharf today. Say a little prayer for those brave souls. And Nora and Erik are at a medical conference in Lake Tahoe. Nora's sister has Danny."

Pairs. Selena was struck by the realization the once tight single-parents coffee group had become a loose confederation of married friends who got together when new blended and extended family commitments allowed.

And she was the last staunchly single person standing.

"And Ellie and Peter?" she asked before she could examine how she felt about being left behind. "Is it your ex's weekend to have them?"

"Yes. Tom and Catherine are taking the kids to look at prospective summer camps."

Selena was pleased to see Margo finally speak of her custody arrangement without a trace of stress.

"So you have my undivided attention," Margo promised, "and Robert's on call if we need him."

As if on cue, Robert brought two cups of coffee, a double mocha with vanilla whipped cream to Margo and espresso for Selena. "Your usual, ladies. Apart from the dog and pony show, Selena, how's it going?"

"Fine. Only if you don't count the dog."

"Oh, that sweet baby," Margo cooed in exaggerated admiration. "You can't stay mad at him."

"You don't live with him. And my neighbors aren't as forgiving as you two." Selena sipped her high-octane drink. "I know I wasn't a dog-savvy person when I agreed to take him, but who knew he'd grow this big?"

"You didn't notice the size of his paws when we found him?"

"You did?"

"Well, it occurred to me…." Margo suppressed a grin.

"What's the latest?" Robert asked. "Besides the exhibition here this morning."

"This week he ate the cushions on my sofa." Selena shuddered to remember. "And the mail. Five days running. I was so worried about the possible effects—on him—I took him to the vet for X-rays. Dr. Wong says Axel has a cast-iron intestinal tract, if you're interested. Then I received three calls from neighbors about his barking. And, last but not least, yesterday he ran off two students from the dance studio next to Sam's. I owe for their missed lesson."

"He may be bored," Margo suggested.

"How can he be bored when he has Drew for a constant companion? And the two of them never stop moving."

"Does Drew walk him every day?"

"Walk? Hah! They run everywhere. It's only a matter of time before they knock someone over, and I have a lawsuit on my hands."

Robert sat on the arm of Margo's chair. "Sounds like Axel needs an obedience class."

"Obedience. What a nasty word," Selena replied, her free artistic nature rebelling. "I don't want to break his spirit."

"But if he breaks his leash once too often, he's going to land in the pound," Margo protested. "And then how will Drew feel?"

"Awful. Simply awful. Me, too."

"You always say you love controlled chaos. Sounds like it's time you take control of your dog before a solution is imposed upon you. One you might not like."

Margo had touched a nerve. She knew just how much Selena hated being backed into a corner. Being told what to do and how to do it.

"I may have a solution," Robert said. "I have a friend with an older brother who's a dog trainer. Or psychologist, I'm not sure which. But he has an impressive list of clients. I could get his number for you."

"A dog shrink?" Selena was skeptical. "Sounds a little too California even for me. Is he on the level?"

"Absolutely. I've met him. He's as no-nonsense as they come. Besides his private consultations, he rescues and rehabilitates stray and feral dogs."

"He doesn't sound flaky," Margo insisted. "He sounds compassionate."

Robert rose to wait on a customer. "I'll get his number for you before you leave."

Selena remained unconvinced. "I really think Axel will grow out of it," she said to Margo. "Don't they say that from eight months to three years dogs are adolescents? So he's really Drew's age. The two of them are growing so fast they can't control their own bodies. And I don't expect Drew will be on an emotional roller coaster forever. He'll mature and settle down. So will Axel. Nature has a way of sorting these things out."

"If you say so."

"You're giving me that look."

"What look?"

"The one that says I'm being stubborn."

"You said it, I didn't."

Selena sighed. Her friends often said her stubborn nature didn't always serve her best interests. "I'll call this dog shrink. But if he shows the first sign of training the joy out of Axel, he's gone. I may not want my sofa in shreds, but if I'd wanted a robot, I would have bought one of those electronic pets."

Robert came back with a name and phone number on a slip of paper. He gave the paper to Selena and a rather soulful kiss to Margo before returning to the counter.

Margo's expression turned dreamy. "What a lovely man."

"The dog shrink?"

"No, silly. Robert. And he has really nice friends. Just say the word—"

"No, thank you! Not everyone is cut out to be part of a couple. Two males in my life are enough, even if one's a dog."

Margo laughed. "Selena, my friend, someday love is going to sneak up on you and catch you so unaware. I, for one, would pay to see that show."

"How about you pay to see a more likely show? When Axel makes short work of this—" Selena glanced at the slip of paper "—Jack Quinn."

* * * * *

Piraeus, Greece

"THERE SHE IS, Stefan. *Alexandra's Dream*." David Anderson squatted beside his new son and pointed at the dark blue hull that towered above the pier. The cruise ship was a majestic sight, twelve decks high and as long as a city block. A circle of silver and gold stars, the logo of the Liberty Cruise Line, gleamed from the swept-back smokestack. Like some legendary sea creature born for the water, the ship emanated power from every sleek curve—even at rest it held the promise of motion. "That's going to be our home for the next ten days."

The child beside him remained silent, his cheeks working in and out as he sucked furiously on his thumb. Hair so blond it appeared white ruffled against his forehead in the harbor breeze. The baby-sweet scent unique to the very young mingled with the tang of the sea.

"Ship," David said. "Uh, *parakhod*."

From beneath his bangs, Stefan looked at the *Alexandra's Dream*. Although he didn't release his thumb, the corners of his mouth tightened with the beginning of a smile.

David grinned. That was Stefan's first smile this afternoon, one of only two since they had left the orphanage yesterday. It was probably because of the boat—according to the orphanage staff, the boy loved boats, which was the main reason David had decided to book this cruise. Then again, there was a strong possibility the smile could have been a reaction to David's attempt at pocket-dictionary Russian. Whatever the cause, it was a good start.

The liaison from the adoption agency had claimed that Stefan had been taught some English, but David had yet to see evidence of it. David continued to speak, positive his son would understand his tone even if he couldn't grasp the words. "This is her maiden voyage. Her first trip, just like this is our first trip, and that makes it special." He motioned toward the stage that had been set up on the pier beneath the ship's bow. "That's why everyone's celebrating."

The ship's official christening ceremony had been held the day before and had been a closed affair, with only the cruise-line executives and VIP guests invited, but the stage hadn't yet been disassembled. Banners bearing the blue and white of the Greek flag of the ship's owner, as well as the Liberty circle of stars logo, draped the edges of the platform. In the center, a group of musicians and a dance troupe dressed in traditional white folk costumes performed for the benefit of the *Alexandra's Dream*'s first passengers. Their audience was in a festive mood, snapping their fingers in time to the music while the dancers twirled and wove through their steps.

David bobbed his head to the rhythm of the mandolins. They were playing a folk tune that seemed vaguely familiar, possibly from a movie he'd seen. He hummed a few notes. "Catchy melody, isn't it?"

Stefan turned his gaze on David. His eyes were a striking shade of blue, as cool and pale as a winter horizon and far too solemn for a child not yet five. Still, the smile that hovered at the corners of his mouth persisted. He moved his head with the music, mirroring David's motion.

David gave a silent cheer at the interaction. Hopefully, this cruise would provide countless opportunities for more. "Hey, good for you," he said. "Do you like the music?"

The child's eyes sparked. He withdrew his thumb with a pop. *"Moozika!"*

"Music. Right!" David held out his hand. "Come on, let's go closer so we can watch the dancers."

Stefan grasped David's hand quickly, as if he feared it would be withdrawn. In an instant his budding smile was replaced by a look close to panic.

Did he remember the car accident that had killed his parents? It would be a mercy if he didn't. As far as David knew, Stefan had never spoken of it to anyone. Whatever he had seen had made him run so far from the crash that the police hadn't found him until the next day. The event had traumatized him to the extent that he hadn't uttered a word until his fifth week at the orphanage. Even now he seldom talked.

David sat back on his heels and brushed the hair from Stefan's forehead. That solemn, too-old gaze locked with his, and for an instant, David felt as if he looked back in time at an image of himself thirty years ago.

He didn't need to speak the same language to understand exactly how this boy felt. He knew what it meant to be alone and powerless among strangers, trying to be brave and tough but wishing with every fiber of his being for a place to belong, to be safe, and most of all for someone to love him....

He knew in his heart he would be a good parent to Stefan. It was why he had never considered halting the adoption process after Ellie had left him. He hadn't balked when he'd learned of the recent claim by Stefan's spinster aunt, either; the absentee relative had shown up too late for her case to be considered. The adoption was meant to be. He and this child already shared a bond that went deeper than paperwork or legalities.

A seagull screeched overhead, making Stefan start and press closer to David.

"That's my boy," David murmured. He swallowed hard, struck by the simple truth of what he had just said.

That's my *boy.*

"I CAN'T BE PATIENT, RUDOLPH. I'm not going to stand by and watch my nephew get ripped from his country and his roots to live on the other side of the world."

Rudolph hissed out a slow breath. "Marina, I don't like the sound of that. What are you planning?"

"I'm going to talk some sense into this American kidnapper."

"No. Absolutely not. No offence, but diplomacy is not your strong suit."

"Diplomacy be damned. Their ship's due to sail at five o'clock."

"Then you wouldn't have an opportunity to speak with him even if his lawyer agreed to a meeting."

"I'll have ten days of opportunities, Rudolph, since I plan to be on board that ship."

* * * * *

*Follow Marina and David as they
join forces to uncover the reason behind
little Stefan's unusual silence,
and the secret behind the death of his parents....*

Look for
From Russia, With Love
*by Ingrid Weaver
in stores June 2007.*

Mediterranean ## N I G H T S™

Tycoon Elias Stamos is launching his newest luxury cruise ship from his home port in Greece. But someone from his past is eager to expose old secrets and to see the Stamos empire crumble.

Mediterranean Nights
launches in June 2007 with...

FROM RUSSIA, WITH LOVE
by *Ingrid Weaver*

Join the guests and crew of *Alexandra's Dream* as they are drawn into a world of glamour, romance and intrigue in this new 12-book series.

Romantic SUSPENSE

Sparked by Danger,
Fueled by Passion.

This month and every month look for
four new heart-racing romances
set against a backdrop of suspense!

Available in June 2007

Shelter from the Storm
by RaeAnne Thayne

A Little Bit Guilty
(Midnight Secrets miniseries)
by Jenna Mills

Mob Mistress
by Sheri WhiteFeather

A Serial Affair
by Natalie Dunbar

Available wherever you buy books!

Visit Silhouette Books at www.eHarlequin.com   SRS0507

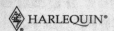

HARLEQUIN®

INTRIGUE®

ARE YOU AFRAID OF THE DARK?

The eerie text message was only part of a night to remember for security ace Shane Peters—one minute he was dancing with Princess Ariana LeBron, holding her in his arms at a soiree of world leaders, the next he was fighting for their lives when a blackout struck and gunmen held them hostage. Their demands were simple: give them the princess.

Part of a new miniseries:

LIGHTS OUT

ROYAL LOCKDOWN

BY RUTH GLICK
WRITING AS
REBECCA YORK

On sale June 2007.

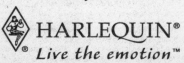

HARLEQUIN®
Live the emotion™

REQUEST YOUR FREE BOOKS

2 FREE NOVELS PLUS 2 FREE GIFTS!

◆ HARLEQUIN®

Super Romance®

Exciting, emotional, unexpected!

YES! Please send me 2 FREE Harlequin Superromance® novels and r
2 FREE gifts. After receiving them, if I don't wish to receive any more bool
I can return the shipping statement marked "cancel." If I don't cancel, I w
receive 6 brand-new novels every month and be billed just $4.69 per book
the U.S., or $5.24 per book in Canada, plus 25¢ shipping and handling p
book and applicable taxes, if any*. That's a savings of close to 15% off t
cover price! I understand that accepting the 2 free books and gifts plac
me under no obligation to buy anything. I can always return a shipment a
cancel at any time. Even if I never buy another book from Harlequin, the t\
free books and gifts are mine to keep forever.   135 HDN EEX7 336 HDN EE

Name	(PLEASE PRINT)	
Address		Apt.
City	State/Prov.	Zip/Postal Code

Signature (if under 18, a parent or guardian must sign)

Mail to the **Harlequin Reader Service®**:
IN U.S.A.: P.O. Box 1867, Buffalo, NY 14240-1867
IN CANADA: P.O. Box 609, Fort Erie, Ontario L2A 5X3

Not valid to current Harlequin Superromance subscribers.

Want to try two free books from another line?
Call 1-800-873-8635 or visit www.morefreebooks.com.

* Terms and prices subject to change without notice. NY residents add applicable sa
tax. Canadian residents will be charged applicable provincial taxes and GST. This offe
limited to one order per household. All orders subject to approval. Credit or debit balanc
in a customer's account(s) may be offset by any other outstanding balance owed by o
the customer. Please allow 4 to 6 weeks for delivery.

Your Privacy: Harlequin is committed to protecting your privacy. Our Priva
Policy is available online at www.eHarlequin.com or upon request from the Rea
Service. From time to time we make our lists of customers available to reputab
firms who may have a product or service of interest to you. If you would
prefer we not share your name and address, please check here. ☐

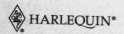

HARLEQUIN®
Super Romance®

COMING NEXT MONTH

#1422 COULDA BEEN A COWBOY • Brenda Novak
A Dundee, Idaho story

Tyson Garnier is a stranger to Dundee—and to his own infant son. The baby was neglected by his mother, so Tyson paid her off to get full custody. Now he needs a temporary nanny, and Dakota Brown is perfect. She's completely unlike the kind of women Tyson usually attracts. She's poor, a little plain, a hard worker. Who would've guessed he'd find himself falling for someone like *that?*

#1423 BLAME IT ON THE DOG • Amy Frazier
Singles…with Kids

An out-of-control mutt. A preteen son. Dog trainer Jack Quinn. These are the males in Selena Milano's life. The first two she loves. The third? Who knows? But he sure does make things interesting.

#1424 HIS PERFECT WOMAN • Kay Stockham

Dr. Bryan Booker is the perfect man. Ask almost every woman in town—including some of the married ones. Even Melissa York is hard-pressed to deny Bryan's charms. Not that she can afford to be interested…since he's already said the only way she can work for him is if they keep everything professional. But is he going to remember that?

#1425 DAD FOR LIFE • Helen Brenna
A Little Secret

Lucas Rydall is looking for redemption. His search leads him to his ex-wife, Sydney Mitchell—and the son he didn't know he had. But his discovery puts them all in danger. To save his family, Lucas must put aside his fears and become the man his family needs.

#1426 MR. IRRESISTIBLE • Karina Bliss

Entrepreneur Jordan King is handsome and charismatic, and he's used to getting any woman he wants. Until journalist Kate Brogan catches his eye—and refuses to give in to her obvious feelings for him. Because the way she sees it, he's just like her father: a no-good philanderer at the mercy of his passions. So all Jordan has to do is convince her he's utterly irresistible.

#1427 WANTED MAN • Ellen K. Hartman

Nathan has a secret. One he has to hide—which means leaving his old life behind and not telling a soul who he really is. But how can a man with any honor even think about getting involved with a woman as wonderful as Rhian MacGregor?

HSRCNM0507